GUARDIANS
OF THE
AFTERWORLD

GUARDIANS
OF THE
AFTERWORLD

STAFFORD BETTY

www.whitecrowbooks.com

Published by White Crow Books, an imprint of White Crow Productions Ltd.

The right of Stafford Betty to be identified as the author of this work has been asserted by him in accordance with the Copyright, Design and Patents act 1988.

A CIP catalogue record for this book is available from the British Library.

For information, contact White Crow Books by e-mail: info@whitecrowbooks.com.

Cover Design by Astrid@Astridpaints.com
Interior design by Velin@Perseus-Design.com
Cover image: Temple of Conception by Freydoon Rassouli

Paperback: ISBN: 978-1-78677-254-1
eBook: ISBN: 978-1-78677-255-8

FICTION / Visionary & Metaphysical

www.whitecrowbooks.com

To my wife, Monica Ayuso, PhD, whose careful reading of the text, dug out of a busy teaching schedule as a professor of English, led to changes that crucially improved this book. For this, and for all the other good things she has brought to my life, I am deeply grateful.

CONTENTS

Preface

This book is more than a work of fiction. It grew out of contemporary consciousness research, a movement taken seriously by a growing number of scholars and seekers worldwide, including myself. Many people are content with their religion's view of life after death. Others are just as convinced there is no such thing as an afterlife. For people at either of these extremes, reading this novel might lead to discomfort or disdain.

But for people who aren't at all sure what's coming but hope it's "The Good Place," perhaps even a place where we are reunited with our loved ones, this book could be eye-opening. The laws of this world, its differences from the afterlife scenarios of the world's religions, and its rationality and 'amazingness' stand out. All that happens to the novel's characters is supported in a general way by evidence. The details of the story are fanciful, of course, but the world in which surviving persons find themselves owes as much to research as to my imagination. Something like this is the world I think we will all enter, whether Christian or Buddhist or atheist or whatever, when we die. As "the dead" see it, we are pilgrims on a very long march.

1

The Galaxy

The home planets of Numen and Sephia stood on opposite sides of the galaxy, as far removed in character as in distance. Numen came from Sirius, a small planet with light gravity and thin atmosphere, a world in which wonder, philosophical speculation, and science marked the superior person. Sephia's much larger planet, Pollux, burdened its inhabitants with a heavy gravity that kept them closer to the surface, where they excelled in architecture, medicine, and the visual arts. Their physical appearances had nothing in common. Numen's body was spectrally thin and shimmered silver with a subtle blue tint; Sephia's was block-shaped, short, and brown. But their physical bodies belonged to the past. Death was behind them. The astral worlds of spirit, sphere on top of sphere, heaven worlds and hell worlds and every gradation between, was their present domain. They had died their last deaths. Now they would be helping others die theirs.

Their teacher, whose true name was unpronounceable and its meaning baffling to beings at her students' level, introduced herself as Fruva. She came from one of the galaxy's oldest inhabited planets, which began forming 12 billion years ago and had been harboring advanced intelligent life for millions of years. This was not the first time she was called to train Earth's astral leaders. She knew its past stretching far back into prehistory and had trained Divinus and Prima, their predecessors. She had molded her body and clothing to look like an earthling's: light almond skin, coffee-colored hair, and a face with high cheekbones and eyes that told of a serene joy tinged with an ancient wisdom steeped in struggle. She wore a simple tan tunic.

She had brought them to the fourth level, or sphere, of the afterworld they would be guiding and managing. A broad grassy meadow with sprigs of yellow and blue wildflowers dappled the ground. A narrow, winding stream linking three ponds trickled over small rocks. The air was warm, salubrious, and sunny. Birds flitted about, and butterflies frolicked in the breeze. A forest of pines, cedars, and spruce surrounded the meadow. Beside the central pond three benches, weatherworn in appearance, stood like a triangle with space between the legs. This was the open-air classroom Fruva had arranged for her students. They had finished their preliminary studies and were ready for takeoff. Both had mastered the universal tongue spoken in the afterworld and English as well. Numen had picked up Chinese and Hindi, Sephia Spanish, Arabic, and Swahili. Teacher and students hadn't met each other until now.

After the introductions were made, Fruva began: "As you know, your training is near an end. I've brought you here for a final test, followed by launching. You are not alone. All over the galaxy leaders are replacing the old guard; there are limits to every term. Planets with intelligent life like ours are spangled across the universe with its trillion galaxies. Ours, the Milky Way, is only one. Do your minds boggle at the thought?

"Space continues to expand. Suns and planets continue to mature or disappear. Joy and beauty alternate with pain and grief. Death and birth do their everlasting dance. Power, for good or evil, struggles in a locked battle. Now it is your turn to govern, to see that the right balance is kept. Each of you is praised for heroism in your history books. Now you will be tested. You have longed for such a test, even at the loss of contact with your loved ones on your home planets. Though recruited, you first volunteered. You give your galactic Mother and Father a joy that renews their termless life together. Such joy, such pride in all you have accomplished to get this far, such eagerness to see what you are yet to do, that is what they feel and rejoice in. And in my own way, so do I. I am honored to be your teacher.

"On physical planets we are hemmed in by the limiting speed of light, but here we are, spirits free of that ball and chain. You loved and governed your physical bodies until they gave out. You were born in pain, refined by struggle, and succumbed to death. You strove to understand your plight, settled for makeshift theories, even imagined you grasped the grand design of the great Ur-Being, the unfathomable Source of the

Universe, the Eternal, the Creator, whom many earthlings call God. Do you remember, you especially, Numen? Do you not now smile?

"The whole point of creation is to fill it with beings who grow in happiness. You can help realize this goal—that is why you are here. You are an essential part of the process. If you carry it out in the right spirit, you will grow into masters, like those you are replacing.

"As you know, universal policy handed down from the Creator requires the new Guardians to be alien both to each other and the planet they co-govern. In that way old alliances leading to favoritism are forestalled and fresh perspectives better ensured. In addition, your very strangeness will disquiet those tempted to control you. This will not be understood by most of your—shall we call them subjects?

"This is the home stretch. You are about to take your place as Earth's new Guardians."

2

The Afterworld

Projecting a hologram in space, Fruva created a place of great natural beauty, "Earth at its most beautiful," she said. She fashioned a rushing stream tumbling zigzag over mossy green boulders through a forest of yellows, oranges, and reds, "the gorgeous colors of decay at winter's onset. The sun is weak during fall and normally you would feel a chill in the air, but I will keep it warm for you. How do you like it?"

"I can't relate to it," said Sephia. "We don't have what you call autumn on my planet. We have rainy and dry seasons, stormy and calm. But this is beautiful in a strange, wondrous way. Strange, yes, very strange.

"Its beauty is precise, detailed, different from the colors that flow and melt into one another on Sirius," said Numen.

"Before going any further," Fruva said, "You'll need to rearrange your body. As you appear now, you look nothing like an earthling, even less like each other, and that will not do at all. Look over there at the hologram. There they are, a man and a woman hiking, enjoying Earth's natural beauty. They are dressed in tight-fitting clothes as if it were summer so you can see their forms more clearly. They are pivoting so you can see all sides of them. And they are smiling. There. Look carefully. Now, imagine your body, including clothing, looking like theirs. This will be your new body; your astral or spiritual body. Study it carefully. When you are ready to shift your shape, let me know. You will do it through willpower and imagination, with me encouraging and guiding you."

They began the transformation under her instruction. Their new bodies felt strange and ill-fitting. Sephia's was lumpy and unnaturally stretched in places, Numen's narrow as a stick but baggy. Numen asked if he could keep the beard he wore back on Sirius. Fruva teased them good-naturedly as they rearranged the ethereal substance. Many minutes passed as they struggled against the subconscious pressure to slip back into what was old and comfortable. Finally she declared it was "good enough for now." Their new Earth suits had stabilized.

"Do you have any questions before we move on to the final test?"

"I have a question," said Sephia. "When I first saw Numen, I found him exceedingly—strange. And I suppose he felt the same about me. I'm grateful you've helped us look more like each other. How are we— how are Numen and I supposed to relate to each other?"

"A delicate question. It's essential that you be friends. It's our hope that as you work together you'll grow closer. But all that's necessary is to live and govern in harmony. If love develops, it will make your lives much happier. Any further questions?"

"The light, this wonderful light that surrounds us," continued Sephia, "it seems to know us, as if it's conscious in some strange, wonderful way. It has a motherly presence. I bask in it. It seems to love me, oh so tenderly, yes, to love me."

"Wonderful it is, but spirits feel it differently. You sense it as motherly because you are motherly yourself. The cruel-hearted feel it as a penetrating force to fear. But yes, it's conscious. A conscious atmospheric Presence. Unlike the physical sunlight of planets."

"This whole place is exhilarating. Birds. Look at them. They seem to know us too. Look at them overhead, swooping down, now back up. Thousands. As if greeting us. Or putting on a show for us."

"How you delight me, child! You and Numen, our quiet friend, will be responsible for all the nine billion astral spirits gathered here, and sometimes even those spirits weighed down by a physical body down on the planet. Don't worry. Guardians aren't required to do any more than their best. Their ultimate contributions will be limited, but they should think big. You'll need ambition, courage, compassion, and, above all, wisdom to make the right decision. Once made, enforce it. But don't fear changing your mind if new evidence surfaces. Don't waffle; don't dither. Have confidence in your judgments. They will be far superior to the calculations of Earth. This is no democracy.

And you'll need to be kind to yourself when you fail—most of your successes will be partial. Just as important, you'll need to know when to take on a burden and when to let it go. You'll never find enough time to do all you want."

3

The Priest

"Let's take a break and stretch our limbs." Fruva looked at Numen struggling in his new body. "Your body looks unstable." Squirming as if he had melons in his pockets, he said, "It feels lumpy. I don't seem to be able to keep things in place. They wobble around."

Fruva smiled. She had seen it before. "I think that's because you never got into the habit of using muscles back home. You wispy beings didn't need many in your thin atmosphere. Will them away. Will those lumps away. You can do it, Numen." She studied him with a mixture of amusement and compassion, then said, "Well, we're going to finish your training with an exercise. Cases like this will work their way through the ranks all the way up to the Capitol, where you will live and rule. This one had minimal impact on the wellbeing of the planet as a whole, which should be your primary concern; but your predecessors too often let themselves get involved with individual cases. Whether they should have is the main point of the exercise.

"Meet Monsignor Pascal Debrisson, a Catholic priest. There he is—in the hologram. He was asked to tell his story in detail, which he did. I've studied it carefully and memorized it for dramatic impact—it's in the archives. We'll especially explore his psychology. Keep your eyes on the hologram as the story develops. He pastored an oversized Catholic church in California's Central Valley. Have you studied Catholicism, Numen?"

"Yes. It reminded me of my own planet—quite similar, right down to a celibate priesthood and a view of God that excluded the female." "I don't know your planet. I wonder: did it grow out of a culture that looked on females as inferior?" "It did. But Catholics at least have a goddess they call Mary." "Careful. Catholics don't like the name 'goddess' for their Mary. It implies she's the equal of God. But they do call her the mother of God."

Numen's brow furrowed. "The mother of God? That implies—hmm, I'll have to go back to my notes."

Fruva laughed. "Well, as I was saying, our priest, Father Pascal, was pastoring a church. You will see it there on the hologram with its steeple bearing a cross. It had flourished under his leadership over the last eight years, and not even the rumors of his having a long-lived affair with a mysterious woman in a nearby rural town alarmed the faithful or seemed to trouble his bishop, his boss. They loved their bushy-haired, goateed, middle-aged pastor because they knew he loved them. He was assisted by an earnest but mostly ineffective priest who spoke poor English and, with Pascal's encouragement, kept his sermons mercifully short. A large woman, Gladys Bunch, the office manager—large not only in girth but in helpfulness and devotion to the parish, there she is—kept the books and his personal schedule.

"All over California the Catholic Church was losing attendees at Sunday Mass, that's their ritual, to NFL football games—you'll discover that earthlings love sports to the point of addiction. In recent years, weekly attendance had become increasingly optional, with the Catholic God no more to be feared than a doting and adaptable uncle. But attendance at the ten o'clock service that Pascal led spilled out the front door—such was his popularity. In one of his sermons he told the story of how his backyard was overrun with possums, one of Earth's less appealing wild animals, who ate the citrus fruit that grew there, and how he trapped them and released them in the foothills nearby, where they would flourish in a natural state. His point was that the Church existed to win back the faithful to a natural state away from the seductions of TV ads, video games, and endless texting. What started out as a joke gradually became a routine practice: The Monsignor's closest circle spoke of themselves as 'Pascal's possums'.

"On a hot Monday morning in early September, Pascal pulled his red and gray backpack out of the closet, filled a half-gallon plastic bottle with cold water from the refrigerator, slapped together two meatloaf sandwiches made from leftovers at a memorial service from the previous

Thursday, and put them, along with a bag of trail mix, into separate pockets. He gave his phone a last-minute scan to make sure there was no emergency, then texted Gladys that he would not be coming into the office. He thought about mentioning where he was going but decided not to. 'See you tomorrow morning,' he ended. After debating whether he would need a jacket, he stuffed it into the backpack. He always brought a book wherever he went and threw in *The Mountains of California*, a book written by a great American naturalist named John Muir. With spirits high, he turned his fourteen-year-old Nissan Altima, that is a car, onto the 99, that is a highway. When he reached the 190, another highway, and turned east toward Springville, he realized he had forgotten his phone. 'Damn!' he exploded.

"It had been three or four years since he last hiked the trail from Hidden Falls north along the Tule River gorge. He and his best friend, Malachi Fruhling, Jewish rabbi of the local Conservative synagogue, loved this little known sector of the Sierras with its ancient, massive redwoods—they thought of it as their undiscovered Yosemite—a national park celebrated worldwide for its beauty—and never failed to marvel how such beautiful country, with its modest campground nestled under a soaring grove of redwoods stretching along the bank of the river, could get such little notice. You see a picture of the gorge there, and there is a typical redwood, the largest, grandest, tallest tree on the planet. On this late morning only five cars were parked in the lot, and a couple of overnighters preparing their fishing gear next to a yellow tent were the only other evidence of human presence. Pascal would be hiking in solitude, a thought that thrilled him.

"Hiking north along the gorge, which opened to the west on his left, with the river far below swishing and gurgling around boulders, and mountains stretching up to the heavens in the blazing blue sky, their tops rocky and devoid of vegetation—there they are—Pascal felt the usual exhilaration of being surrounded by such grandeur. Looking to his right, he saw a few redwoods mixed with the more numerous pines and cedars. They stand like giants guarding their smaller brethren. He exercised almost daily at a nearby gym and did not have the least trouble climbing the winding trail. There, see how beautiful it is.

"After three miles he reached a bridge over the river formed a century earlier by a fallen cedar tree. He did not feel safe on it and turned back. He found a rocky shelf extending out over the river fifty feet below and sat down. He noticed two eagles circling far out over the gorge. He swallowed three mouthfuls of water and ate one of the sandwiches as a breeze dried his sweaty white cotton pullover. He sat for an hour and enjoyed the scene, forgetting the business of his church. He loved the craggy peaks, the forest of green spires striving upward toward them, the river below, and the warm breeze passing through trees overhead. *Thank you for all this, Lord,* he prayed to his God. His soul expanded in gratitude for such a magnificent sight. He felt specially favored as if singled out. His lips turned upward in a smile. He thought about reading a few pages of his book but decided against it. Not even Muir could make it better.

"He decided to take an inland trail back to the Falls. He had seen it on a map and had always wondered what it would be like but never explored it. As he walked south along it in silence, he wondered how far the redwoods extended up the slope—he could make out only two from the trail. He decided to leave the trail and bushwhack his way farther up the slope. Working hard as he climbed eastward, he came across a lonely giant soaring in solitude 250 feet. He wondered how many humans had ever seen it and talked to it as a friend. There he is, sending his thoughts out to it. Up the steep slope he went farther until there were no more redwoods; then he turned south and hiked parallel to the trail back toward the Falls.

"A half hour later he reached a point so steep that the only chance he had was to turn back the way he had come or travel straight down the slope to rejoin the trail. Disliking the idea of retreat, he decided to head down. He made steady progress, then found himself slipping on the leafy, rocky duff of the forest floor. He was terrified when his boots failed to grab hold and stop his slide. Before him a flat rocky shelf stuck out like a tongue of granite. He landed hard on it, his heart racing. Let's call it a ledge. Look carefully at it, all around it, out beyond it, to the left and right of it, down below it.

"He understood that for a few seconds he had been in mortal danger. He closed his eyes, took deep breaths, and calmed himself. Now he was safe. He thanked God for saving him. He decided to go back the way he came and rejoin the trail.

"He looked down over the lip of the ledge at a collection of smaller rocks fifty feet down, jagged and hostile. He looked to the left, then the right, and realized there was no exit either way. His only way out was to climb up the slope he just slid down. He looked up and saw how steep it was. The first ten or so feet were at least 45 degrees off vertical before it leveled off. Did he have the strength to climb it? Would the crumbly soil give him a footing? It had been slippery enough on the way down. But he had no choice. Look carefully at the slope, Numen.

"Pascal looked up, said a prayer, and began the climb. He scrambled up three feet, then slipped back down. He took off his backpack, took a few deep breaths, said another prayer, and tried again. He noticed some weeds, reached up and clung to them, but they came loose. A sprig of a tree he had not noticed offered hope, but it too gave way under his weight. He made no better progress than the first time. Over and over he tried until he dropped back on his ledge shaking with exhaustion and fear, his hands bloody and his pants ripped at the knee. He looked again left and right. Had he missed something? Was there a gentler descent he had not seen before? There was to the left, but it would take two or three steps, and attempting those would send him fatally to the rocks below. Feeling increasingly desperate, he looked outward and studied the branches of nearby pines that surrounded the ledge. Could he leap out toward one of the branches, grab it, and shimmy down the trunk? No, they were a little too far out. He realized he was trapped. Trapped on a ledge that stuck out ten feet like a giant flat-topped mushroom over certain death.

"Trying to steady his nerves, he began to consider how far he was from the trail. No more than a quarter mile he guessed. Maybe much closer. Could he yell loud enough to be heard? But a wall of cedar, pine, and fir stood in the way—as you can see. And the trail didn't get much travel, and it was a Monday, a weekday. Then he realized, *Good God, I forgot my phone! I never forget my phone. Dear God, help me.* He prayed with rare intensity. Please note the fervor with which he said this prayer.

"He stood, looked again left and right, up and down, to see if he had missed something. He had not, but it was hard to accept his situation. It was simply too absurd. He was just a few feet away from freedom, he could see the slope level off ten feet above the ledge, but he could not reach it. It seemed as if he were caught in a nightmare. What if no one traveled the trail—the very inland trail he shunned because it lacked the beauty of the river? Did anyone ever use it?

"He calmed himself and took stock. Possibly not today, but almost surely the next day or two someone would find him. He would yell, just keep yelling until somebody heard. He began to yell. "Help! Help! Help!" Then he stopped and listened. The shrill cry of a hawk high overhead was the only answer. Then he yelled again, three times. Nothing.

"He looked directly up, saw an opening of sky, and watched a jet fly noiselessly across. He told himself that a helicopter could spy him if it ever came this way. He let himself hope that Gladys would know what to do, as she always did. She would wonder why he was missing his appointments, something he never did, and call 911 to get help. Maybe not the next day, but surely by Wednesday. He could hold out. He had his sandwich and some water. And she knew he hiked with his friend, the rabbi. And the rabbi knew where his favorite spot was. They would find his car in the lot and begin a search. Men would scour the slopes, and he would yell his lungs out. Or maybe a helicopter would fly over and see him. But, wait a minute; did he really tell her? Did he really tell her? He was not sure. A dread settled over him as he remembered not telling her where he was going or even what he was doing. No, he had not told her. Then what might she assume? Maybe that he was visiting a relative or driving over to the Coast or playing golf. Or hiking, yes— but where? He had never told her about Hidden Falls. *Good God, she doesn't know. No one knows.*

"He forced himself to face reality. At some point a forest ranger would notice that his car was still where he had seen it before, perhaps a week earlier, and report it to the police. By then the authorities would know he was missing and put the puzzle together. A search would be organized. They would begin looking for his body in the river after assuming he had probably fallen in and drowned. But they would also cover the slopes, and maybe, just maybe—no, no one would think to look for his ledge. Why would anyone leave the trail? What reason could there be? By then he would be dead anyway. Instead they would assume he hiked farther north up the main trail, and after two or three days, finding no trace, would end the search. He would go into the annals forever as a missing person. His only chance was to keep yelling.

"That is what he did, never letting more than ten minutes pass before trying again. A gentle wind blew the tops of trees, a sound he had loved all his life. How ironic, he thought, that he might die amid so much natural beauty—he, an acolyte who found God in it more readily than in a church. A church, his workplace. Nature, his hearth. He felt betrayed. Fear gave way to bitterness, and he called out, not in anguish, but in anger to the God who did this to him.

"Here is some background on Pascal. He had attended a Catholic high school in Fresno and Jesuit Santa Clara University in the Bay Area. A class in physics left him with no doubt that the universe had been evolving for almost 14 billion years. The professor implied that the Big Bang had happened on its own with no one's planning or execution. One of his classmates, a girl, challenged this assumption: 'But how could something so stupendous just happen? It took a whole bunch of engineers and architects just to build this campus, and it's a measly feat compared to the universe.' Pascal followed her to the Student Union after class and asked to speak with her. He told her that was exactly what he had been thinking and that he admired her for daring to speak up.

"'Daring?' she said. 'Where I come from that's what we do.'

"She wasn't especially beautiful by conventional standards and had a rather large mole just above her lip on the right side. Her broad forehead spread out over lively blue eyes and cheeks slightly scarred with acne, and her long reddish-blonde hair was gathered in a pigtail. He noted that her breasts were small and her hips nicely rounded over a lean waist. He liked everything about Sydney Harris, there she is, from the start, her quick wit and analytical mind even more than her looks. He thought she might be attainable and asked her out, and she accepted. Eight months later, by the time they graduated, he had slept with her; it was his first time, and he was passionately in love with her. But he had not been her first, a fact that gradually emerged one night during an argument and that at first worried him. He wondered if she were still attached to the 'other guy,' and she assured him she was not. A month later he brought up marriage, and to his surprise she resisted. She said they were too young and he would first have to get his graduate degree in environmental engineering. He begged her to reconsider. He argued that she could work in her field of graphic arts, her major, while he was in school; then they could raise a family. When she further objected, he grew desperate, then angry, and questioned her love for him. Out of control, he began yelling and claimed she was still in love with her first boyfriend. Shocked and revolted, she blasted back that she 'just might be.' In a fury he drove her back to her house and let her out. After a harrowing week passed, he phoned her, remorseful and ready to apologize. But she had 'moved on.' There was no dissuading her. He had lost her for good.

"Over the next six months he wrote a barrage of love letters and drove past her house hoping to see her. Some nights he parked in front of it just to be close to her as she slept. On one occasion long after midnight, a car drove up. As she got out, he heard a man's voice indistinctly. The next day she phoned and asked him to stop stalking her. The word *stalking* shocked him and called him to his senses.

"Pascal had enjoyed his theology and philosophy classes at Santa Clara and wondered before he met Sydney if he might become a priest. Now that she was gone and his world commingled with grief, its good times reduced to beer bashes with his buddies, and with no obvious way to meet 'the right kind of girl' as he waited for his engineering program to start, he began to play again with the idea of becoming a man of the cloth.

"Five years later he was working for a firm requiring him to develop guidelines for the disposal of hazardous materials. As important as this work was, it struck him as utterly incongruous with his real interests. His math and engineering courses had been challenging, his professors and colleagues supportive, and theoretical solutions intriguing, sometimes even fascinating. But on the ground, sometimes in mud, sometimes on treeless baked earth, often away from home, they lost all their glamor. Often his work amounted to matching science to impractical governmental regulations. Thoughts of the priesthood again rose after a long dormancy.

"He requested a leave of absence and studied the various novitiates where priests go for training. Jesuits, Benedictines, Dominicans, Franciscans, and diocesan priests—he studied them all and chose to stay home. Five years later he was ordained in the Diocese of Fresno, where he had been serving ever since.

"Back to the ledge.

"With night falling, Pascal stopped yelling. What could he do now? He remembered a movie about a man stranded in a sinking yacht in the Pacific after it rammed a truck-size container that had fallen off a ship. The man was busy trying to save himself: repairing the hole in the hull, bailing out water, studying maps to see where he was, organizing emergency equipment. But Pascal, unlike this man, could do nothing. All he could do besides sit and think was try to get comfortable and stay warm as the temperature dropped. He thanked God he had at least brought his jacket and worn long pants and that he still had a half bottle of water and his sandwich. He lay on his side curled up to keep warm on the mostly flat rocky surface with his backpack serving as a pillow to see if he could get comfortable. There he is. He thought about how hungry he was but knew he had to fast until morning. He knew how to fast: it was a discipline he had undertaken willingly many times. He thought of it as something that priests should do to experience God's undeserved blessings.

"Now, as shadows overcame the remaining daylight, he began to think about the people who would miss him. Tuesday mornings were always busy. Margery Dunn, head of the Altar Guild, would be dismayed not to find him waiting in his office. And Bill Chavez was coming by to arrange for his father's funeral.

"His mind wandered off to Sydney. She had divorced her husband and called him out of the blue one day. She would be happy to see him, she said. This was a little over four years ago. Her son had moved out, her daughter was in college in Colorado, she said. Yes, he wanted to see her. It had been 26 years. Twice since his ordination he had been tempted to abandon his vow of chastity, but he buckled down and got through it. One of the reasons was his memory of Sydney. He knew it could not be as good. It would cheapen what they had. Another was the grace of God after fervent begging for the strength to resist.

"But this time he wavered. She had come to see him in his office. She looked good for 49, her hair dyed reddish blonde, the color it had always been, her eyes as lustrously blue as ever, her figure still trim, her facial skin smooth. Look at her. It was not long before she was in tears. 'I should never have married him,' she said. 'After Chandler, that's our son's name, I knew I'd made the wrong choice. But I didn't permit myself to know. Do you know what I mean? I didn't permit myself to know. Then came Anne, and I threw myself into being a full-time mom. Life became bearable even though I knew he was unfaithful. We fought a lot. In a way I can't blame him. I was pretty bitchy. But I was bitchy because I didn't love him. All this time I never stopped thinking of you, never stopped thinking of the wrong choice I'd made. What it would have been like having kids with you. I know I shouldn't be saying this. I really don't know why I'm here. Except to say I'm sorry. I was stupid.' That's the way he remembered their first meeting after all those years.

"Sitting on his rock facing death, he squirmed inwardly, vacillating between justifying his decision to take a lover and condemning himself for breaking his vow. He knew other priests who had a 'special person,' perhaps a woman, perhaps a man, in one case another priest. He had always judged them harshly—until he became one of them. Now his judgment turned to compassion. They were lonely; they had no idea what they were signing up for in seminary surrounded by friends jumping through the same hoops on the way to ordination. Like teammates, they endured each other's hardships, the families they missed, the sex they had renounced, because they were together. Now it was different. Buddies were hard to come by. In seminary their teachers warned them not to get too close to their parishioners for fear that a secret shared with a special person could lead to jealousy and resentment with the unfavored. Too often loneliness resulted. The soft hoot of a solitary owl somewhere in the shadowy forest seemed to confirm what he felt.

"He used to think that celibacy was a proper requirement for priests because it set them apart for the special respect they needed to inspire in their congregation. If they could give up sex, they had 'street cred,' 'skin in the game,' as Father Hempstead put it in seminary. These are colloquial expressions, Numen, denoting authenticity. Celibacy also prepared them for a life of selfless service, with no natural family to distract them from their spiritual duties. And celibacy served as penance for personal sin.

"He had learned his lessons well, yes, he had, but after Sydney things were different. He told himself that all he had to do was not get discovered and not give her too much of his time and energy. He convinced himself that the role he played as a priest was as strong as ever. He was dependably in his office, said Mass most mornings, worked hard on his sermons, presided at baptisms, weddings, and funerals, and was especially valued as a confessor. And now he understood first-hand the lure of the flesh.

"Now, sitting on his rock, all he needed was God's approval. Hugging himself for warmth as twilight gave way to darkness and stars shone in their places in the heavens, he imagined himself seated before God. *Heavenly Father, have I been a good priest? Have I served you well? Can you overlook my sin? We know that Peter was married, and some of the other apostles.* Then he remembered the difference between being married with all its responsibilities and having a lover. *But I would have married her, you know that. And you know how I love her, have always loved her. The love is real, from the heart, not glandular. It's just that— oh my God, how stupid of me trying to explain this!*

"Hungry and cold, he felt the old anguish he had put aside returning. *God, let me live! Let someone hear my cry! Don't let me die alone out here, my flesh pecked away by cormorants.* He then turned philosophical. *But why do I care what happens to my body anyway? And why do I want so much to continue living? All along I've believed, and preached, that the next world is better than this one. Why am I not rejoicing? Why don't I see this as a first-class non-stop ticket to heaven? Come, Pascal, make your peace with death. Eat your sandwich and drink the rest of your water. Resign yourself to dying, the sooner the better.*

"He took real solace in these thoughts, for he had a deep conviction of the world to come. He had read books about the near-death experience, several written by Christians, and all of them said they didn't fear death any longer. They had died, they said, seen the world to come, and welcomed it. He found their testimony inspiring and credible.

"He felt exhaustion rushing at him and curled up in a ball, his head against his backpack. He wriggled to find the best position on the rock with its subtle indentations. He tried to ignore the cold and hunger. But in place of the world to come he thought of the remaining sandwich as he fell asleep. There he is, curled up.

"The night brought a chill unlike anything he had ever known. Curled up more and more tightly in a ball, he fell in and out of sleep with a different dream remembered after every reprieve from the cold. The dreams featured frightening beings staring down at him. Even so, they were better than the waking cold and the waking ambush of death.

"He woke up freezing in full daylight, grateful that finally he had managed to sleep deeply. Even in his predicament it was possible to feel a kind of early-morning happiness. He heard a rustling sound above him and sat up. Did he imagine it? No, there it was again. Hope surged through him and he cried out, 'Is someone there?' He waited, but no one answered. He stood and called again. Now the same sound, though closer. Above him. He looked up. A whiskered white-tipped mouth on a round head with pointed ears and two pale yellow eyes stared down at him just ten feet away. Fear shot through his whole frozen body as he stared back at the animal. He was prepared to die by starvation, not by a cougar's mauling. There is the animal staring down at him. He remembered to wave his arms and make a loud noise. The animal backed off.

"This different kind of terror awoke in Pascal a different kind of passion for life. He had to admit he was no Christian welcoming a martyr's death followed by heaven as he faced lions ready to tear his body apart. Desperate for an escape, he looked up at the embankment and dug his hands into the soil just as before. Up he went a couple of feet, then down he drifted as the soil crumbled and gave way, his hands burning with pain as wounds from the previous day reopened. He again faced the horror and hopelessness of his position. It occurred to him that the cougar was eyeing him as a future meal. Would he be back the next day?

"The struggle left him feeling intensely hungry. He opened the backpack and began eating the sandwich. He told himself he had to save half for later but could not stop eating. He followed it with three big gulps of water. He reminded himself that a great swath of humans since the beginning of history had starved to death; he would be joining them. Or would he? Muir wrote of an incident much like his: Trying to climb a sheer cliff, he found himself with no way to hoist himself farther up and no way to go back. Almost miraculously a rock he hadn't noticed appeared and he was able to grip it and climb to safety. He remembered another story he had read: shining spirits floated down from the heavens and led a Dakota Chippewa freezing to death to safety. And mountaineers told of a mysterious 'third man' not a member of their party miraculously appearing and rescuing them. Pascal believed in what common people called miracles but did not think of them as violations of the natural order. He believed that spirits were as much a part of nature as rocks and trees. For him they were real and available. He had never thought they would be available to him, but now he considered it. He imagined one prompting a hiker to come his way or at least take the upper trail where his cry could be heard. He prayed fervently for help. A half hour later he let fly the day's first cry for help. A windless still was the only answer.

"Longing for warmth, he began to consider the sun's path. He was on the east side of the gorge, so it might be as late as 11 o'clock before the sun rose over his mountain and warmed his rock. He thought of doing pushups but decided it would be wiser to preserve what precious calories he had left. He sat on his rock huddled in a tight ball and shivered.

"He began to wonder between shouts if what had happened to him was supposed to happen. Was there some lesson to be learned? Had God ordained it? To be only a few feet from a climb to freedom but without hope of achieving it seemed too strange to be a random event. It seemed like a form of torture, intended, calculated. He remembered a story about a hiker who had fallen and gotten his arm wedged under a rock he could not move, and how the man had to choose between cutting his arm off and dying where he was stuck. Just bad luck, Pascal remembered thinking at the time. But back to God. *Heavenly Father, if it be in your will, let someone hear me!* He shouted help three more times and waited.

"He wondered if he were being punished because of Sydney. If he vowed to give her up, would God save him? Supposing He did, would he later regret the vow? Would he be able to live by it? And what of Sydney if he did? How fair would that be to her? He made up his mind not to vow, not to bargain. Even if it meant dying without knowing the vow would have worked. He decided he would die as he had lived: with his love for Sydney intact, not betrayed. He had participated in quite a few deathbed conversions, even given the Eucharist to cowardly souls wanting insurance against hell. They disgusted him. No, he would die as he had lived and trust in God's mercy. No bargaining for him.

"But who or what was this God he called out to anyway? Who was this Heavenly Father? The vast power behind the creation of the universe with its trillion galaxies stretching back 14 billion years? Or was He some lesser God, perhaps a lesser deity assigned to minister to Earth? Who was it that heard his prayer for help? He wondered if prayers to God were intercepted by angels or saints closer to him, caring for him as a person. Could the Creator of the universe really make time for him while suns were exploding or being sucked into a black hole? He told himself it was easy for Jesus to pray to his Father because Jesus' universe was tiny.

"Pascal had been struggling with these questions ever since one of his parishioners, a physicist, brought them to his attention. He prayed to God anyway, hoping that his prayers were heard, but by whom he wasn't sure. Seated comfortably in his swivel chair facing his little bedroom altar, which he decorated with fresh flowers from his garden, he would reach into his depths for the God within and thank him for his life. Then he would begin the requests, which he addressed to a motherly being. This was not the Virgin Mary, but God's motherly face; in time he grew comfortable addressing God as his Heavenly Mother as well as Father. He would pray for the strength to live up to his calling as a priest and pastor, to be compassionate and patient, to listen well, to counsel wisely. He prayed for health—his first colonoscopy revealed precancerous polyps. He prayed for parishioners by name who asked for prayer. He did a lot of praying. Sometimes he found himself praying absentmindedly and spurred himself back into attention.

"Seated now on his ledge, he listened to the faint dee-do-do of a chickadee close by and thought how lovely its sound was. More distantly a woodpecker was rat-a-tat-tatting away as if to awaken the forest from its nightly slumber. Wistfulness settled over him at the thought of missing these common sounds, taken for granted until now.

"He had no energy left for a cry. As the day brightened and warmed, he lost hope he would be rescued. His mouth was sticky with thirst. He allowed himself one big gulp, the last, from his water bottle. The warm day faded—he could already feel the chill stealing over him. As the sun set, Pascal gave up hope and prepared himself to die."

Fruva ended her story and the hologram vanished.

"What a story," Sephia exclaimed. "How did you gather such intimate knowledge of this man? You seem to know his soul."

"As I said, it's in the records for anyone to read. He was its author. There is nothing I had to add."

"So we can assume he died," said Numen.

"He did, but don't be too quick to assume you know how. He might have survived and died later of some other cause. He might have died only a year ago. Anyway, it's in the records. If you're curious, you can consult them, though it would be a waste of your time."

"So you are saying we shouldn't let ourselves get involved with individuals like Pascal."

"Sephia, would you agree?"

"Yes, but I'd want to. How could you not? You'd end by caring for him as if for a best friend."

"Well, let's see. Let's assume the case was carried all the way up to you. Remember, you'll be occupied with planet-wide calamities—war, terrorism, earthquake, and the like. These individual cases will reach you by the thousands, and their suffering will tempt you to get involved. But should you? Should you take this case into your own hands and try to rescue our unlucky priest?"

"He is a good and worthy man," said Numen, "and he has a good impact on many people. He's more than just any old individual. Maybe we should get involved."

"All right, then what would you do?"

"Well, to begin with, I'd try to influence a hiker to take the upper trail. Maybe I'd prompt him to be curious about the same thing as Pascal—he can't be alone in his love of those trees. Then I'd influence him to turn south. But there might be an easier solution. If Pascal's whoops could be heard from the upper trail, I'd try to instill in the hiker a curiosity about what those whoops meant. If the hiker heard a cry for help, I would bombard him with a feeling of compassionate concern. I couldn't control the outcome, of course, but I would give it my best. That's what I'd be inclined to do."

"You are certainly thorough, Numen! But is that what you *should* do? Bear in mind that Pascal failed to take the necessary precautions. He didn't tell Gladys where he was going and carelessly forgot his phone. And he hiked alone. The Creator has designed a universe as a training ground. Mistakes have consequences, including death. Anything less than that and we would not take the lesson seriously. Do you agree? Is that not the way it was on your planet?

"It was."

"And consider this. Death might look like a brutal outcome when faced with it, but we know otherwise. All of us have died, most of us several times—you and Sephia and even I, though in my case it was so long ago

I have almost forgotten—but here we are. *Alleluia,* as Christians like Pascal cry out every Easter. Here we are indeed. Do you want to deprive Pascal of his alleluia—reward him with death for his carelessness?"

"Well, I have to admit it's a complex situation. You're painting death as both the ultimate disaster and the ultimate reward."

"So what would you do?"

"Well, his death would hurt many people who were not careless: his parishioners, even Sydney. He does a lot of good in his little world. He would be sorely missed. Earth needs more people like him. So for that reason I would stick to my first impulse."

"You surprise me, Numen. I am quite impressed. But tell me, would you reprimand him for having a girlfriend in defiance of his Church's statutes?"

"Hmm, I'm not sure—No. No. That rule probably does more harm than good."

"That's debatable. So you choose to rescue our wayward priest?"

"Yes, I think I do."

"What are the chances you would succeed?"

"You'd have to tell me. I don't have enough experience at this level."

"A wise answer. At your level, power, though short of control, is higher than you have ever known. You could probably tempt a passing hiker to climb that mountain. But it seems like an awful lot of effort to give to an individual, even a dedicated servant like our priest, when whole societies are in a state of disruption. Just before you arrived, a new war sprung up when a large country invaded a smaller neighbor. Millions of prayers are flying up to heaven from all over the world. All the time. So you see why, as good a man as Monsignor Debrisson is, you would have been wise to hand off this case to one of your many assistants. Teach your assistants to solve problems at their level. They'll need your guidance and constant encouragement, but don't do their work for them. What would you do, Sephia?"

"Honestly, I'd be tempted, like Numen, to help him myself."

"Spoken from a good heart. But be careful. Earth will test you in ways you have never imagined. You'll be confronted with immense problems. It's a planet of extremes: tremendous wealth accumulated by a single individual greater than the combined wealth of whole countries. Athletes with salaries a thousand times higher than teachers. Saints who wear a mask so as not to harm a passing mosquito and fanatics willing to kill millions of men and women to get their way. Governments that devote tax money to protect a small lizard from extinction and arsonists who gleefully burn down pristine forests with the strike of a match. Earth is a planet badly out of balance. Forces within it, both physical and psychological, threaten its existence. Wars are common, always going on somewhere. Soldiers who fight them are valued as heroes willing to sacrifice their lives. What for? Oddly, not only for their country, but their religion. But the planet has great potential if only you can redirect that heroic spirit."

"It sounds like a planet with a death wish," said Numen wistfully.

"Not quite. It also has millions of exceptionally good souls in the making who will be your allies. All throughout the universe the forces of light are waging war against darkness. Our Parents' hope is that light will prevail in the end—even the demons must be won over. Since our Parents are perfect light, the balance is set up to give the light a slight edge. This is referred to by Earth's largest religion, Christianity, as "God's mercy"—an inspired teaching."

"This is all rather frightening," said Sephia. "I feel a kind of dread at the thought of what's ahead."

"Well spoken. Eight billion souls on that magnificent round carpet we call Earth—look at the hologram, see its continents and seas."

Fruva slowly rotated it, first latitudinally, and then longitudinally, though by now they had studied it so often they could name all the countries. "Seventeen billion altogether counting our world and theirs. From the fate of an individual to that of the whole planet—such is your responsibility. I am always on call if you need me in a pinch."

Wide-eyed with awe they looked at their formidable teacher, as if begging her not to say more.

The expression on her face changed. "Have you noticed," she said in a hushed voice, "have you noticed how still it suddenly is? No breeze, no birds, just a heavenly still." She paused so that they could listen, then continued, "Ah, my children, it's time for us to part."

They seemed stunned. Then Numen recovered and said, "Please, before you go, can you tell me about the ultimate Creator—not our Galactic Parents, but the beginningless Origin?"

"Ah, our Ur-Parents, the Mystery within the mystery. About them it's better to remain reverently silent, Numen. Feel free to call them God, or the Divine Couple, or the Force behind the Big Bang. Remember, none of us comprehends more than a bat squeak of our true nature. Now, children, I must take my leave."

Without touching them, she gave them a loving look and faded out of sight.

4

Journey Over Earth

The Guardians, or Regents, were introduced to their new world at an inauguration ceremony. The site was a vivid-green grassy plain sloping down to a pond with a small island in its center. The setting resembled a fan-shaped roofless amphitheater, but instead of aisles dropping down and separating the seating into seven pie-shaped sectors, wildflower-bedecked hedges did the separating. Delegates from each of the spheres occupied the various sectors, with the seventh sphere flanked by the other six on either side. A forest of firs, spruce, oak, and dogwood stretching up the side of a mountain range until they reached a height that gave way to jagged, snow-dappled crags of granite, reminiscent of a Yosemite or the Italian Dolomites, formed the backdrop. Waiting for the ceremony to begin, the delegates, about 17,200 in all, could pick out villages on the slopes or even hikers on the trails that linked them and provided pleasure for nature-lovers. The splendid setting provided high excitement for the audience, all handpicked as a reward for meritorious service.

On the islet Sephia and Numen stood. The astral technology that might have beamed every facial line of Numen's austere face or every accent of Sephia's mellifluous voice as she gave the address was banned by ancient tradition. Their people would get to know them later.

Sephia didn't expect much from a purely ceremonial speech that had no real impact on astral affairs and kept her speech short. Even so, a silvery cloud formed over the islet when She reminisced about Pollux, her beloved home planet, and then declared her love for her new people. Looking to the side at Numen, she sang out, "We are Earthlings!" The crowd erupted with shouts of support as doubts of being governed by an alien seemed to vanish, then gradually lifted off toward their proper spheres and homes.

Others wanted a closer look and surged forward. Three flew across the water surrounding the islet and were ushered back with a warning. A dozen or more called out their concerns and were gently silenced. Smiles of encouragement and gratitude greeted the new governors.

Finally the organizers took Sephia and Numen in tow and escorted them to their new homes at the top of the topmost sphere, the seventh.

Work began in earnest the next day with a tour of Earth. Five spirits were chosen as guides: Simone, a French geologist; Morgen, a German environment scientist; Rudra, an Indian criminologist; Ying, a Chinese technocrat; and Masako, a Japanese executive in a social media company in Japan. They would show their new governors Earth's biggest challenges. Secretaries were present to record the events, but no other media were allowed.

They took off the next day. From the start everyone missed the much lighter gravity of the astral world as closeness to the Earth's surface weighed them down. It reminded Masako's secretary of the "bad old days," as she put it.

"Down there is frigid Antarctica, white and gleaming," Simone said. Do you see that portion of the continent that has broken off from the mainland? That concerns us. It tells us the ice is melting and will lead to a rise in sea level. Many of Earth's coastal cities are beginning to take the threat seriously, but not fast enough." She looked at the Guardians. "We think this could lead to serious disruptions during your regency." The expression on her face was businesslike, bordering on severe.

They flew northwest toward a vast floating mass in the middle of the Pacific Ocean. "You're looking at plastics that humans use to package food and just about everything else under the sun," said Morgen. "Plastics don't dissolve."

"So it's a kind of pollution," said Numen.

"That's exactly what it is."

They continued west across the Pacific to China and flew over Hong Kong, then farther west over Guangzhou. "Take a look," Ying said, "at the land of robotics and sweat shops. Ten thousand human ants make shoes for a fat American company in that factory down there. Do you want to go inside for a closer look? It would not be pleasant.

They dipped down and entered the building through the roof. Hovering, they watched.

"They work 12-hour shifts to save money. A tiny house to raise a family is their dream. See how their backs are bent over. It's grueling work. Is there a better way? It won't be long before robots take their place and save them the labor. A good thing, right? No, because it will cost them their jobs. This was my country. This is China's problem today."

"What can we do?" said Numen.

Ying shrugged his shoulders while the secretaries made mysterious jottings directly onto their astral brains.

They moved further west toward Afghanistan and hovered over a scene of horror where the blood of 200 Shia Muslims had been shed three days before. Now it was Rudra's turn, and he spoke with passion. "This is what can happen when fanatics hitch their suicide belts to their bodies. Were the killers taking back property stolen from them? Or maybe their women had been raped or their cattle poisoned? What do you think? No, none of these. Their victims were being punished for their beliefs. They didn't believe the right thing, and for that they were slaughtered."

"Back on Sirius we murdered too, but not for that," Numen said. He looked over at Sephia. "Good God!" he said under his breath.

They turned back across the Pacific to the United States and hovered over a house in Los Angeles. Now Masako spoke: "Down there is a boy named Kado, my great grandson, born after my death. I follow his progress. Or I should say his stagnation. You see, he spends most of his waking hours on his phone. When he's not gabbing with strangers he meets on internet forums, he's playing video games. His father, my grandson, signed him up for karate to get him out of the house, but he showed no interest and refused to go to practice. He said he didn't like the other kids. The same for baseball. The same for piano lessons—no discipline. All he wants to do is play video games on his phone. Now he refuses to go to school because online education is available. Do you think he's happy because he gets his way? He's depressed and doesn't know why. My son, like most Japanese, has always had a strong work ethic and has no idea how to instill it in Kado. He doesn't exercise and is overweight. He doesn't care. He is their only child. What is one to do?"

"How sad," said Sephia.

"Many of our astral guides give up on kids like Kado," said Masako. "Their prompts are treated as distracting mental flotsam by these kids and discarded. There is only so much rejection the guides can take."

"Can we go inside?" said Numen. "I'd like a look at the boy."

"Let's hope we find him tuned into his teacher on the phone."

There he was, eyes devouring a game, flashing avatars engaged in combat, fingers zipping across the controls.

The orientation continued with different guides for the next nine days. Stories of success were also included—a reforestation project in California's Sierras, a makeshift emergency room in Haiti operated by Doctors Without Borders, teachers and their students in Uganda excitedly opening crates of donated books, a taxi fleet of three-wheel EV rickshaws waiting for customers in New Delhi, prison inmates practicing meditation in a classroom at San Quentin, a social worker in Nigeria talking to women about birth control options. But most of the attention was directed at Earth's endless problems.

5

The Capitol

~

The new Guardians, also known as Regents, had spent many years in their own planets' afterworlds and had a general idea of how they worked. They had distinguished themselves as leaders and excelled in conflict resolution. They had descended into the shadowlands of their afterworlds to counsel addicts who feared the light of the heavenly spheres. They had lived in lovely homes that suited their status, but nothing like the grandeur of the buildings and grounds that made up their predecessors' estate.

The immense main building referred to as the Capitol stood at the highest point of the seventh sphere, the crown of the astral world. The building was shaped like America's Pentagon back on Earth except that it had four instead of five sides and stood nine stories high. Each side of the square stretched for 270 yards under a pitched roof with long rows of mahogany-framed dormer windows of stained glass. Inside the square was a courtyard that wrapped round a towering dome-topped structure referred to as The Temple. Chartres Cathedral, steeples and all, could fit inside with room to spare. Divinus and Prima had lived in this space, the heart of the Capitol. It was assumed that the new Guardians would too.

Inside the first three floors of the square were meeting halls of various sizes and temporary housing for as many as a thousand visitors from all seven spheres. Colorful murals, tapestries, and framed paintings decorated the interior walls, with hardly a space left empty. Sculptures, fine crafted furniture, and many other decorative features set this floor apart as the place where large assemblies from all over the Astral, and sometimes beyond, gathered.

The middle three floors were divided into hundreds of spacious offices that looked out onto flower gardens, winding brooks, fishponds, grassy fields, and forests farther out. Each of these rooms displayed murals of scenes from Earth arranged by themes. The waterfall room, the temple room, the mountain room, the sculpture room, the bridge room, the lake room—two hundred such rooms showed Earth at its finest. There, the Guardians' closest assistants and cabinet members did the work that ran their world.

The top three floors were meditation chambers. The furnishings were nonlinear, with a beauty abounding in curves and colors unknown to Earth. Spirits preparing for advance out of the Astral into one of the heaven worlds—an event known colloquially as "takeoff"—occupied these spaces. Artists descending from the upper worlds where they lived had projected scenes of nature found in those heights to inspire spiritual work. As many as 320 aspirants used this venerated space.

Outbuildings, some made of precious stones with turrets and verandahs for viewing, or with trellises laden with flowering vines covering walkways, dotted the grounds. "This is the Capitol," the greeters, their faces beaming, had told Numen and Sephia when they first arrived. They hoped to dazzle their new Guardians with its beauty, and they succeeded.

6

War

Sephia and Numen never felt comfortable living in the palatial Capitol building. Its grandeur felt strange and ill-fitted for their private sentiments. Instead they made their home in a smaller structure they referred to as "the cottage" that once housed the head gardener and her family. But they found the Temple useful for another purpose. On top of the dome was a small, hardly visible, open-air platform they called their "special place." High enough to overtop the surrounding trees and buildings, it allowed a panoramic view of the landscape stretching into the distance. In restful moods they would sometimes fly up to it and stand, amazed that all this beauty was theirs to enjoy and rule. The terrain could be compared to the Lake Garda district of Italy with its cypress and pine forests, its olive and citrus trees, its clear azure blue lakes, steep mountains, and villages nestled in valleys or spread out in strips along the length of a clinging meadow. As they turned slowly around and scanned the horizon in every direction, they saw, even with their heightened vision, only a tiny fraction of their world. One of the beauties of the Astral was its sheer size. So far out was its outermost sphere that it covered an area 61 times greater than Earth's land and sea mass. "So much space!" Sephia sang out. Only in the Shadowlands close to Earth was there congestion.

As time allowed, they explored the lands modeled after the less temperate zones of Earth. Africans enjoyed thick forests of tropical foliage, Inuits the snows that they loved and named in its many varieties, and herders endless grasslands that was home to them. Even desert regions flourished, and whales and dolphins plowed through the oceans that lapped at the astral shores. Whatever the inhabitants desired and were willing to preserve—the landscapes and seascapes, the buildings and their furnishings, astral arts and technology, even the weather—was available. Learning and discovery replaced the dirty work of Earth. No digging in the soil or pruning with shears was required. Every forest and dell, every river and sea, every mountain and plain had been created by imagination and willpower. Imagination, industry, and teamwork had produced this amazing world, with every generation passing it a little better to the next.

Yet this world was not heaven. Many souls lacked the curiosity or dedication or humility to learn, and a paralyzing self-made laziness left many stricken with boredom. Others occupied themselves with the events of Earth and failed to outgrow their mundane fascinations. They missed the nightly news, football scores, gym work, even soap operas. They couldn't wait to discuss the latest shooting or politician's fall from grace or the latest styles in shoes or even tee shirts with their friends: anything to fill the tortoise-like tread of time. A few sank into the Shadowlands, where gunless gang warfare and grating, angry music prevailed, the only weapons being insult, hatred, and pointless competition. Time hung heavy, and rebirth on Earth often seemed the best way out. When unwilling to wait for an appropriate set of parents, many began considering any mother that came along. The most desperate flung themselves into an animal's womb, anything to escape the unbearable drag of time.

It saddened Numen and Sephia when considering such waste. What caused such lethargy, such lack of curiosity? They thought that in most cases a traumatic childhood event on Earth was the cause: a child disease, a battering father, a terrifying witness to a mother's rape, violent bullying, slow starvation when the rains failed, relentless neglect, any of a thousand things. It stunned the child into a permanent state of victimhood. When they died, young or old, they brought with them a paralyzed will. They were not bad people—they didn't belong in the Shadows—but they didn't function smoothly in the Astral either. Numen and Sephia regarded this as one of the most challenging problems they faced. But what could they do about it? Over and over they exhorted the healthy to love the victim into freedom.

All this beauty and comfort, this release from the deadening work of Earth—yet so many wanted nothing more than to go back there and do it all over again. Numen and Sephia had never experienced such torpor. They wondered what their Galactic Parents must think when they see it.

Sometimes it wasn't torpor that concerned them but its opposite. Many souls held convictions that drove them almost to a frenzy when challenged. Such was the case when Russians and Ukrainians clashed over Putin's war, which was raging when the new Guardians took up their post. It would be their first big test as Guardians. They had been at their new post a bare two months.

News of Earth was televised all over the Astral—not directly, as if the planet's technology could be taped for an otherworldly audience—but with the help of an array of astral scouts that covered the planet, country by country, region by region. These scouts—or sentinels, as they were sometimes called—patrolled their region and reported back what they found. In this way news of the entire Earth, not only one's own country, was accessible and viewable using the same psychic technology that Fruva used to project scenes on her hologram, though on a much larger scale for general viewing. In this way news of the war reached the Astral's entire population. In addition, soldiers and civilians killed in the war brought their own tales.

The purpose of scouting the planet was to facilitate spiritual aid, not excite factions and rivalries. Sephia and Numen got news of squabbles, then hatreds, then clashes as Russian and Ukrainian partisans lobbed psychic bombs at each other following their deaths. The Guardians had witnessed such wars in the afterworlds of their own planets and seen the damage to basically good souls that such warfare wrought. Many souls caught up in the rage found themselves catapulted toward the twilight regions of the Shadowlands. Recently arrived victims of the war were especially vulnerable.

As the madness spread, Numen and Sephia wondered how to get the two sides to reach agreement. "What a way to begin our regency!" Sephia bemoaned. They debated with each other and fretted over what to do. Whatever they decided would carry risks. If it succeeded, it would cement their authority. If it failed, it would threaten it. In the end they decided to formally address the entire astral world.

They chose a spot where a famous peace memorial, a towering obelisk where 85 heroes from Earth had been sculpted from the ether and held in place by the will of the people. The heroes, 43 men and 42 women, were intertwined on the column as it rose 250 feet toward the sky. Some, like Lincoln and Gandhi, were well known to Earth's historians.

Others, in the majority, were completely unknown. The greatness of their lives became known only after their death.

The Guardians wore garments heavy with symbolism as they stood in front of the great column. Numen's featured broad horizontal stripes of white, blue, and red, the color and design of the Russian flag, in descending order; Sephia's gown the blue and yellow of the Ukrainian flag, also in descending order. They stood holding hands, their bodies so different in appearance, his elongated and thin, hers short and sturdy.

They had memorized and rehearsed their speech. At the nod of the technical director's head, Sephia began.

"Friends, Numen and I greet you warmly yet soberly on this day. Many of you have been following events in Ukraine since the Russian president, Vladimir Putin, invaded that country. Some of you have taken sides and passionately defended one side and condemned the other. Full-scale psychic grenades molded of hatred are being slung back and forth. Hospices designed for the newly dead are being turned into emergency centers for victims of these brawls. In many of our homes a favorite pastime, watching the news, has occupied our citizens to the point of addiction."

"We are concerned," Numen continued. "When we arrived here, we found an advanced planetary surveillance system in place. We were told it helped our world follow the events of the world you left behind at death and that it allowed you to keep in touch with the communities your loved ones lived in. In other words, it served as an outlet for a healthy curiosity about your former homes. In this way, we were told, it kept your kin close to you and facilitated the transfer of healing energy and love to them. More generally, it served as a portal for well-rounded, wholesome entertainment."

"But look what is happening now," Sephia continued. "This war has ballooned into a distraction from the work you are responsible for. Please understand: We're not opposed to entertainment. There are a thousand ways for us to enjoy ourselves over here when our work is done. We are not even opposed to following the war if it doesn't consume us or excite conflict."

"To follow it with compassionate hearts heavy with sorrow is one thing," said Numen. "To get caught up in the blood lust that makes you celebrate the slaughter of your enemy is quite another. And that is what we see around us now."

"Please understand," Sephia went on. "We know the issues. We see the terrible wrong that Mr. Putin is doing. Invading a weaker country that borders yours is never excusable. Ukraine has a right to be outraged. To fight the invader, even at the risk of death, is an understandable response. And the courage to die in battle for a just outcome is praiseworthy and can even be heroic. But there is another side—there always is. Russians will tell you that Ukraine is an artificial country. If you have Russian friends, ask them to explain. They are likely to say that Lenin, then Stalin, then Khrushchev ceded territory to what is now Ukraine, and that Putin is only trying to take back what was Russia's to begin with."

Numen continued: "But these arguments shouldn't concern us. Here is what should. A fair number of cities and towns in Ukraine are uninhabitable, and that list is growing every day. Oil depots and chemical plants are burning. Clean water plants have been blown up. Rivers and wetlands are being laid waste. Harbors are being mined and the global food supply blockaded. Smoke and ash hover over bombed out cities. Bridges and trestles needed to move populations and supplies have been wrecked. The carbon footprint left by armies at war is skyrocketing. Half the country's infrastructure has been levelled, with worse to come as Russia destroys armament sent to the front by Western allies, and the West responds by sending more. Meanwhile nine million Ukrainians have fled their homes, many of them living in countries that welcomed them at first but now want them to go home. Worst of all, there is all the violent dying, soldiers and civilians alike. They die daily in the hundreds."

Sephia: "Ukrainian president Zelenskyy refuses to meet with Putin and discuss a truce. 'Give me liberty or give me death,' said an American hero during their revolution. This is Zelenskyy's policy. Is it a wise and good one?"

Numen: "Dear friends, this is not your war. If you feel you must get involved, then send down your prayers to one or the other president. You might get quite specific. Prompt Putin to resist using a nuclear weapon, which he is threatening. Or prompt Zelenskyy to at least meet with Putin, as the Pope is urging. Nothing might come of it, but at least it would be a start. Send your prompts if you feel they will do some good. Nuke them with appeals to peace! They might make a meaningful difference. Otherwise get back to work. Your home is not Earth, but here in the Astral. I say again: This is not your war."

Sephia: "We especially appeal to victims of the war who have recently joined us. Do not yoke yourself to the ringleaders of this mayhem. Rather, seek out victims on the other side, even those you might have killed if you can find them. Let them see your contriteness. Embrace them if they allow it. Endure humbly whatever emotion they throw at you. Help them digest this truth: You killed them because you were born to your parents and they to theirs—there was never anything personal. Do not allow an accident of birth—whether you were Russian or Ukrainian—to govern your attitudes. The Astral exists to take you beyond that."

Numen: "Forgiveness is critical. No one who persists in hatred can find a home in the Astral. That person will gravitate toward the Shadows. Dear friends, you were made by your Creator for the worlds of light."

Numen and Sephia, wearing their robes, turned and embraced each other. As they did, their bodies seemed to merge, and the contrasting colors of their robes, the colors of the flags of the two countries, faded and disappeared, leaving only a glowing, pulsating white robe with purple at the edges encircling them.

Not all citizens were won over by this appeal. Some scorned the closing symbol of merging bodies and called it a "parlor trick."

"Without boundaries there is no stability," wrote a popular astral journalist, who claimed that for the Guardians to even mention the Russian point of view was an insult to a ravaged, invaded population.

Sephia, who had conceived the "parlor trick" and persuaded Numen to join her, was disconsolate for days.

"It's all right. It'll blow over. Give it time." These were Numen's words of comfort. He hadn't seen this soft side in Sephia emerge so prominently. He was touched by it. His feelings for her deepened.

1

The Children's Religion

Anotoriously difficult case reached the Guardians' attention in their fourth month. It would be the second case to test their wisdom and power, with far-reaching consequences covering the entire astral world. Great numbers were closely involved in the outcome, and passion was already running high. It involved religious instruction for children. How should it be carried out? Basically three options were on the table. Should children be brought up in the religion their parents would have raised them in if they hadn't died? Or should they be brought up in a broad-based faith recommended by astral scholars who deplored religious exclusivism? Or should they be raised with no religion at all?

The Court consisted of eleven jurists serving as advisors to the Guardians. Attorneys were to argue the case in front of them; then the jurists would discuss the case with the Guardians and try to reach a decision. As the executives, Sephia and Numen—listening, enquiring, confirming, refuting, whatever they were inspired to do—would then render their judgment. If they couldn't agree between themselves, the case was hung. This is what happened when the same case came up for Divinus and Prima during the last months of their regency. Their failure to agree created turmoil throughout the astral world and almost led them to divorce each other. In effect Earth's afterworld had been poorly governed for the seven months leading to the new Guardians' installation.

The case had arisen in one of the many Muslim sectors. A decision would shape policy well beyond a single Muslim sector or even beyond the religion of Islam as a whole. Christians were especially watchful. Many who took an interest in astral governance for its own sake but had no skin in the game, no relatives affected and would find the goings-on fascinating as high-quality entertainment. And journalists by the hundreds from all sectors and spheres would be following every twist.

The astral world that Sephia and Numen governed—life after death as it really existed—parted in fundamental ways from the way Earth's religions usually pictured it. If Great Uncle Jeff were a Christian on Earth, he was not a Muslim or Jew or Hindu or Buddhist. He viewed them as wrong in some fundamental way. But when the same Jeff died and found himself in the new astral environment, he would eventually realize that quite a few of his former beliefs didn't add up—for example, he couldn't help but notice that all those people he thought would go to hell lived in the same world he lived in, and all those other people who thought he would go to hell had been just as wrong. Or that the afterlife wasn't at all like what he had been told: Where was God with Jesus at his right hand? And so forth. So he would make inquiries and discover, further, that many souls around him had discovered a new kind of religion—one that rewarded or punished souls not for their beliefs but for their character. Known as the Universal Religion (UR), it appealed widely to those who thought religion important but needed revision. Such was the environment that Numen and Sephia found themselves in.

The Court assembled in a complex outdoor structure of trellises that stretched up to a ceiling composed of spreading flowers of many colors, shapes, and scents. The setting was especially pleasing and harmonious.

On the stage the thirteen stood. Numen, tall, slender, and austere, wore a cobalt blue tunic belted at the waist. Sephia, short and rather stocky, with the usual lovable glow on her roundish face, wore a free-hanging gown of alternating small patches of golds, browns, and beige. They stood at the center between the others, five women and six men, wearing clothing as varied as their multihued characters. Facing them, also standing, were the petitioners and their advisors. Behind them stood thousands stretching back beyond the cover of the canopy, while others hovered closer in under the ceiling of flowers like bees next to nectar.

The case involved a six-year-old Syrian boy named Kamel who had died when a bomb destroyed the home of a friend he was spending the night with. His guardians assigned him to a school for first-graders, where he learned the universal language and received a typical education for kids whose lives were cut off early. He had progressed normally under loving instruction and was a happy kid.

A leading Sunni imam who rejected the "redesigned curriculum," as he called it, demanded that the boy be removed from the school and placed in a madrasa where he could learn the Quran and not be "turned into an infidel." He argued that family came first, and, since his parents were Muslim, Kamel should be too.

One of Earth's leading theologians, who spoke on behalf of the Universal Religion, said that the whole idea of infidels was an "artifact of Earth" made obsolete by a more enlightened point of view. Placing a child in such a school was indoctrinating him in an ideology that belonged to another world. "The same can be said for any other religion that makes exclusive claims to the truth, not just Islam," she said. "Where we are now, we know better."

The final position was argued by a man who, on Earth, was a German-American nuclear physicist and Nobel Prize winner. "Our world, like the world we left behind at death, would be better off with no religion at all. There is no need for religion where we are. Its only use was to reassure us that life went on after death. Now we know for a fact it does, so what is its use? Be done with it, I say."

The three positions were argued at much greater length, but the gist of each was as reported above. At this point the spectators withdrew, and the thirteen went into a long huddle of uninterrupted deliberation. Two days later the petitioners and the crowd reassembled to witness the cross-examination by the new Regents.

They wore the same attire except for two details: Sephia had fashioned for herself a green sash tied around her waist, and Numen had imagined for his head a skullcap resembling a Jewish yarmulke. Many in the crowd looked at each other quizzically, wondering what it might mean.

Numen began by asking the imam, who wore a white turban and a long, flowing white garment covering his body from neck to ankles, if he were surprised to find he now occupied the same world as infidels.

"Yes, I was at first, but then I understood the Quran to be speaking of the world beyond this one. That's where the great separation will occur."

"Where in the Quran does it say you would be living in the same afterworld as Hindus, Buddhists, Sikhs, Christians, and Jews when death came?"

"It doesn't say. But it doesn't say otherwise. Men are fallible, even our scholars. Now we know."

"Could it not be said that everybody in this world is your brother? Look behind you. Men—women too—are eager to hear what you have to say. They stand together as friends, they come from many different traditions. You see it with your own eyes. Do you not see them as equals?"

The imam doggedly clung to his point of view. Finally Sephia broke in: "Sir, you seem to be making a sweeping claim, not one limited to what's best for little Kamil. I thought your argument was that the boy should be brought up in the religion of his parents. Using that logic, you should insist that if Kamil had been brought up by Christian parents, he should be brought up Christian. Would you agree to this?"

The imam shook his head. "I don't care what happens to Christian boys." His voice quivered with impatience and a trace of anger.

"Well, we do." Then she smiled at the imam and added, "I hope you will learn, too."

With that pointed remark, gently delivered, Sephia won the hearts of more than a few in the crowd.

After a brief intermission, the Guardians listened to arguments for the next position, the Universal Religion. Sephia conducted the cross-examination woman to woman. The petitioner, oddly, had fashioned for herself glasses although no one in the astral suffered from loss of vision. Her appearance and bearing suggested intelligence and erudition. "Your position," Sephia began, "claims that religion belongs in our world, but one that's been, how shall I put it, that's been cleaned up—one that avoids disputes over obsolete doctrine and emphasizes the development of good character instead. Can you summarize it?"

"First, UR says we're accountable for the actions we take. India's religions call this the law of karma. We are rewarded for good behavior and punished for bad. This law makes us stop and consider: Should we choose what we selfishly desire, or should we also act for the good of others? No society, physical or astral, can survive long without such a law. Second, a true religion makes plenty of room for this law to work itself out. From the suffering of those deep in the shadows to the joys of the great masters in the highest heavens—every degree of excellence or failure is noted and accommodated. Third, a true religion tells us the universe is governed and loved by an unimaginably powerful, good, and wise Creator."

"So you offer this as a consolation to the imam—you might call it a replacement—for the religion he loves?"

"I'd call it an improvement, a huge improvement. Our divine Parents love all of us, not just a portion."

Sephia, concerned that the imam and other Muslims in the crowd would feel they didn't get a fair hearing, said, "Not just a portion. But some people don't feel loved unless others unlike them are excluded. They don't trust universal love. It leaves them feeling no more special than anyone else. Even children pine to be first in their father's affection. Doesn't the imam have a point?"

"In a way, yes, but look how narrow his perspective is. He assumes that souls like himself are more lovable than others. This is the ego speaking. This is the very thing we must outgrow. To tell our children, the little Kirans in our keep, that they are more special than other children because they belong to this or that religion is simply untrue. Not only that, it's poisonous. On Earth it has led to many wars. In our own world it takes the soul in the wrong direction—back down to Earth instead of up into the heavenly realms. Or even worse, down into the darkness of the shadowlands. We have a solemn obligation to give Kiran the best education available, not the one his parents in their ignorance prefer. Would you feed him stale bread when fresh is available?"

Widespread applause from the gallery greeted this last comment, but there was also some hissing.

Another brief intermission and flashing of information on holographic monitors followed. Then the scientist wanting to abolish all religion took the stand. He was wearing coat and tie, as if still bound to the habits of Earth. After he summarized his earlier presentation, Numen began the questioning: "You admit scoffing at religion when on Earth. You looked at the promise of an afterlife as ridiculous. How did you feel after landing here?"

"Frankly, I was embarrassed. I was wrong, yes, it was embarrassing. How could I have missed something so obvious once I got here? But I was delighted to find myself still alive, even to find some of my old scoffing colleagues. We had a party to celebrate our ignorance." (Much laughter.)

"It might be that you missed it because you hated religion, and since religion came with an afterlife, you rejected that too."

"I'm afraid you're right. Not very scientific, eh?"

"I admire your honesty. The reason I point this out—"

"—I know perfectly well where you are going."

"—is that this bias might be resurfacing."

"I don't think so. As I see it, religion on Earth exists to take the terror out of dying. But life over here doesn't end at death, and we all know it, so what's the point?"

"Do you remember her third point?"

"About God, you mean?"

"About an all-powerful Creator who had a purpose for creating the universe—"

"—in other words, God, yes, I noted it well. But I don't see any evidence of such a being, do you? Does anyone? So why encourage such a belief? In this more advanced world we should be putting the ignorance of Earth behind us. What especially troubles me is the expectation that we should worship such a being. I see that as an absolute waste of time and an assault on our intelligence—and autonomy. I refuse to genuflect to a phantom. We shouldn't encourage Kiran to do it either."

"I respect your need for autonomy. But all these religions, their many faces, teach our children there is such a being, an eternal Parent. Who mentioned worship? In the Universal Religion worship is optional. You might enjoy the way it's done here. It's not what you scorned back on Earth."

"The fact is that in our schools the children are taught there is such a being, a primal parent behind the Big Bang. There is no evidence for such a being."

"Is there any evidence against it?"

"No."

"Thank you. Do you have any objection to teaching our kids about the Big Bang?"

"Of course not. That's good science."

"But is it good science to tell this much to a child but leave out a creative intelligence behind it? Wouldn't that imply that the Big Bang happened on its own?"

"Well, it might have."

"What happens when a child asks the teacher if there was a creator? Surely that question would come up. It always does. What do you propose telling the child?"

The scientist paused a minute. "Tell him we don't know."

"And when the same budding philosopher then asks, 'But doesn't everything have a cause? How could the universe just create itself?' What do you tell him—or her?"

He shrugged his shoulders and shook his head. "I would hate to discourage such wonderful curiosity in the child. I would tell him he has a point and leave it at that."

"Thank you, sir?"

The cross-examination continued longer into the day. Finally, each of the positions was summarized and the crowd dispersed after much applause, as at the end of a concert.

"It went well!" exclaimed the jurists as they reassembled. "It went so well." An air of deep relief flowed out of them. "You stuck to questioning, not proclaiming. Divinus made a fatal mistake," said one of them. "Divinus saw everything with such clarity that he couldn't help dictating the verdict in advance. He's a brilliant soul but came across as biased. Prima couldn't manage him."

"By the way," another said, looking at Numen, "Why did you wear that skullcap? You looked like a Jew."

"Oh, that," he chuckled, "in my prepping for this career, I became fascinated by the Talmud, the way the rabbis reasoned. It reminded me of myself. So I took pleasure in looking the part. I had no idea anyone would notice or care."

The thirteen went into a final huddle to discuss what they heard. Unlike Divinus and Prima, Numen and Sephia were of one mind. "But we would be disappointed if any of you feared speaking out because you saw it differently," said Numen. "The physicist made a good point about worship. We would never require that. But if a child wanted to worship, we would show them how and where it's done, and even escort them to the nearest temple."

"Should their teacher be allowed to bring it up?" asked one of the jurists.

"Yes," said Sephia, "but not recommend it. But their astral mom or dad, or any other adult, or one of their friends could. Anyone but the teacher, who should remain neutral. Speaking personally, Numen and I feel that worship can be a wonderful way to lift the spirit and advance toward higher realms."

All over the astral world, layer on top of layer, with its 9.1 billion residents and vast spaces, spirits had followed the event on their telesets, some in the privacy of their homes, others where they gathered with their friends in their clubs, sodalities, or guild houses. Many kept up with the goings-on in one of the many telegazettes, most of them using the universal tongue, others, mostly new arrivals, the various languages of Earth.

Most of the residents awaited the formal announcement with high anticipation. Everyone had seen pictures of the new Regents, but few had heard them speak or watched their bodies in action. Rumors and speculation based on their histories in faraway worlds fascinated the observers.

Sephia and Numen had agreed to divide the announcement between presenting the facts and describing their personal views. Their advisors suggested a more veiled approach, but Sephia held out for transparency "even if it makes us vulnerable." The more cautious Numen, by now trusting her charisma, supported her. They stood amid thousands of children, aged two to twelve, assembled in seated rows beneath a spreading bower of climbing vines in a glade that gathered them together into an enormous single embrace. The children wore uniforms by grade level that covered the colors of the rainbow.

After the introductory formalities, Numen told the world what happened. "You see these children here, gathered from all over the Earth. Their parents mourn them, their friends miss them, the whole planet weeps for the loss of their talents. So many stories, all of them needing an education, the best we can provide. Behind them stand their teachers."

After referring to the distressing events that led to the recent confusion, he came to the point: "After careful consideration, with input from all sides, we concluded that indoctrinating our children in a religion patterned after Earth, while not without benefit, was not the best we could offer. In the astral world we are closer to the Source; we see things more clearly than on Earth. Death is a portal into a more spiritual environment, a light that blesses us. There is much that our children missed by not having a long life on Earth, but the narrow religion practiced by their parents is not one of them. We decided to spare our children this descent into ignorance. We decided, after careful consideration, against the view represented by our good friend the imam."

With that said, Numen looked at Sephia and nodded.

"Back on Pollux," she began, "we had very little spiritual experience and no idea that a world like ours even existed. Astral worlds? Heavens beyond? I had no idea. What a thrill to discover them. Learned, more advanced souls who preceded us were our teachers. They spoke of even diviner beings who were their teachers. I wanted to meet those beings. By some weird fluke of fate I got that chance. That is when I met our Galactic Parents. That is when I first met Numen. That is when we were given our present assignment, our mission of service. That is when I heard from our Galactic Parents, a source I could trust, that the universe didn't emerge out of nothing but was designed and created and is now loved by our Ur-Parents, our ultimate Father and Mother, the supreme Source. And here is the most astounding thing

46

of all: inside each of us is a speck, an atom of that Being. We call it the soul. This wonderful Being fills the entire universe, every planet, every galaxy, every one of us.

"I ask you: Why should this truth be hidden from our children? The Universal Religion tells them about it. We believe and hereby decree that our schools will adopt it.

"Some of you will be dismayed. You hold out for no religion at all. 'Spare our children this dreaded blight,' you say. But I ask you, where is the harm? The harm coming from the wrong kind of religion is lacking here. No one is threatened with hell or the Shadows because of their beliefs. Those among you still clinging to those old habits of hate and exclusion are like wounded falcons being nursed back to health but still afraid to fly. We think that believing in a divine Source—our Ur-Parents, our God—leads to hope and joy. It enchants the universe. It makes it lovable. But no one is obliged to believe it or practice it. Nothing bad will happen to a soul who rejects it."

"But for those who accept it, may you become like angels. For them, happiness is being in the presence of something greater, something that calls forth awe and wonder. Angels don't praise our heavenly Parents because they are expected to or out of fear if they don't. They praise because they can't help themselves. Praise is the language of delight. Praise is the noise that happiness makes. Would we deprive our children of the knowledge that leads to praise?"

Sephia turned back to the children, lifted her outstretched arms, and said, "May your hearts be filled with praise. May you rest in the knowledge that, in the end, all is purposeful under the watchful eye of the Eternal."

At this point the crowd broke into sustained applause. The older children closed the event with a song of gratitude for the Guardians.

8

A Little History

From the start Sephia felt embarrassed about occupying their mountaintop palace. She was a lowlander by nature and found it difficult to think of herself as better than others. Numen found his surroundings congenial and tried to argue Sephia out of her scruples. "It doesn't mean you're better than others, only that you've achieved more."

On a holiday they were enjoying each other's company in the privacy of a stroll through the east garden with its groves of flowering trees. In the light gravity of the astral world they almost floated along the garden's winding paths, glad to be free of the arbitration courts that took up their time during the first months of their regency. Making peace between rival factions and special pleaders of every imaginable sort left them feeling weary. They might be the appointed rulers of this afterworld, but they were not omniscient. Instead they second-guessed themselves continually and depended on consultants who were better informed but often hid their biases.

As Fruva hoped, Sephia and Numen began to feel a growing affection for each other. In their physical lives they had come close to perfecting the art of putting the common good ahead of their own. It almost seemed that they had matured into lovable beings.

As they glided along, Numen told Sephia the story of his ascent to fame. Sirius lacked the safeguards against emotional upheaval found on less spiritual planets, where a denser gravity acted as a kind of protection against wild, unchecked emotion. When anger turned to rage on Sirius, there was no telling where it would end. When a conflict over a border between its two most powerful countries reached a frenzy, a world war seemed frighteningly possible. War on Sirius would not be fought with bombs and bullets but with lasers. Both countries had perfected the technology and were loaded with weapons—enough to destroy the planet six times over. The advanced civilization that geniuses of every kind had built over seventy thousand years was threatened with doom. At the time, Numen presided over the equivalent of Earth's United Nations. He mixed raw candor, powerful charisma, and a pledge to sacrifice his life if a compromise were not reached, and the opposing sides came to their senses.

Then Sephia told her story. On Pollux her reputation as a heroine was built on the back of an equally risky action. For its entire recorded history, an underclass of Polluxians had been bred and harvested as food for the rest of the population. At first the basis of selection was a stiff, unbending, scaly tail that stuck out in such a way as to require an opening in the back of the clothing. Children who were cursed with this deformity, which emerged with puberty around the twelfth year, were forcibly removed by the police and sent to camps where they were fattened for slaughter. The flesh of these unlucky victims was universally regarded as not only delectable but as enhancing sexual performance. Every child was inspected on their fifteenth birthday to ensure that the tail had not been surgically removed. Removal was a capital offense, and few parents were willing to risk it.

For centuries reformers had been trying to shut down the camps—thousands spread all over the vast planet—but failed. When Sephia's son developed a tail, she surrendered him to the authorities, then experienced a spiritual crisis so severe that she started a podcast calling for reform. As the podcast gained in popularity, her fame grew until it covered half the planet. After years in and out of prison, her relentless calls for reform led to the closure of the camps.

"What an amazing feat. Did you save your son?" said Numen.

"No. But I found him in our afterworld when I passed. We didn't believe in an afterworld, so I was astounded to find him—I was surprised enough to find myself!"

"Did it stick? Did the reforms hold?"

"Yes. From what I've learned, it's like slavery on Earth. A consensus gradually emerges and there's no looking back. The reform holds."

"The same on Sirius. Realizing what mutually assured destruction meant for the planet made everybody wake up."

They walked along whatever path caught their fancy, happy in the warm, salubrious light. Birds twittered and sang their songs while bees buzzed among the flowers. Monkeys swung overhead from branch to branch while chipmunks scurried across the paths' velvety green grass. Numen and Sephia reached a height that provided an unobstructed view of their astral world. Clusters of little towns tucked into forests and undulating meadows stretched out below. Snow-capped mountains stood farther out, with hamlets hugging their slopes. The pellucid air made the panorama vivid and sparkling. Yet it lacked the clarity, the perfection of higher worlds, worlds they had voluntarily given up so they could serve a lower one—their new home, Earth's afterworld.

"Do you miss the world you gave up?" Sephia said.

"I do, but I knew what I was getting into. How about you?"

"Same as you. No, I wouldn't trade it. The challenges facing us tomorrow—that's what we came for."

"I have much to learn from you, Sephia. You delight in service. I don't find it so congenial. You'll have to keep me on track."

"Isn't that what wives have always done for their husbands?" She looked at him hesitantly, wondering if she had gone too far. By now both were comfortable in their new astral bodies. Both chose, after experimenting with different appearances, a stately, dignified, pleasing appearance of 35 years.

They walked along. He was always half a step behind and to the right of her. He liked the way she turned her head to the side just enough to see him. He liked the way her light brown hair bobbed back and forth through a silver hair clip down to her shoulders. There was something very innocent, even youthful about her. He found it hard to believe that she was the great soul that led to her selection as co-Guardian of their new world.

9

Dowry

Fruva had made it clear that deceased spirits living in the Astral could influence conditions on a physical planet like Earth. That was the main point of the exercise with Fr. DeBrisson. Almost as important was whether it was wise to. A case arising in India during their second year on the job would test their mettle in both respects. It began with a petition brought by 22 Indians—male and female, high and low caste, Hindu and Sikh—who had put together an impressively thorough video about a man named Manbir. For the interview they met on the Capitol grounds on a sloping lawn overhung by trees resembling flowering mimosas. A woman, whose name was Naina, was to be their speaker. She had kind brown eyes on a wheat-colored face and wore the traditional sari, with blue and red geometric patterns printed on a golden background. The Regents had spent months studying Earth's various cultures and histories, including India's, but they weren't experts. Once the formal introductions were made and a cordial atmosphere established, they didn't hesitate to ask for more information about India's customs, and the petitioners were happy to comply.

Naina stood and faced the already standing Regents, while the rest of the petitioners sat or sprawled on the lawn behind their leader.

She began by asking the Regents what they knew about the caste system, and both answered they knew it existed but not much more.

Naina then turned to the video and activated it as a moving hologram, just as Fruva had done with the Monsignor. "We'll touch down in Haryana State in North India. There. We are in a village. You see it spread out before you, pleasant, green, with misty purple mountains in the distance. Meet Manbir—there he is, brown-faced and bare-footed, his clothes old and faded, with that forlorn expression. He is the victim of an unbalanced culture, a tragic victim. For every 54 men in his village there are 46 women. Millions more like him are found all over India. These are men who want to marry, have children, raise their status in their family and village, share their life with a wife, give their parents grandchildren, but cannot find a match. Now he is 38 and lacks the wealth to attract a girl. In the local marriage market he is a 'lesser man,' a 'loser.' What can you do about such cases? That is what we are asking you. He often cries out to Krishna, his God, for a miracle. Can you deliver that miracle?"

Sephia's smooth brow knitted as she remembered Fruva's warning not to get involved in individual cases. Reluctantly she said, "Please understand. We have greater concerns, whole societies to guide. Uprisings and wars. Natural disasters. These occupy our time, not individuals like Manbir, however much we might sorrow for him. I am sorry, but, well, I'd send him loving energy and hope that consoled him. I think that's all I, we, would have time for. I'm terribly sorry."

"Please, please hear us out," she continued. "Manbir is a type." She looked all around at the gorgeous scenery that surrounded her, the huge trees, the trimmed paths that entered the enclosure from three sides, a spire in the distance. "Take this Capitol, a magnificent collection of buildings on grounds fit for a sovereign. It's located at the highest point of the seventh and last sphere—the level closest to the true heavens. This is your home, as it should be. You and—" she looked at Numen, "keep order in this wonderful world. You guide your assistants, including your cabinet, and through them your world, our world. But also Manbir's world. Not only Manbir. But Manbir's world. From this perspective, is there anything more you might do?"

"I get your point," said Numen. "There is an imbalance between the sexes all over India. Manbir is just one of millions of victims. But tell me what created this imbalance, this deficit in the number of females. Then maybe we can find a solution."

Sephia and Numen looked at each other, then back at Naina.

"Parents of the bride must pay a dowry to attract a good husband. And that costs money they don't have. Baby boys are celebrated; they bring money to their family when they marry, but baby girls cost their family when they marry. They must pay dowry to the groom's family. That is the dowry system. So what do millions of poor Indians do? They abort the girl babies and keep the boys."

"So it ends with Manbir having no one to marry. I understand," said Numen.

"It involves a whole culture, a sixth of the planet's population. Can you help us?"

"How exactly?

"If we knew, we wouldn't be here."

"Is it a matter of a faulty religion?" Numen asked.

"Not really. Mainly bad politics and poor enforcement. Anti-dowry laws exist in India, but there isn't the will to enforce them. So what can you do? You have great spiritual power at your disposal, some would call it divine grace. Can you put this grace to good use and start a revolution?"

"Excuse us for a minute." He and Sephia walked a little way down one of the paths out of hearing. They came back with more questions, but at least they knew what they were dealing with. It all boiled down to dowry laws. Not even that. Just poor enforcement. They reentered the enclosure.

"We know that India is a democracy run by a prime minister, that much we do know," said Numen.

"Yes, Narendra Modi. Along with Parliament and the Supreme Court."

"But Narendra Modi is the elected executive, the supreme authority, the leader. More than anyone else, Modi runs the country. Modi enforces the law. Is that correct?"

"Yes."

"This is what we will do. We will send down strong prompts to Mr. Modi to enforce the dowry laws."

"We'll throw all our energy into urging him to take the problem seriously and start enforcing the law," added Sephia.

"With all due respect," said Naina, clearly annoyed, "you need to get rid of Modi. He's a man—he'll never feel what we feel. We have a better solution. Send your prompts down to a woman who can defeat him in the next election. Women take family issues seriously. Men don't. We know who the right woman is. We'll guide you if you let us."

"Not so fast," said Numen, shocked at Naina's tone. "Is she the only woman? Would other Indians favor someone else?"

Naina looked back at her colleagues, who shook their heads as if the idea were preposterous. "No, only one."

"I take it there are millions of you," said Sephia. "Your collective energy as much as ours is needed to bring off the result you seek. Don't expect a miracle."

"We do expect a miracle," Naina shot back. "We are all connected to the One Mind that pervades the universe. We can make things happen by willing it. You and your husband are the tip of the arrow, and we are the feathers. You must think big or nothing will get done." Then she turned toward the hologram and reactivated it. "There, look at him now. He is smiling. His wife is wearing a lovely blue and beige sari. Two children are standing between them. That is our goal. Not for him—for him it's too late—but for millions who will follow."

Sephia was torn between compassion for all the unfortunate Manbir's of India and Naina's overbearing attitude. She calmed herself and said, "Naina, we are not omnipotent. Millions of other minds will push back against yours. Vast forces, both down on Earth and here above, heave it this way, then that. We have no control over Earth. All we can do is influence it, with no guarantee of success. Often it's wiser anyway not to interfere. Life can be very tricky. Rushing into things is never a good idea. But we will definitely consider what you say. Dowry is truly a disaster, but there might be better ways to undo it than making a woman prime minister. Let's put our heads together and meet again soon. And bring the woman you favor."

Naina's disappointment vanished as soon as Sephia asked to see the anointed savior, and the petitioners left mollified.

10

Gaia

Probably the greatest surprise awaiting many well educated, scientifically literate, usually atheist residents of the Developed World was waking up to a world beyond death. The British poet Philip Larkin and Finn Urho Keranen were typical victims of the prevailing creed. Hundreds of seminars awaited the newly dead—classes with names like *A Flawed Epistemology* and *Where Science Went Wrong* were available. Others explored long-scorned religious beliefs: *Forgotten Truths* and *Spirituality Is Not a Dirty Word* were popular. Another surprise was discovering that the laughed-at Gaia hypothesis, fancied by New Agers and other free thinkers, was no illusion after all. The Earth visible to all was the body of a living soul that dwelled invisibly within it. Gaia was her name. She had many assistants but no husband or children in the ordinary sense. She considered all humanity her offspring and looked after them as best she could. But her power was limited, and her personal needs sometimes clashed with the wishes of her children. Many referred to her as "the hag" or "the devourer," but others called her "Mother."

Sephia and Numen knew from the beginning of their reign that Earth was a living organism, and it was widely rumored that she could be bargained with, though enquiries brought forth contradictions, some saying she could help, others not. Sector representatives brought their complaints to the Guardians, pleading that they do something. It was up to the cabinet to sift through them and select the most urgent. Thoroughly briefed, the Guardians would then approach Gaia. This would be their first meeting.

It took place on the shores of the Dead Sea, the planet's lowest land point. Gaia's astral complexion was the color of clay, orange with streaks of brown, her hair thick and black. Her dress was yellow and gold, the color of a sunflower. Her waist was tied tight with a sage green belt. Her overall figure was shapely, well-proportioned, and statuesque. The word amazon fit her well, except that her eyes were those of an angel—compassionate, kind, benevolent.

"You must understand," she said minutes into the meeting, "why I have bought you here to this hot, desolate place. This is a single pore of my body, a deep, disfiguring pit. I cannot change it by wishing it filled in. Keep that in mind as we move ahead."

"What should we call you?" Sephia said. "Is Gaia your real name? Some call you Mother."

"Gaia will do well. You are their mother, not me."

"Thank you, unworthy though I am."

"And if you don't mind," said Numen, always the curious one, "is your present appearance your natural shape? Or is it the appearance you chose for this meeting?"

"You are perceptive. No, my natural shape bears no resemblance to what you see. And my size is immense by your standards."

"How immense?"

She laughed. "Doesn't your soul fill your whole body? The planet is my body."

"Ah. Forgive my stupidity."

"Not at all." She gave him an engaging smile, as if to calm any nervousness he might feel over her size.

Down to business, Numen began with a complaint coming from Pakistan. Working with holographic images, he ran through a series of pictures showing the devastation of a recent flood. Buildings crashing into a raging river, bridges collapsing, children being swept away, a third of the country underwater, 800,000 livestock lost. "We don't question the need for floods and droughts, but rainfall in Sindh, the desert region of Pakistan, reached nine inches in a few days. This was unprecedented, unimaginable. These are poor people living in mud huts. Why these extremes? Isn't Pakistan part of your body? I mean no offense, but can you not control it?"

She studied him for moments without speaking, then said, "I see your concern. But there is very little I am willing to divert from its natural course. There are several reasons for this. Think back to the time you grew old, when your old body wouldn't do what you wanted it to. Think of me like that. The wind that mortals feel is my breath. The cyclones and tornadoes that violently destroy my children are like coughs I can control only with the greatest exertion. The moisture that rains down from the clouds is my sweat, which I could control only by limiting my activity. The earthquakes that ravage cities is my gut, about which I have almost no control. This is the way it is with me. Part of the problem arises from the very children who do the complaining. In recent years whole cities are smothering me with their pollution and heating up my seas. This leads to more violent storms and floods like you see in Pakistan. My whole body is heating up as if with a fever. Can you understand my predicament?"

"I hadn't thought of it that way. Still, is there nothing you would be willing to do, even on a small scale? Or is it—forgive me my bluntness—that you are too feeble?"

"It is a bit of both. While Pakistan was flooding, five hundred miles to the east India was in drought. I could have interfered with the weather patterns, but it would have required tremendous energy, with no guarantee of success. Both populations would have thanked their gods. But meanwhile there are a dozen other places calling out to their gods for special consideration. I cannot come close to doing it all. What can I compare it with to make you understand?" She looked out at the still warm water of the sea. "Look out at that. It's so salty that no fish can live in it, only bacteria. That's what your planet would be like if it were not for me. My job is to keep it living, even healthy. This is no easy task. If I abandoned it, it would die, like that sea. No, my calling is not to arrange conditions to fit the wishes of humans. So, with rare exceptions, I let my body—what you call nature—take its course."

"I hate being pushy. But a needy crowd is waiting to hear from us when we get back. You mentioned other reasons."

"Yes, overriding everything is the huge banner spelling out the rules of the game. The same ones that govern you. They all come down to, 'Do Not Interfere.' Isn't that your mandate?"

"But there are exceptions," Sephia pleaded. "You cannot know the suffering of these wretched people."

"Not in any special way, that is true. But I do know that the great river that brought the devastation, you call it the Indus, has flooded like this too many times to count. Children are taught it in their history books. Yet precautions are ignored."

"But people—"

"Besides, human tragedy brings out not only the worst but the best in human nature. It teaches unity. People help each other in ways not imagined during normal times. It jostles them, even bad men, into action that astonishes them. Extreme weather brings suffering in the short run, but progress in the long."

"You paint a rosy picture, but so many die."

"Dear sister, everybody dies."

"But—"

"Over and over they die. But life is not extinguished. I provide them another entry point. That is my calling. My job is not to keep people from dying but to keep the planet healthy."

"So you are not interfering at any point at the moment?"

"I am always interfering in ways that I am allowed."

"Now I am confused. You just said—"

"I cannot stop my body from taking its natural course, but I can combat those who try to alter it."

"What do you mean?"

"Spirit on spirit is allowed. Spirit on matter is not. But there are hoodlums who interfere where they are not allowed."

"What do you mean?"

"Demons lack the power to create a hurricane or tornado, but sometimes they find the strength to change its direction. They latch onto it and target a region or a community or even a neighborhood. I send them sprawling and howling and cursing. But there are far too many for me and my assistants to catch them all."

"Good God. So we can never know whether you put them to rout or not."

"That's right. And it's better you didn't. Dear sister, imagine the tumult if you did, and if you told everyone where I succeeded—and where I didn't."

"Yes, that would be bad. So you have a big heart."

"Yes. But also the big picture. The total picture."

"Can you help us understand more about it?" asked Numen, breaking in like an over-eager child.

Gaia laughed from the belly. She began to speak, then began laughing some more. Finally she said, "Numen, I have heard you are always pushing, so eager to understand. What a blessed trait. One day you might house a planet of your own. Then you'll understand."

11

Depression

Delegates from all over the Astral had been carrying their grievances to the Regents almost from the day they arrived. Judging by their persistence, two especially stood out: malnutrition and famine in Africa, and the epidemic of depression and despair in the developed world. Recent deaths confirmed what long-time citizens in the Astral had known for a long time. Many of them watched Earth helplessly as their loved ones died from one or the other. These watchers came in groups to the Capitol to demand action: "How can we put an end to this?" That was the plaint Sephia and Numen heard over and over.

The first was as old as civilization itself and seemed to have no remedy, but the claim that progressive elites in the West were dying of melancholy despite every material advantage presented a novel challenge that might have a cure. The Regents decided to act on this and arranged a conference.

The scene was a grassy open space, a lawn where the dead who flooded the Astral's overcrowded hospices during the First World War had been assembled and registered. Now, more than a century later, the Regents were expecting a medium-size crowd to watch the action. What drove tens of millions of prosperous people, many at the height of their careers, to take antidepressants? Why did so many people of means hate their lives so much that they overdosed on sleeping pills or swallowed fentanyl or put a gun to their mouth rather than face another day? Why was insomnia afflicting a third of the adult population who were dog-tired and needed nothing so much as sleep? Why did kids prefer the fantasy of nonstop video games over healthful outdoor sport or the society of real people? What caused depression on such a broad scale? These were the questions Numen and Sephia hoped the delegates could answer.

Theories abounded. "For many people, time that used to be spent solving everyday problems goes unused," said one delegate. "Think of our ancestors: they had to wash their own clothes by hand, they had to go to different stores to buy the food they needed, they had to go to the bank to get money or pay the bills, they had to travel to libraries to get information. They had to write letters on paper and mail them at post offices or drop them off at letter boxes. Further back they had to walk or ride a horse to get places. Even further, they had to clear the land of trees and grow their own food. They had to sew their own clothes and darn their children's socks. They had to cut grass with scythes and play games in the fields they cleared. A doctor might be a day's travel away. There was not enough time to be bored. Now there aren't enough meaningful activities to do and too much time on hand. Like a clammy fog that never lifts, an unbearable boredom too often sets in, with deadly consequences."

Another was television. One of the theories was that TV ads promoted a rosy sense of the world that was unreal. They promised exotic vacations with beautiful mates to enjoy them with. They displayed shiny new cars, gorgeous clothing, unaffordable jewelry, athletes making prodigious salaries with all the glitz that with them, and free sex. All this led to discontent with what one had. Another theory was that television led to isolation. "Earlier generations," said another delegate, "had to find entertainment by visiting neighbors, sitting on porches, and trading stories. But television had more interesting stories to tell and in time replaced the neighborly visit. A self-imposed isolation was the result. People grew more cut off from each other and lonely."

Another theory said there was too little time for leisure rather than too much. Another identified declining educational standards due to underpaid teachers, another too few good jobs with adequate pay. Another claimed it was demonic attachment or possession leading to schizophrenia or bipolar disorder. Another the loss of religion.

This last captured the widest attention. Philip Larkin, widely acclaimed as Britain's greatest post-World War II poet, made an impassioned presentation blaming "the godless, secular culture" he grew up in as the overriding cause of the pessimism, cynicism, and unhappiness gripping the Western world. He died in 1985 and spent the next eleven years "mashing my way through the Shadowlands," as he put it. His presentation riveted the audience:

"Early in life I was made to feel that religion and all it represented was nonsense. As I put it in one of my poems, Anglicanism was a 'vast moth-eaten musical brocade/Created to pretend we never die.' God, eternal life, an afterlife where good and evil are rewarded and punished, angels and saints, all of it was magical thinking. Can you imagine my embarrassment, even my anger, when I woke following death and found myself in a world with spirits, with angels and saints, with widespread, almost unanimous belief in a Creator? Can you imagine how appalled I was to find that I, Philip Larkin the nonbeliever, the sometimes scoffer, was not only alive in a world of spirit but was himself a spirit? How could I have gotten it so wrong? That is what I asked myself a thousand times? How could this have happened? I know the answer now. I know it all too well. It was the culture I grew up in. It was our most prestigious scientists telling us that the universe had evolved all by itself, that people who believed in a God who created it were fools, at best deluded theologians, not worth taking seriously. And I didn't take them seriously.

"As I look back at my life, I see how the rejection of religion stifled my natural ebullience at a young age. I remember an early meditation on the meaninglessness of life in a godless world. I wanted to be thought of as smart, to think of myself as smart, even if it required me to believe in a barren, unloved universe that condemned us all to an endless nothingness at death. 'No touch or taste or smell, nothing to think with, nothing to love or link with. Not to be here, not to be anywhere, and soon; nothing more terrible, nothing more true, the anesthetic from which none come round.' That's what I wrote in my poem 'Aubade.' Horrible thought. I saw it all too well, yet foolishly endorsed it."

"Even if this bleak thought were true, we would derive no comfort from knowing it. All we could get from it was the satisfaction of not being duped. So we partied on, told ourselves we were happy, that death was nothing to fear since it vanquished all regrets. Yet even as we told ourselves this lie, the skull, as William James put it, was all along grinning in at the banquet."

Philip stood aside. Urho Keranen, a Finn who had prided himself on his "principled" opposition to the Christian teachings he had grown up with, took the podium. "I am grateful for Philip Larkin's heartfelt confession, but his views are as different from mine as a Helsinki winter from a Southampton summer day. Like Philip, I rejected my Christian upbringing early in life, and for some of the reasons he mentions. Like him I had my self-respect as an educated man to consider. But I never suffered from the anxious dread he describes. I accepted death as the end of life and was grateful for the life I had, for it was a good life: nurturing parents, a good marriage, two successful children, a satisfying career as an engineer designing ships, and a retirement party that left me in tears of gratitude. You might say I was lucky and that a different set of circumstances would have led to a life experience more like Philip's. But I would deny this. I looked upon life as a banquet staged by a generous host and death as its end. To resent death would be like blaming the host for not extending the banquet indefinitely.

"Now, as it has turned out, the banquet has in fact been extended! And I am happy for it. But I do not fault myself at all for failing to see the future. In fact I pride myself for not seeing it. The evidence we had at the time pointed in the opposite direction. In other words, it would have been wrong for me to see things as they were, and it was right to see things as they were not. Which brings me to my point: I do not believe we are meant to foresee a future life. I do not believe that was our Parents' intent. It would have enfeebled us, distracted us from the work we needed to do in the present on our planet. For that reason I will discourage every attempt to seed the planet with 'intimations of immortality,' as your Wordsworth put it, and as Philip would have us do.

"Finns are a hearty lot. Our winters are brutal and long lasting. We have adapted. Do not ask us to lapse back into a second childhood, a jacuzzi of hot moisture that saps the energy out of us. Leave us alone. Then, when it is time, we will discover, not that we made a mistake, but that a completely unforeseeable and wonderful surprise was awaiting us."

And with that Urho stepped aside.

An American tycoon and billionaire told how he worked hard all his life and enjoyed seeing his businesses flourish and make him rich, but was distressed that he couldn't awaken ambition in any of his three sons, one of whom took his life. "Did my wife and I raise him wrong? We gave him everything he needed, every advantage, and it ended with him having nothing he had to work hard for—we robbed him of every incentive. For him religion might have helped. It might have inspired him to become a philanthropist, to labor as a servant of the poor. He might have done much good by following Jesus' gospel. We didn't even give him that. So what am I saying? For me, I didn't need religion. My life was full of meaningful work and the pleasure of having power over a great many people. But for him, let's just say I didn't know how to guide him. I was the worst of fathers. His mother had religion and took him to Mass until I bullied her out of it. So I am ambivalent. Religion can be good for some but a waste of time for others. Those are my thoughts."

Chico Xavier, a spiritist medium and author revered as a saint by his fellow Brazilians, spoke next. "First let me say that my thoughts aren't worth much. On Earth, spirits spoke through me and wrote my books, hundreds of them. They guided my hand and wrote correct Portuguese even though I quit school at fourteen and went to work to help feed my family. They had two goals. They wanted to prove their world existed, and they wanted to help suffering people on Earth. I was an instrument in their hands. Much of my time was taken up channeling letters they wrote to grieving parents and grandparents. These sad people found comfort hearing that their loved one was alive and in a good place. If you take this away, depression follows. So I stand with Philip."

After more speakers had their say, a woman with a face and aura reflecting a rare degree of compassion took the podium. Sephia had persuaded the woman to close the convocation as a way of bringing it to a proper close. The woman was the Catholic saint Mother Teresa of Calcutta. She was no longer the bent-over old nun in her white habit with blue stripes, but youthful, erect, and glowing. When an advanced spirit descended from one of the true heavens to teach, there was always a flurry of excitement. "Let us not talk of outcomes," she said. "We should bring our message to the suffering souls of Earth in any way we can. And that message is that life never stops. What souls do with this great truth varies from soul to soul and is unpredictable. We should leave the rest to God."

Over the following weeks thousands of volunteers scoured the astral communities for ideas to bring back to the Regents. A Muslim businessman from Gaza, where unemployment had reached 50%, said, "Discourage reincarnation. Then we could roll back Earth's population and reduce the unemployment rate." A French woman described herself as an atheist who had nostalgia for the Catholicism she practiced as a child. "Make religion more attractive by making it more rational," she said. "Get rid of virgin births, an all-male Trinity, Christ's return to Earth, and all those other medieval dogmas. Keep what's essential and true." Other ideas ranged across a broad spectrum. A man who lived alone in the forests of British Columbia suggested getting rid of the internet and all social networking. "Destroy it!" he howled like the wolves he lived among. "Then everybody will be so busy surviving that they won't have too much time on their hands."

But how was all this to get done? Chico Xavier called for spirits to bombard mediums at a pace unparalleled in human history. "The spirits who came through me in Brazil made a big difference in that country. It's the most spiritual country in the world. I'm communicating through my old friends back there. The rest of the world is beginning to pay attention." A college professor from Wales agreed with Chico's optimism but for a different reason. "The young are beginning to reject materialism. All that's needed is for enough of the old guard, the baked-in materialists, to die. We don't need to do anything. It'll take care of itself."

In the end there was no consensus. The conferees went away with a better understanding of the problem but with no solution. One muttered to a friend, "At least we're not as likely to repeat our stupidity if we reincarnate."

"What do you think, Numen? We didn't have much to offer," said Sephia as they flew home.

"I found myself agreeing with most that was said. Everyone made a valid point."

"But the truth is the truth, and for me the nun spoke it. You don't agree?"

"I do agree. But physical planets disguise it. It's up to us to break the disguise. That's the challenge that makes life so worthwhile, so much fun."

"So you think the Creator intended it that way."

"I do. Don't you?"

12

The Suicide Game

Delphus, one of the eleven, was noted for his unusual insight into the afterworld's problems and how to fix them. Among Numen and Sephia's advisors, he seemed the most likely candidate for promotion to a higher world. He took on the appearance of a man nearing 70, an unusual choice. Back on Earth he had blemishes of dark pigment on the side of his forehead, and he kept them in the Astral to ward off vanity. But, strange to say, he enjoyed gambling, a habit carried over from day-trading on the Earth's stock exchanges. Since money didn't exist in the Astral, he dealt in the currency of prayer. He bet on spirit helpers as a man on Earth might bet on a horse and had organized an astral game with millions of followers. The object of the game was noble and profoundly serious, yet at the same time it brought pleasure in an odd, questionable form. There were winners and losers. Played like chess, one on one, you won by toppling a devil-doing spirit trying to claim a victim on Earth. You lost by failing. The competition inspired intense dedication in the players, long bouts of intense prayer, even confrontations with the dark spirits doing the mischief when possible; thus the nobility and ultimate seriousness of the game. Players were rated by their record of success and failure. Masters evolved over time; as in taekwondo, degrees were awarded, the highest being the tenth. Many different playing fields developed: child abuse, rape, murder, theft, character assassination, cruelty, infidelity, and the many kinds of addiction. Delphus' favorite game was suicide. Spirit guides brought him the candidates. His competitor would choose one of them and leave him the other; Delphus, the more skillful player, or "knight," always allowed his opponent first choice. Since inventing the game, he had managed to steer 80% of his "patients" down on Earth away from the fatal choice. His opponent knights triumphed 53% of the time. Delphus had lived in the Astral 64 years.

When the new Guardians first learned of his prowess, they were mystified. A year into their term they asked for a private interview at his residence. He showed them the gorgeous murals on the inner walls of his home, then invited them for a walk through the woods and meadows that made up his property. They walked side by side along a wide path that weaved desultorily through the buoyant light, with Sephia in the middle. A warm breeze soughed through the trees to the accompaniment of birdsong.

"Dear friend," Numen began, "as you must know, we value your advice more than we can say, and we have often noted and even wondered at the joy that seems never far from you. And your sense of humor has brought us many a smile in the months we have known you. But we are puzzled by the—by the game, the sport you make of suicide. We are aware of your effective service to souls contemplating the deed, but, well—"

"What he's saying," Sephia broke in, "is that you seem to be playing with death. You seem to be trivializing something that should inspire deep uneasiness over what's about to happen. It's like—I learned this from my study of Earth's maxims—like fiddling while Rome burns. I think that's how it goes. We want to hear how you justify the game— if I'm not mistaken, you do call it a game."

Delphus stopped walking and turned to face the Regents, who also stopped. "I do call it a game. We get pleasure from success, from winning. Why shouldn't we feel pleasure when we repulse a demon? But pleasure is not the aim of the game—it's a byproduct. We play to rescue. That's our goal."

"That's well and good," said Numen, "but you seem to be competing not with a demon, but with fellow brother or sister spirits playing the game. You tabulate the results, you keep records. There are winners and losers. There are even champions and medalists. All this does is puff up the ego. Isn't our goal to advance beyond that? Shouldn't it be enough just to know you've succeeded, and a troubled soul lives to see another day?"

"You've got a point, Master, but we're not as advanced as you'd like us to be. To get the utmost out of us, it helps to create a competition." He gesticulated with his arms and hands, extending out from his body. "Competition builds character. Don't you agree?"

Numen looked at Sephia. "He has a point."

"I don't think so," said Sephia. "Competition builds skill, it develops craft. But that's different from character. Character comes from one thing: service. You can't trick yourself into being a servant. You can't turn it into something that gives you pleasure. Service is always difficult."

"At our level, yes," Numen added. "It becomes easy once we ascend. When service becomes natural, then we are ready to ascend. Ease is a mark of maturity."

"But at this level," said Delphus, eagerly breaking in as if sensing a kill, "we are *not* mature. That's the very reason for competition. We've still got too much Earth in us. Craft, skill, call it what you will. The point is that competition works with souls at our level. It makes us work harder. It brings the best out of us. As a result demons are routed and suicide thwarted." Delphus beamed. "Do you see my point?"

Numen smiled, chuckled, and then shook his head. "You're relentless, friend, irresistible. I need to confer with Sephia. We need to think it over. We'll get back to you soon. In the meantime, carry on." Again Numen shook his head in puzzlement.

Back home Numen and Sephia tried to reason their way to an agreement. Long ago both had mastered the art of listening to opposing points of view and either arriving at a compromise or graciously conceding to the opposition. They were gifted peacemakers and usually brought the opposing sides to a compromise. In large part it was this skill that led to their appointment as regents. But in this case they were pitted against each other, and compromise seemed out of the question. Either the game went on or it was terminated. They were still far from agreement.

"Back on our planet," Sephia said, "there is an animal that carries a somewhat disagreeable odor. Not like the Earth's skunk, which has a revolting spray. This animal, known as a zharka, has reddish-brown fur and three stripes down its back, rather like a giant chipmunk. Its green-eyed head is shaped like a fox, and it moves with the impressive stealth of a fox, but the odor of its stripes is off-putting. Delphus is like the zharka. He is very handsome, almost as if enjoying a royal pedigree, but his game leaves a foul odor. The astral world is less lovely because of it."

"Hmm, allow me to use a different metaphor," said Numen. "Do you remember how we talked about the geranium flower on one of our orientations? Our guide used it as an example of Earth's ambiguity. Do you remember? You thought it smelled bad, but I was intrigued by it. The guide said it was used in perfume. I think Delphus is like the geranium. Think of his games as perfuming the afterworld by lessening the number of suicides."

"A clever analogy, husband. Usually you're the idealist, but now you've turned pragmatist. I'm not persuaded. Delphus is doing the right thing but for the wrong reason. There is no virtue in what he does. He has left the highway of ascent and turned down a backroad leading to a dead end. Better if he had done the wrong thing with a good heart."

"Better for him perhaps, but not for his customers," Numen shot back.

"Customers?"

Sephia visited Delphus in his mansion in a final effort to change his mind—such was her confidence in her growing powers. But she failed. As a compromise she and Numen thought they might restrict the gamers to one case per year but then changed their minds. Neither was happy with the outcome, but in the end Numen won Sephia over. "A suicide is worth more than a game," he concluded. Delphus had his way.

13

A Classroom Visit

Tens of thousands of secular public schools for orphaned children covered the astral world. They served all ages, from pre-kindergarten to high school, just as on Earth. But there was a difference: They doubled as homes, and teachers served as vicarious parents. It wouldn't be exaggerating to say that all the kids were being home-schooled. Discipline problems surfaced less often than on Earth since physical diseases didn't exist and the environment was ideal. Still, a small subclass of kids came into the Astral with memories of terrifying abuse. Many more had died of starvation or disease in countries where poverty was endemic. This latter group comprised by far the greater number of kids. Relatively few came from the affluent West. What all the children had in common was an astral intellect that excelled their physical intellect . The damage done to the children of Earth by alcoholic mothers or abusive fathers, all the scarring that trauma produced on the children's fragile psyches, took its toll in the Astral, but not directly on the astral brain. The kids progressed much more rapidly than on Earth.

The children differed greatly in the memories they brought from Earth. In this area scarring often ran deep. Every school had experts specializing in psychology—and love. For it was love that these damaged children needed—and got.

"I have to get out of this castle on the hill," Sephia told Numen one day after a long meeting on Earth's troublesome gender issues. "I'm going to drop in on a school, a school for ninth graders. I need some fresh air."

Numen seldom showed surprise; he was the one with the cool head with everything under control. But surprised by this announcement he was, and it was clear that he had reservations. "But you're this world's governor. Would that be fair to the teachers—just to drop in?"

She laughed. "How evasive you can be, husband. Your opposition has nothing to do with my being fair, but everything to do with the extra burden I'll be placing on you." She lowered her head but lifted her eyes, her lips lifted slightly at the ends into a canny grin.

He smiled and said, "I'll manage." She often got her way, but never by pressure.

She chose, almost at random, a 14-year-old's class in a sector that hovered high over London. The 26 kids knew who she was and had given her permission, through the head teacher, to ask some "hard questions."

When she stepped into the classroom wearing her traditional robe of Earth colors, they rose in awed respect. Yes, it was really she, the very being they had seen often on their telesets since her arrival seven months ago; the one they had written reports on, with stories to tell about her lives on a planet called Pollux, where she saved children with tails from being eaten by cannibals and had an earlier career as a teacher of 15-16 year-olds. Most of them had heard the stories. She was the one that people sometimes colloquially referred to as "the Goddess." And now she stood before them. They scarcely believed what was happening.

"Relax, young friends," she began, her motherly smile radiating a welcome that at once put them more at ease. "I know you're expecting me to tell stories, but I'm here to listen to yours. What are your stories? Where did you come from? What brought you here, and where do you see yourself going? Come, come, don't be bashful."

A tall thin boy gingerly raised his hand.

"What is your name?"

"Howie."

"Howie. Tell me, is the story you are about to tell known to your classmates, or will we all be surprised?"

"It's a deep dark secret," he exclaimed with a big-eyed guffaw and a rather goofy smile on his face. His classmates turned toward him— he sat in the back row. "Naw, not really. I just wanted to break the ice."

A collective groan followed.

"Sorry. We all know each other's stories, but Fiona's is the best," he said.

There was no mistaking where she sat, as all eyes turned toward her. Her light brown hair was pulled back into an ordinary ponytail, but her intense eyes caught Sephia's attention and suggested a history that was unusual. "Fiona, don't feel obliged, but if you're willing—"

"It's okay," she said with a quick nod of her head.

A breeze blew into the classroom, which was surrounded by open windows and roofed by a large spreading oak that let in thin, wavering streaks of sunlight.

"I got here about a year ago, so I have more experience of Earth than most in the class. That's about the only thing special about me. Except maybe that I could see spirits. Ever since I can remember, I could see a special boy who visited me from time to time. He was about my age, maybe a little older. He just kept showing up from time to time. It was strange. I felt sure I knew him from somewhere but didn't know who he was. And of course he was dead. I mean—I mean he was like we are now."

"Dead," chuckled a boy who seemed amused by the irony of being dead and alive at the same time.

"So he was here when you came over," said Sephia.

"Yeah."

"Did you meet him? Was he waiting for you?"

"Yeah. He was overjoyed. You see, he didn't expect to see me for a long time."

Sephia waited for her to continue.

"I died of a brain tumor. He told me he was my twin brother, but he was stillborn."

Another pause. "What happened next," said a voice.

"He told me we had loved each other in a previous life but were both married to someone we didn't love. We were wild about each other and violated our vows, hurting our spouses and destroying our marriages. He died shortly after his divorce while I continued to live another thirteen years, always missing him. As soon as I died, we made plans to live together happily, blissfully, forever in the Astral. But our guardians intervened. They approved of our love, not our passion. They arranged for us to live together, not as lovers, but as twins. We would share our lives as brother and sister in a new life, which was both reward and punishment. It wasn't what we had dreamed of. But it was something good, something very good. They saw it as a way of curing us of an unhealthy, reckless passion. That was the plan, the plan that our guardians came up with. But, as you see, it didn't work out that way."

"Does the story end there?" said Sephia.

"No. When I died a year ago, he was waiting for me. When I opened my eyes after I woke up, there he was, looking into my eyes. I had come home, he said."

She paused and gathered her thoughts. "He was farther along than me. I had to relearn the universal tongue and begin a new life here. And we went to different schools." Puzzlement registered on Fiona's face. "He wanted us to take up our lives where they left off, but for me the passion had cooled. I was more interested in a new life with a new set of friends. It seemed as if the thirteen years I spent on Earth with my mom and dad but without him had freed me to—I can't explain it, but I'm glad of it."

"Do you keep in touch?"

"He sees to it that we do. You know, it was a shame he died at birth. He might have found what I found."

"What was that, Fiona?"

"That I was done with Earth. I want to move on."

Sephia responded with a smile that touched even the rowdiest boy. The class couldn't have known the smile had been reared and refined in a higher world, a world Sephia would reenter when her present term of service expired.

The class was now relaxed, and student after student shared their stories. Most dreamed of a new life on Earth, a restart, the one that fate had deprived them of. Even those who had died of starvation hungered for another adventure in flesh. One boy joined Fiona in her wish to avoid it. Sephia listened intently as she peered into the souls of these children—each of them, as she put it to herself, a tiny droplet of divinity at play in a universe of infinite possibility.

14

Gender

One of the many planet-wide problems brought to the Regents' attention concerned sexuality. By many accounts sex on the planet, at least in the West, was increasingly decoupling itself from love. It was an accepted way for total strangers to link and have pleasure. Many people condemned this development and linked it to the loss of traditional moral values bred by religion. Others were concerned with a different kind of decoupling. People in larger numbers than ever before wanted to be decoupled from their very bodies. Men and women did not want to be what their biology dictated—some even chose surgery to reverse their sex. Others thought of themselves as "gender fluid"—they identified themselves psychologically as male for a while and female at other times. They said that switching back and forth was completely out of their control and had nothing to do with their physical gender. Sephia and Numen were left with the impression that all this was causing widespread unhappiness, including high rates of suicide among those affected.

"All over the planet disturbed people, especially teenagers, are mutilating their bodies to anatomically reverse their sex," a leading sociologist said at one of the Guardians' open sessions. "I am asking if there is something we can do about it."

The Guardians collected input from all sides and eventually put together a task force to address the problem. It included recently deceased trans people who hated their biological sexuality, doctors who had performed surgeries on some of them, scientists from various fields with their "solutions," and psychologists who had done research on the probable causes of "gender dysphoria in a wide variety of cultures.

Numen and Sephia became convinced that the problem was universal and required their attention. "What could be the cause of such a deviation from the usual course of evolution?" So they wondered. "In every world we are familiar with, the bodies of male and female are designed to procreate the race. That there should be a few deviations is not surprising. But so many—why?" They called for a hearing and staged it in the grand mansion they refused to live in. "Maybe the building will be good for something," Sephia said.

Twenty-two experts gathered in the "great hall," more like an indoor arena than its name suggested. Divinus and Prima had designed it for just such a purpose. Media of every kind were present—a daring experiment in transparency for such a volatile subject. Earlier Prima had called in artists to patch and redecorate the neglected mosaics. She enjoyed watching them hover like hummingbirds next to the discolored, drooping scenes as they psychically restored them to their original design.

The Guardians orchestrated a program that had experts and experiencers alternating their presentations topic by topic. Some of the experts had been famous in their days on Earth. Adrienne Rich and Ian Stevenson were two of them. Religious conservatives who deplored the "break with nature" could be depended on to butt heads with social scientists who called for a complete divorce between one's "physical equipment" and one's "true nature." Trans people would describe what it was like being at war with their own bodies, and surgeons would describe what they did to "reverse the gender" of their patients. Gays would describe the pain of being cast out from their families to live as exiles in their society, even at the risk of death in some non-Western countries. Psychologists would offer theories about "gender dysphoria," ranging from uneasiness to distress, and might even suggest possible solutions "that could be passed down from our world to theirs." Putting together the panel and staging the event demanded more resourcefulness than any venture the Regents had so far undertaken.

The panel sat in their robes on a recessed stage in two semicircles, the nine experts in the first row and the thirteen experiencers in the second. They looked out at the regents seated side by side, with their cabinet members to their left and right. Behind them 130 invited guests, most of them reporters and historians, fanned farther outward and upward. A raft of technicians tasked with bringing the event live to the astral world had taken their positions near the ceiling of the hall.

A biologist began the program by stating the obvious: "From a strictly evolutionary view, the male and female bodies have been designed to propagate the species, so it's natural for men and women to have sex in the normal way—that's how you get to the goal." Anticipating resistance, he parried that it was also normal for the sexes to cohabit for pleasure alone. "But the anatomical, complementary structure of the male and female bodies dictate how to arrive at the pleasure."

A venerable Tunisian cleric and an evangelical American, both astral veterans, vouched for the conservative view, declaring that it was "unwise" to deviate from the "visible plan of the Creator."

The famous feminist and lesbian Adrienne Rich, who died in 2012, gave a brief account of her life: marriage, three sons, divorce following therapy, and eventually how she came out as a lesbian. "Cohabiting with a man was unnatural for me, not the other way around." She told how she had been a victim of her culture's compulsive heterosexuality—that was the phrase she used. "I was force-fed by my culture to enjoy sex with a male because anything else made me a deviant. Once I saw the lie, I devoted my life, my essays, my poetry, my passion, to celebrating homosexual love."

One of the experiencers in the second row waved her hand so frantically that Numen recognized her, "I know it's not popular, but I must speak. How could the Creator design a person who wanted sex with somebody of the same sex, resulting in a couple who couldn't reproduce—a person whose nature, if followed by all of us, would lead to universal extinction? I say that the Creator has never made such a person. Homosexuality is a either a sickness calling for therapy or the result of demonic possession calling for exorcism."

A disciple of the radical feminist Judith Butler, still alive on Earth, rose in a state of obvious agitation. "What an argument! For God's sake, Earth is overcrowded. Let's hope that more and more of us choose not to reproduce. Good for the Creator, I say, for making us like we are!" She then paused and gathered herself. "It's what you desire, what you are drawn to, that's what determines your gender. To listen to your soul, to follow it, is to behave naturally." She labeled a person's gender a "social construct not tied in any way to the body you bring into the world." She said that the speaker's "simpleminded view" led to the persecution of gay and lesbian people, "even to death in some cultures." She expressed shock that homophobes were allowed to live in the Astral, then apologized for the violence of her emotions. Calming herself, she concluded, "If a woman is drawn to a woman, or a man to a man, that is nature speaking. The body has nothing to do with it. Follow your desire."

By now the Regents' well laid plans had crashed. Spontaneity and passion had taken over. "Shall we let it run?" Numen whispered to Sephia. She looked at him and nodded. Numen was skilled at conducting Q & A sessions and felt up to the challenge. They had become moderators.

"We need to open the discussion to the trans experience," Numen said to the panel. "Dr. Graf, most of the astral community needs help on the subject. I know I do. How do you define a trans person?"

Dr. Herbert Graf was a Welsh therapist specializing in gender dysphoria, especially for the trans population. "They feel they are in the wrong body. Males say they are females, females say they are males."

"To most of us this seems very strange. How do you account for it?"

"Back on Earth many studies have been done. Brain scans reveal nothing that might predict a trans. Their brains aren't different from cisgendered people."

"Cisgendered?"

"*Straights* in other words."

"Okay. Then what about upbringing?"

"A deadend. Countless studies have been done on siblings raised the same way, even twins. It's a mystery. I think that's something we can all agree on."

"But there has to be a cause, right?"

"Right. We just haven't discovered it yet."

Anvit Malhotra, a social scientist from India who died in 2019, spoke next. "This is all very interesting, but I think we are here to see what we can do about the problem. The fact is that 31 percent of transgender people in India commit suicide, and 50 percent attempt it before their twentieth birthday. The same percentage for Australia, and 48 percent in Britain. For example, they cut their wrists or burn themselves or violently bang their heads against a wall. These people are suffering."

One of the experiencers in the second row, a black woman who looked about 25, waved her hand urgently.

"Go ahead," said Numen.

"Yes, we are suffering. I was one of those trans suicides. But why did I do it? Not because I began living as a woman. That's what I wanted. It was because I was ostracized. I lost my family, my friends, eventually my career. I was one of Nigeria's first trans females to come out, and I paid dearly for it."

"Did you have surgery?" said a young white man sitting next to her.

"I wanted it, but that would have been too radical. So I lived as a woman despite having the organs of a man."

"I fared better in America, at least at first," said the same man. "And I did have surgery. I hated my female body. They took tissue from my forearm and molded a—the male organ. I even had my uterus and ovaries removed. But I needed a prosthesis for sex. Despite everything, I wasn't happy. I had mutilated my body. Women looked at me and were turned off. I began to wonder if I'd made a mistake. I wondered if it might have been better for me to make my mind match my body than my body match my mind. Could I have learned to live with my female body? I was totally confused. One day, four years ago, I jumped off the top of a building."

Another hand from the second row shot up. An Asian woman said, "The two of you make it seem like being trans is bad. Aren't there happy trans people?"

"Sure, you'll find them back on Earth," said the man with a choked-off laugh. "They're the ones who didn't jump."

"We chose these two for the panel," said Numen, "because they give us insights into the suffering of trans people, not to skew the findings."

"And because we know it's exceptionally widespread," Sephia chipped in.

"There are many happy trans people," said the Asian woman. "My granddaughter is one. Some are satisfied with hormone therapy. Others go all the way and remove their birth organs. It's up to them."

Numen was eager to move the program along. "Dr. Geneviève D'aubert, we chose you because of your work with gender fluidity in Paris. What is gender fluidity?"

"Too beautiful to be a scientist," Sephia whispered to Numen in jest.

"First let me say that I'm not gender-fluid. I'm as straight as a steeple on a French cathedral. A person who rejects the solid certainty of being a boy or girl, a man or woman, is gender-fluid. She might feel like she's a woman one day and a man the next. The feeling might shift from moment to moment. Or she might feel like a mixture of the two. Her gender sloshes around. Or should I say *his*? Look into the closet of a gender-fluid person and you'll see quite a variety of clothing: dresses with frills and tight tee shirts with scary insignia. Mental health professionals report that such a person is happier being fluid than being shoehorned into a male or female identity."

"Do gender-fluid people have the same high suicide rates as trans people?" Numen said.

"I don't know. My guess is that they are happier so long as they are not forced to be a *he* or *she*. Quite a few Hollywood starlets reject those pronouns and insist on being called *they* or *them* in English." Geneviève paused, smiled, then added, "Grammar is not their strong suit."

Another on the second row stood and announced himself as gender-fluid "before I knew there was such a term, or even such a concept." His curly blonde hair and sensitive face suggested the ambiguity he felt. "I was born a male and came out gay and lived to 67. *Gay* never felt quite right, but it was the best I could do. You see, I liked thinking of myself as a girl, then a lady. It pained me to look in the mirror at my flat breasts. I even missed having a period. Then the next day I would feel great looking like the man I was, hair on my chest and a muscular build. Some days I felt an engulfing melancholy wondering why I never felt comfortable being one or the other. I never figured it out, but I never felt life wasn't worth living."

Canadian Dr. Ian Stevenson, who died in 2007, still hadn't spoken. Regarded back on Earth as the world's foremost reincarnation expert, he was most known for his research on young children, ages two to five, who claimed they remembered previous lives. Stevenson and his associates studied 2,500 such cases from all over the world and in half matched the children's memories to real people whom they remembered being. In many cases memories were extremely detailed and included a recollection of the previous person's death. Why did Stevenson wait until it appeared the program was coming to an end? Had he resolved to save what he regarded as the best till last—like a giraffe grazing on treetops. He said he had evidence that explained the prevalence of gender dysphoria down on Earth. He thought that acceptance of this evidence as genuine by astral spirits might even lead to fewer suicides. The audience—panelists, guests, and especially Numen and Sephia—were all ears.

Stevenson was unexceptional in appearance. Middle-aged and lacking any trait that might make him stand out, he was not handsome in the way that most males made themselves in the Astral. It was easy to imagine he felt no need to improve his broad-browed facial structure or brighten his eyes or lips. He wore a plain beige robe, the only trim being blue piping around the collar. He lacked the usual signs of even a modest vanity.

He began by saying he assumed that most of the audience accepted reincarnation, unlike on Earth where many did not, and described a typical case in Myanmar of a four-year-old girl who missed her children and her mother from a previous life. She remembered the names of her three sons and the name of the village where they lived until she died of malaria at age 27. He told how he took her by rickshaw to the village and watched her navigate the curving lanes to the house where her sons, now teenagers, lived with their father and new wife. She recognized them at once even though they were three times her height and called them by their pet names. She didn't want to leave and screamed when taken back to her own village. Gradually she learned to accept her new life and by the time she started school had mostly forgotten the old memories.

"But we are interested now in less typical cases," Stevenson went on. "Many children remember being the opposite sex of what they are now. A mother is now a little boy, a father a little girl. Now this is what's interesting. In almost all these sex-change cases the child exhibits traits typical of the previous sex. A boy plays with dolls and enjoys dressing in girls' clothes. A girl dresses in boys' clothes and enjoys playing boys' games. In most cases the children eventually accept their anatomical gender, but sometimes they don't. These typically grow into unhappy misfits.

"So maybe you can see where I'm going. Back on Earth I came to believe that the various types of gender rejection were caused by a sex change between incarnations. The great research on gender dysphoria over the last fifteen years back on Earth has strengthened my belief. Interviewing cases here in the Astral, especially suicides, has further strengthened it. I am not saying that sex change is the only cause, only that it is the most likely cause. That brings me to the central concern of this conference: What can we do to ease the suffering that drives people, mostly young people, to kill themselves? If the Regents can allow us time, I would like to hear your reactions."

Numen looked as if taken by surprise, but Sephia nodded encouragingly.

"I am intrigued," said one of the first-row panelists. "So it's not brain chemistry, as our materialist sages back on Earth assume. It's the habits of a lifetime. It's psychology, not chemistry."

"Well put. Anyone else?" said Stevenson.

"Can I ask a question?" one of the invited guests said.

"Please."

"Is all this gender-questioning or gender-denial natural? Or is it a perversion?"

Stevenson pounced on this question: "It's as natural and normal as the desire to switch genders. Back on Earth many claimed that homosexuality was an abomination in God's sight. I hope you can see it's not unnatural and it's not an abomination. It's a condition growing out of curiosity over what it's like to live as a member of the other sex. The male answers this question by incarnating in the body of a female. And vice versa. Is there anything unnatural or unhealthy about such curiosity? The only question is: Is it prudent?"

"Why shouldn't it be?"

"It leads to so much suffering, including frequent suicide. That's why."

"But what can we do about it?" cried out one of the cabinet members to Sephia's right.

Stevenson continued: "Maybe nothing, but maybe a lot. I'm optimistic. Let me be clear. Here in the Astral most of us dive back into flesh, and some of us elect to change our sex. I am not opposed to this, but it does represent a future danger. Suppose we could discourage reincarnating souls from undergoing a sex change, advise them to be content with their present sex—better to perfect that mode of existence rather than muscle into the other and risk so much unhappiness. Do you follow me?"

A woman in the back stood up, shocked. "I lived my life as a contented lesbian, and you are telling me I was a man in my former life and was a fool to come back as a woman. I am appalled at your homophobia and think you should excuse yourself from the panel and retire from active life in the Astral. Why do we have to listen to such garbage?"

A hubbub was about to break loose when Stevenson raised his arms and cried, "Please hear me out. There is another way. Hear me out, I beg you."

The audience calmed, and he continued. "There is another way. We can train those who want to change their sex. We can acclimate them to a sex change before they reincarnate. We all know that many switchers end up rejecting the sexual preference they sought in the first place. The whole point of the sex change is to see what it would be like to live as a woman after living as a man, or live as a man after living as a woman, with all that goes with it. I believe that such a change has great potential for soul growth. Most of us know this—it's just that we haven't known how to prevent the old habit from sneaking in and taking over. Then there is a graver problem for the trans soul. Some find themselves hating their new body so much they mutilate it and reverse its sexuality. All this, we believe, and believe we can show, leads to a great deal of misery and stalls the natural progress that the soul hoped for in the first place. As I was saying, I believe proper schooling can ensure this won't happen. This will entail living for a time in the astral body of the intended new sex. In this way we can thin out the old habit, the direction of the old passion. If successful, homosexuality or a trans lifestyle will be forestalled. But it might be simpler than that. We forget as time passes. Rather than rush back into the womb as the opposite sex, but with all the habits of the previous sex still intact, wait. Wait for the old habits to become less dominant, go dormant, so to speak; wait for them to fade away, as all things do if given enough time. Then enter the womb. My team and I have compiled preliminary evidence suggesting that gender dysphoria might be caused by something as simple as being in too great a hurry to dive back into flesh. Better to wait and start out fresh with, so to speak, a clean slate."

"But I wouldn't want a clean slate, don't you see? I loved my life as a lesbian," said the same woman. "You won't be experimenting on me!"

"You wouldn't be under any obligation. If you wanted to enter the world as a lesbian, that would be your right. I am not opposed to lesbianism if it is desired. But it seldom is. Homosexuals typically find themselves in a state of confusion or even shock when they realize their condition. All too often this leads to unhappiness. Poll after poll back on Earth as far back as thirty years ago show that gay males and females are three times more likely to attempt suicide then straights. Facts like these are my touchstone."

He paused as if to catch his breath, then looked directly at Numen. "I am asking the Regents"—now he redirected his glance toward Sephia—"to set up a worldwide campaign under my leadership for the reduction of sexual dysphoria on Earth. This is not a moral crusade. My heart goes out to those many people, mostly youth, who kill themselves rather than endure the stigma that leads to family rejection and peer bullying, and that in many cases is caused by self-loathing apart from social persecution. I do not judge them in any way; rather I feel compassion for them."

As he sat down, voices on both sides filled the room. Stevenson's proposal was so unlike anything ever seriously considered on the Astral, let alone Earth, that everyone wanted to hear more—to praise or censure, endorse or attack, enlist or anathematize. Sephia and Numen meanwhile sat and listened. Finally they rose together and called for quiet. "We will take all you have said, all of you, into consideration. We are deeply grateful to each of you, both experts and experiencers, and to you"—they turned and faced the guests—"for your comments. We will conduct a worldwide poll to gauge the feeling of our people, most of whom will be entering flesh in the next fifty years, perhaps as a member of the opposite sex. Dr. Stevenson's proposal, whether it yield fruit or wither on the vine, is important for us to consider. How it will be received we cannot say. Encourage those who missed the program to view it. And let us give thanks, as always, to our Cosmic Parents for the great gift of existence—male or female, straight or gay, confident or confused."

15

Music

Back on their home planets Sephia and Numen had enjoyed the music unique to those worlds. Thirty-one months into their regency they had sampled many different musical styles beloved on Earth but alien to them. It took a little time, but Sephia grew fond of the traditional music of Earth's various cultures, from Japan's mystical flute music to the Andean panpipe music of Ecuador. But her favorites came from religion, such as India's ecstatic bhajans praising Krishna and Handel's *Messiah.* "Every day I shall give thanks unto thee and praise thy name for ever and ever": Those words from one of Handel's anthems, sung by soprano, made her shiver. As she listened to them, and eventually sang them to herself, she thought of the Creator, her Cosmic Parents. She was their devotee, an eternal devotee full of gratitude and love.

Numen made a point of studying the music of the masses, the popular musical styles that new arrivals brought with them from places like Iran and Israel and times as distant as the 1950s. He listened to Enya and the Beatles. He put on a strong face and did his best to understand country music from Appalachia, the poetry of Black rap artists, and the wistful sounds of Chinese rock. In the end his taste veered toward the Western classical tradition, which reminded him of the music he enjoyed as a boy back on Sirius, where he learned to pay the clanger, an instrument resembling the piano in shape but the cello in sound. He fell in love with the music of Schubert and on one occasion attended an astral concert dedicated to the master.

This event led to an unusual episode in Numen's life—of the kind that he had sworn not to get sidetracked by. To his amazement he found Schubert himself at the piano. Schubert—how could this be? He had died over 200 years ago. Numen knew there were malingerers in the Astral who refused to go upward toward heaven or reincarnate, but 200 years? And a genius of such distinction? Numen knew that great painters sometimes stuck around longer than normal: utilizing the body of an artistic medium, they painted pictures back on Earth in their unique style, even signing their name to the picture. They took such pleasure in this strange inter-world exercise that they were reluctant to give it up and move on. Numen wondered if Schubert was similarly addicted to his art, composing rather than painting. He decided to investigate when he got home.

The investigation led to a digression from duty and earned him a scolding from Sephia. "Are you leaving me alone to dedicate that new temple?"

"What new temple, Princess?"

"The Ice Temple. The one over Antarctica? Surely—"

"Oh, for heaven sake, I forgot." He hung his head.

"Well, now I am reminding you."

He continued looking down, his brow furrowed, then back up. "I'm sorry. Schubert is not a spirit I want to disappoint. One doesn't put off a man of such greatness." He fixed his kind eyes on her and shook his head. "Besides, you can do it perfectly well without me. Religion is one of your specialties—you will know what to say. I would be little more than an ornament."

It was true: she loved to worship in any of the various universal temples found all over the Astral. For her, worship unfurled naturally out of her in thanksgiving for the precious gift of life. More than that, it flowed from the memory of her encounter with her Galactic Parents. How could she describe the experience? Words like ravishing, enchanting, awe-inspiring, even frightening came to her. She felt no obligation to attend services. She loved them. They uplifted her, strengthened her. You couldn't keep her away.

The Ice Temple, named for its outward appearance, which sparkled brilliantly like ice back on Earth, was perched high over Earth's Antarctica in an astral zone noted for its vast unpopulated space. A team of Earth's most celebrated astral architects, led by Antoni Gaudi and Zaha Hadid, designed and oversaw its construction. Immense in scale, a quarter mile in length with a roof almost as high, it was designed to hold a million spirits. Its interior was warm, with earth tones of brown, orange, and green—her colors—prevailing. No rain or snow fell on the swirling ice-blue roof, and the temperature was pleasant. A ceiling was necessary to keep members of the assembly lost in adoration from floating upward out of the building. The idea behind the temple's structure, unique in scale and grandeur, was to attract die-hards away from the divisive theologies and practices of Earth's religions into a spirituality all could share. Divinus and Prima conceived and spearheaded the project; many considered it their greatest contribution to astral life. Numen and Sephia were expected to carry it through when they arrived.

Sephia was surprised by Numen's decision, but she respected his indifference to organized worship. Though disappointed, she decided it was fruitless to argue further.

Numen met Franz Schubert in old Vienna, the astral equivalent of the city as it looked around 1910 before the Great War. It reminded Schubert of the Vienna he called home a century earlier when he made music as a teenager with his father and brothers. Numen had agreed to meet Franz in his home, but he wasn't there when Numen arrived.

Schubert touched down in a fluster and apologized for his tardiness. "I never got your name or I would have telepathized you. I thought my anthem would be opening the ceremony, but it had to wait for a speech."

"Don't mention it. You're here now; that's all that matters."

"You are too generous. My excuse is that a huge new temple was being consecrated, and they wanted me to—well, I had to wait until the speaker finished."

"A new temple? Would that be the Ice Temple?"

"You know it? It's quite extraordinary. They got the new Regent to open the ceremony. The woman. Have you seen her? She apologized for her husband, who couldn't get away."

Numen could hardly believe his ears. "Did you like her speech?" he stammered.

"I liked *her*. She was mesmerizing. I had never seen her. I'm sorry for babbling on. What is your name again?"

"Numen. Numen Syzygy." He was astonished that Schubert didn't know who he was.

"Numen. A popular name these days, especially among young people. There must be some rock star down on Earth named Numen. I hope I'm not offending you."

"Not at all. I take it you don't follow current events."

"I don't even keep a teleset in the house. A terrible distraction. My friends tell me what's going on."

As they entered the house, Numen changed the subject. "You are the composer of the *Arpeggione Sonata,* the most beautiful music I've heard since arriving here. I studied and played music on my home planet, which we call Sirius. I was esteemed, but not to the degree that you are. Thank you for agreeing to my visit."

"I almost feel I've met you somewhere," said Schubert, who had kept the small look-alike body he lived in back on Earth. "So you are not from Earth. That is most interesting. What do you do here?"

"I'm just another sojourner on life's endless path."

Numen had fashioned for himself a rough brown robe out of which his brilliant face shone, like a diamond mounted on an unostentatious setting. He had hoped to disguise his eminence.

"Do I know you?" Schubert said. With a quizzical smile on his round face, which had earned him the nickname "the little mushroom" among his friends back on Earth, he seemed to be chasing down an old memory. "But I can't place you."

"Think of me as an inquirer and a friend. I want to understand your music. It's very different from what I knew on my planet, yet its purpose is the same."

"What is that?"

"Joy. Pure joy. Indescribable joy."

Schubert smiled. He knew he had found a friend.

They struck up an easy camaraderie almost at once, with Franz never guessing who Numen was. He had no interest in politics and was barely aware there had been a transfer of government.

When Numen found Sephia at home after the business of the day and told her what had happened, she exploded in laughter. "You never told him?" she gasped.

"Never. Our meeting was not about me, but him. It was better he never guessed."

"But it's dishonest. At some point he'll have to know, and then he'll feel like a fool. Don't you see that, husband?" Then she started laughing again.

By their fourth visit Numen was pretty sure he knew why Schubert refused to move up or down but was unwilling to give his diagnosis. Still, he was itching to do so. Their friendship had arrived at an impasse, in musical terminology a point where a coda was needed.

Numen asked Franz to spell out the difficulty one more time. "Start at the beginning and take us up to the present."

Schubert, sitting on his piano stool with the piano behind him, faced his friend. A golden retriever named Nudel sat on the reddish carpet next to his master. Numen hadn't asked why Franz kept his appearance so un-touched-up. Anyone else so short in stature would have added at least a few inches. Did it imply a lack of vanity? Or was he so engrossed in his music, like Hillel in his science, that he couldn't bother with his appearance? In any case, it didn't matter. The animation as he spoke radiated a personality that didn't need any touching up.

"Part of the problem," Franz began, "is that I never stop enjoying composing my music and can't see any good reason to leave this place. I also enjoy entering the minds of those who are listening to my music, both here and down on Earth. When I get wind of a concert, especially my chamber works, I tune in. Not because I want to hear the music, not because I'm interested in the interpretation, but to feel the love of it in the hearts of the audience—but only a few, those who love hearing it as much as I did composing it, or you felt when you heard the *Arpeggione.* I feel their joy, and it gives me the greatest pleasure. To love my music is to love me. And for me to love them back. I feel absolutely understood, in the way God understands us. And what is better than that?

"But everybody is telling me it's time to move up. And I half believe they're right—because when I'm not composing or not snooping on my patrons down on Earth, or even here, I sometimes feel something like boredom. After all, I've been here for over 200 years. There's not much new here to see. I do appreciate the magnificence of higher worlds, which I've visited. Brahms tells me he has a place waiting for me. He's even shown it to me on a visit I made. Is there something wrong with me? Is it unhealthy to be so attached to the best that's come out of me? Is it wrong to delight so deeply, and for the ten-thousandth time, in those who love what I love? Is my ego holding out against a higher, a more divine experience? Or am I wise to hold on to what has made me who I am? That's my dilemma. That's what we've come to. That's the problem I hope you can help me figure out—you, who seem to understand me so well, as if by some divine gift.

"There are other problems, of course. I've watched music evolve over the years since I left Earth, and I've admired the great geniuses— Brahms, of course, but also Mahler, Wagner, Stravinsky, Prokofiev, and others. Then there're all the new masters over here writing music the Earth never dreamed of. I confess with some embarrassment that I've never loved anyone's music as much as the best that's come out of me, and that continues to come out of me. Please understand that I'm not claiming mine is the best, only that I love it the most. This brings me to the point. The music I heard when visiting Brahms in his world was strange to my ear. Yes, it's exalted in its own way—very exalted, even amazingly exalted—but it's so different from my own sense of beauty that I fear I'd be lost there, that my gift would go unappreciated and dry up. I fear I'd be annihilated in that higher world, extinguished. I really do."

Schubert halted, his face filled with fluster. He reached down and stroked Nudel.

Numen felt his confusion but wondered how he could help his friend decide. He hadn't much experience of Eidos, the world where Brahms lived. Most of what he knew was what visitors from those higher worlds told him. Still, his instincts told him Franz was making a mistake by not ascending. He asked why he hadn't taken counsel from an advanced spirit over there. "It was like talking to an alien," he said. "Oh, and then there are my friends—Schober, Vogl, and Countess Caroline. How could I leave them?"

Friends? Numen wondered why Franz hadn't mentioned them until now. "But you left them once before when you died."

"Ah, yes. But I had no choice. And they found me when they came over."

"Couldn't they find you again if you rose to Eidos? But let's not get sidetracked."

Numen stood up and walked to one of the windows, which opened to a view of cherished old buildings with their steeples and turrets, and the Danube flowing behind them. Farther out he noticed a streetcar moving across a bridge. Streetcars weren't needed in an astral world where bodies could fly, but they were there anyway. He turned back to Franz and sat down. He looked at his friend with affection. "Franz, even souls that reincarnate aren't annihilated. They just take on new bodies and personalities. And they forget their old ones. That really is rather frightening, I admit. But if you go forward rather than backward, you won't be forgetting anything. There won't be any break in awareness. But as time passes, your interests will change, and you probably will gradually forget the old life, the life you're leading now. But you won't feel it as a loss. Probably it'll feel like a gain. It'll free you to grow into the next phase. There is no telling what will happen to you musically. You might learn to love the new sound, or invent something even newer."

"But I'm not sure I want to grow into the next phase. Isn't that what we've been talking about?" Franz seemed impatient.

"Yes, it is. Let me put it this way. Your city is close to Vienna as it looked in 1910, almost detail for detail. Why has it been so preserved? I suspect because the Viennese are deeply attached to it—perhaps too attached, so attached they'd rather not try something new. They're addicted to what they know, and who can blame them? It's still a beautiful city. They even ride in streetcars." Numen then broke into a grin. "Tell me, Franz, do the streetcars rumble as they do on Earth?"

"The streetcars? No, they don't. They're just part of the scenery." Franz smiled at the thought.

"All of us get attached to our past if it's been happy. And making music the way you made it was for you a happy experience. A supremely happy one. All the more because it brought happiness to so many others. What a high it must have been! So you want to rumble some more."

"Rumble some more. I like that. And it's true, I guess. But I lived with a Beethoven complex, never felt his equal. And the world outside my little circle in Vienna neglected me. Some of my best music was discovered in closets and attics many years after I died. Some of it has never been found. I craved recognition but didn't get it. Only after death did it come. And then it came in a flood. I was intoxicated. Intoxicated, I tell you. It felt incredibly good. It was bliss."

"Are you saying you've hung around so long because you still crave recognition?"

"Yes, I suppose so. But it's not for me that I crave it. It's for my music."

Numen looked suspiciously at Franz. "Would you run that by me again?"

"I crave recognition for my music, not for me."

"Franz, what's the difference? You earlier said that to 'love my music is to love me.' In the final analysis you seek fame—through your music. And that's what's keeping you back. In other words, your ego."

Schubert looked slightly miffed. "Well, what is wrong with that? Even God seeks recognition."

Numen looked amused. "He does? I wouldn't have thought so."

"Of course he does. If he didn't, there wouldn't be any relationship with him. How could he value us if we had nothing to offer him—or her?"

"I'm really quite astonished. What do you think God gets from us?"

"He gets our love. It delights him to see that we love him and love the world he made for us."

"Hmm."

"I'm saying that God created the universe not just to give life and joy to us, as if there were nothing to gain except how it would all turn out, as a child might study the movements of ants, but to enjoy a relationship with us."

Numen's brow furrowed. It was as if he were considering some great puzzle he hadn't solved. Then he chuckled. "I should have known you'd eventually turn into my guru!" And he chuckled again.

"Not only that. But I also enjoy sending musical ideas down to Earth, to fellow prodigies like I was, starting as early as five. I work now with three, ranging in age from five to eleven. They don't know where their ideas come from, but I do. It's such fun. And it's giving back what was given to me."

"Are you saying you got your musical ideas from a higher source?"

"The best of them, absolutely, without a doubt, though I didn't know it at the time. There is no way I could have imagined the *Arpeggione*, or all that joyous music in the *Trout Quintet*, or that miraculous slow movement in the *String Quintet*, and so much more. Oh, the pleasure I felt as it poured down from heaven into my head! I shouldn't take credit for any of it. The best ideas came from above. I just recorded them."

"So you were a sort of musical medium."

"Absolutely, I know that now. Brahms knew it before he died. He thought his best ideas came from God."

"Do you think that?"

"I'm more modest," Franz said with a grin. "But I will tell you something that might surprise you. The joy I felt as I composed *was* divine."

Numen looked at Schubert as if he were viewing a semi-divine being and blinked hard. For a few moments there was silence. Then he became aware of birdsong beyond the window, a cuckoo's haunting call.

"What does my friend have to say at this point?" Schubert said from his piano stool.

Numen shook his head with a rapid jerk, as if trying to shake free a solution to Franz's problem. "Well, well, this might change everything. Seriously. I've always hoped I could help free you from this world so you could take flight to a higher. But now I'm not so sure. The highest vocation for all of us is service. And you find joy in serving Earth in this most extraordinary way—by sending musical ideas down to Earth. Like me, and like those Buddhist monks toiling in the Shadowlands, you are working the trenches. You're a trencher, Franz. A true servant." Numen jumped up and embraced the little man, though not so forcefully that his arms slipped into Franz's ribcage.

Franz beamed with delight at being so well loved.

Numen's countenance became serious as he sat back down. "But it's odd that only now, in our fourth session, you've mentioned this gift to Earth's present geniuses. How much of your time does it take?"

"Not much at all. Other composers work with these special beings too. I have to wait my turn."

"Really? So you're saying this vocation doesn't occupy much of your time."

"That's true. I share my musical ideas with other young composers, but they aren't as receptive. It's as if their channels are clogged. So the results are disappointing. It's only the prodigies I really enjoy working with."

"Interesting. So it seems we are back where we started. Should you move ahead into higher worlds where there might be greater joy or stay put?"

"Exactly. What do you advise?"

Numen frowned, stood up, and began to wander around the room, stopping in front of the window. He began speaking while looking out at the Danube, his back to the master. "I really need to think more about this. But I do want to leave you with something. Throughout my life, when I came up against something I didn't want to do, I made myself go ahead and do it anyway. And it usually paid off. I've found that it's usually best to beat back your fear and move boldly ahead into the future. I suspect the higher world you fear is just such a future."

Numen turned around to look at the great man, now his lovable friend, his best friend in the whole astral world next to Sephia. "Can we meet here as usual in a few weeks? Is that all right?"

"I have a better idea," said Schubert. "I'll come to you. Let's meet at your place. Where do you live?"

The moment had come. "At the Capitol," Numen said sheepishly.

"The Capitol? For me that means where the Regents live. What do you mean?"

"That's right."

"The Capitol? So you work for them?"

"Forgive me for not telling you. I *am* the Regent—or, rather, the lesser half."

"What?"

"I must apologize."

"But—"

"Franz, I worried you might have been awed by my rank. I didn't want that. My achievements are small compared to yours. I'm a lucky politician, you're a musical genius of the highest order. I wanted us to start our as equals. Can you forgive me?"

Schubert looked with bewilderment at Numen. "So that wonderful woman at the Ice Temple is your wife?"

"Yes, she is."

Still stunned, he said, "She apologized for you, I remember now, said you had another meeting or something."

"That's right. With you."

"What?"

"Yes, with you. What's another pageant compared with meeting you? I was not about to stand you up, or even be late."

"You must be crazy. You shouldn't have. Numen. Of course. The name of the new Regent. How could I have missed this?"

"Franz, can you forgive this charade?"

"There is nothing to forgive. Are we not friends?"

"The best," said Numen. They looked lovingly at each other. "So we'll meet at my place?"

"I would love that. I am—I can hardly speak."

"So then it's my place this time. The Capitol."

"Wonderful. Thank you. But feel free to cancel if—"

"I will. After all, we have all the time in the world."

"I don't think so," said Franz.

"Why not?"

"You convinced me."

"I did?" Numen eyed his friend skeptically.

"I'm going to ascend."

"No! You don't mean it!"

"I absolutely do."

Numen grabbed Schubert's hands, and together they danced a little jig around the room as Nudel wagged his tail and barked.

"You have no idea how I've waited for this moment," Numen said. "We'll give you a ceremony you'll never forget. I'll wager Brahms didn't have such a sendoff."

The little man laughed uproariously and stammered, "You're a terrible dancer, Numen," then coughed and laughed some more.

"So we meet next week at the Capitol," said Numen. "We live in the gardener's residence. Just ask for the Cottage. I'll be waiting for you outside. Admiring the flowers and listening to the birds. Next to a little brook flowing under the huge Chinese elm. If she's not swamped with business, Sephia will be there with me."

Franz's mirthful eyes shone with joy, as if a dusty, moth-eaten bundle of his music had been found back on Earth in the archives of a long-shuttered museum.

Five months later, to great fanfare, and with a promise from Numen and Sephia that they would visit soon, Franz lifted off and joined Brahms in the heaven world called Eidos.

16

Shade

Proposals that made their way up to the Capitol from inventive minds were commonplace, and the Guardians' assistants debated over what to bring to their leaders' attention and what to cut. "How could our world be made better?" That was the common theme. On one occasion an intruder breached security and alighted on the Capitol grounds.

One of the gardeners found the intruder wandering over the property and brought him to Headquarters, where, at the man's urgent insistence, he was ushered into Numen's office. Taken aback, Numen could tell at a glance the man was no ordinary spirit. With wispy strands of gray-black hair dangling like Spanish moss to his shoulders, he resembled a mad scientist too busy to fix himself up. His dark, intense eyes flashed a warning: This man is on a mission. Numen was intrigued.

Numen asked the man to relax. "How did you bypass the checkpoints?"

"It would be impossible to explain, sir. The technology involved, I mean."

"But what inspired you to ignore laws you must have known about?"

"Desperation. Sheer desperation. We were not content to watch what we had achieved after years of experiment and testing die on the vine."

Numen called Sephia to join them.

"An invention that I'm sure you'd want to know about," the man went on.

"There are legitimate ways to bring such matters to our attention."

"We tried that way and got rebuffed again and again by idiots. They thought we were quacks."

"Who is we?"

"We're not easy to pin down. We make our home at Level 3 in one of the Jewish sectors. We're a tight-knit group, most of us Israeli. Two of us used to work in the Einstein Circle. We keep to ourselves and have been working secretly on our project for years, even before I arrived eight years ago."

"Tell me your name."

"Hillel Rosen."

"What do you want to tell us?" said Sephia, who had just walked in.

"Oh my God, it is you!" the man said, stunned by her beauty, even though she wore her work clothes, a common white robe."

She smiled. "Please be at ease, sir."

"Tell us about your invention and let us decide its merits," Numen said.

"In a word, we've invented shade, shade without a sun. Ethereal shade. It works as if there were a sun, exactly in the same way. If you are under a tree, you will see light shining through to the ground where breaks in the branches permit it, while being blocked when they get in the way. A perfect facsimile of the way shade works on any sunlit planet."

Numen couldn't hide his astonishment, his mouth open in a somewhat skeptical smile.

"Please go on," encouraged Sephia, equally mystified.

"We feel it will bring beauty to our world. It's not that we don't love the brilliant light that shines everywhere. We all feel its uplifting, benevolent presence. We feel blessed by it, even nurtured by it as if it were alive. But we miss the shade of Earth, and we've found a way to spread it across the Astral as if a sun shone from above, and trees and buildings blocked its direct rays."

Numen remembered his first impression of Earth when Fruva projected hikers enjoying a hike. He remembered its beauty. Was shade part of its beauty? He thought so. He remembered the shade of his own planet. It had been a long time since he had experienced shade. "You claim you can create shade without a sun?"

"That is amazing," said Sephia.

"The judges claimed that shade was fit for Earth, not the Astral. We disagreed and put up a terrific fight, but got shut out. We think shade would enhance the astral beauty, not diminish it. It's not as if there isn't enough light to go around."

"It's surprising we haven't heard of your work. Can you demonstrate it here?" Sephia went on.

"Not now. But, yes, once we set it up."

"But you're not suggesting placing a sun in our sky, are you?" said Numen, just to make sure.

"No. Like the light, our shade will be ethereal. It's not the absence of light, just a different form of light. It's been designed to act *as if* there were a sun in our sky."

"And the motive for—"

"—beauty. That's all. Just the beauty of contrast between bright light and less light. As beautiful as the Astral is, it could be even more beautiful." His face and eyes lit up with conviction.

"Where would you want to install your shade?"

"Everywhere."

"Not just in your sector. Not just at your level. But everywhere, in all seven spheres, in all sectors?"

"Yes, why not? Though we are in no rush. We could try it out. In any case, it would take months to get it going with everyone helping."

"I wonder if you would mind placing half of the Capitol grounds in shade and leaving the other half as is," said Numen. "As a test."

"We could do that, but it would be easier to do it at our level."

"Why is that?"

"Because—because working conditions would be difficult for us here. I already feel a little dizzy. The atmosphere is so—well, it feels thin, the light so pure. Almost blindingly pure. We're not used to it. But we *could* do it."

"No, no," said Sephia. "We understand."

"This is a very interesting proposal," said Numen. "I had always assumed that astral light was unalterable, like gravity on Earth. We'll look further into it and get back to you. Thank you. And let your group know of our interest."

Hillel left the meeting with head bowed in gratitude. Despite his daring breach, he was a humble man who sought no glory for himself or his group. The Guardians saw to it that he was escorted home through established corridors allowing access from one sphere to another.

"He certainly has a point," Numen said to Sephia after the day's work. "But on Earth shade is natural, while here it would be artificial."

"But isn't everything here artificial in some sense? After all, our landscapes and buildings are imitations of Earth, and we can rearrange them any time. The only thing that's not is the light. Or so I thought."

"But dimming down our glorious light—that's what it comes to—is, well, I don't know. If you shut someone inside a windowless cubicle, it would leave them in total darkness, wouldn't it? Is that what we want?"

Sephia remembered a conversation she had with Simone during their orientation: that one of the things about Earth, which spirits missed, was darkness. "Some spirits say they miss the night," she said."

"But isn't it odd that something so basic had never been discovered until now."

"I guess they didn't have the technology."

"Shade. Who would have thought it? You know what I'm thinking? This will be the first real test of our authority. A worldwide test. We've got to get it right."

"We should broadcast the idea across all spheres, to see how it's received."

That is what they did. The first reaction was amazement, just as it had been with the Guardians. Then followed a second phase: In general, the old guard who had made their nest in the Astral and liked things the way they were, resisted the change. They imagined a whole raft of bad outcomes: The purity of the light would be desecrated in some way by such a novelty. It might get out of control and blanket the Astral in shade. It would be too much like the twilight of the Shadowlands. How could we see inside our houses? It might not be revocable once in place. It would give rise to a harmful nostalgia for Earth. It would even upset the animals in the astral zoos. And who could say with certainty that it was not against the will of the Creator? Hillel and his company assured the opposition that none of these fears could materialize. As for the will of the Creator, that argument could apply to every change ever made in the Astral.

When the dust settled and wiser heads prevailed, two positions solidified, and most of the population rallied to one or the other. The conservatives argued that shade was akin to darkness, and darkness universally symbolized—on Earth and every other planet—vice, ignorance, secrecy, threat, unconsciousness, and nonexistence. For these and other similar reasons, shade would be even more alien to the higher worlds of the Astral. It would be like a chill wind.

The liberals argued that darkness signified none of the above. Did people who were ignorant or corrupt live in darkness like the blind? Did people really view darkness when unconscious? No. Darkness was a metaphor that could just as well apply to concepts like mystery, privacy, intimacy, and rest—good things. Many plants, like ferns, thrive in low-light situations. Without darkness, all Earth's flora would burn up. The world would not rest and regenerate itself. The stars in the sky would not shine. But their main argument was constructive. The best way to appreciate the virtue of light was to contrast it to its absence. Undiminished radiance might prevail in the highest heavens, but for astral beings as well as earthlings the contrast between light and darkness provided beauty. Shade was darkness' offspring. Imagine a painting without shade, or a string quartet without the cello. In both cases beauty would suffer.

The news outlets quoted thousands of spirits, from centenarians who found fault with shade, as if it were an annoying insect, to orphaned children, who imagined games they could play in it. In the weeks that followed, positions hardened. There was no sign of compromise, as if astral shade might be made less dark than on Earth. It was either the shade of Earth or no shade at all. Calls went out to the Guardians for a decision.

Numen and Sephia remembered Fruva's emphasis on taking a firm stand. It was time to announce the law of the land: there would be shade. "Along with the formal declaration we should stage a worldwide celebration," Sephia suggested to Numen at the end of a day's work. One of their assistants said it would be like the switching on of electricity for a whole town in rural Ireland when she was a girl. "It was like a miracle!"

"Or in this case a miracle in reverse," said Numen.

When the moment came, little children who had no memory of shade stationed themselves under a tree to experience the wonder. They held their hands out as if shade were water and were amazed they couldn't feel it. Then they began chasing each other in it to see what it would do. On a paved opening under trees along the tree-laden banks of the third sphere's most beautiful river, an orchestra of Czechs played *The Moldau*, Smetana's homage to the river that flowed through his homeland. This was the place selected as the site for the official ceremony, with the Guardians attending. It was the first of the spheres to be shaded.

Gatherings of protesters were almost as numerous as the celebrations. Winners and losers both lamented: "This would never have happened with the previous Guardians."

Three months later shade became a universal feature of all seven spheres. Two months following that, shade had become so taken for granted that it almost seemed as if it had always been.

17

Jolene

S ephia missed working with ordinary spirits one-on-one. When doing research on the Catholic pope, the supreme shepherd of his flock, she noted how he went about appointing his bishops. They had to have "the smell of the sheep" on them or they didn't get appointed. "I need to have the smell of my sheep too," she told Numen. "It helps me remember why I'm here." So one afternoon she left the government in his hands and descended into the lowest realm of the Astral, just above the Shadowlands.

She couldn't hide her extraordinary aura with its brilliant glow, but she had no difficulty in lengthening her body and altering her facial features, especially her nose, which she flattened and broadened. She was unrecognizable.

Many more spirits lived at this level than further up. Modest but tasteful houses bordered the streets. Pleasant lawns under trees were unfenced, and the air was fresh and bright. Every two or three blocks a stately school of some kind stood. Lettering in the universal tongue announced what went on inside: Academy of Astral Science, Horticultural Institute, School of Games and Entertainment—these were typical titles designed to broaden interests and build skills. Residents walked along pathways—they were too narrow to be called streets— most of them in twos and threes, but some were alone. Most looked to be in their twenties and thirties, and their faces, while handsome, usually lacked the finely tuned features found in the upper regions. Many had not been long in the Astral.

Sephia attracted instant attention and commentary. One woman dressed in gray and with a yellow-gray aura gaped at her and stepped aside to let her pass. Sephia intuited a deep sadness in her—her hair was unkempt and her dress smudged: rare for the Astral. To Sephia she seemed to be a troubled soul of the type usually found in the Shadows. What was she doing here?

The woman said she had died at twenty-five in a traffic accident and left her six-month-old daughter behind. She was three months out of hospice and hadn't made friends. But she had quickly learned the universal tongue.

"Are you an angel?" Those were her first startled words when Sephia approached her.

"No, darling, no. Here, take my hand."

The woman held it out, confusion on her face.

"Are you lost?"

"I have a house. It's over there." She pointed at one of the houses on the block.

"Is there a park somewhere around?" said Sephia. "Can we go there and talk? Or let's talk now."

"It doesn't matter. No one seems to notice me."

"No one? Why is that? I did. Come. Do you want to fly or walk?"

"I don't know how to fly yet."

"Well, then, let's walk."

"You don't look like the people here. They aren't very friendly."

"Oh, I just think they're wrapped up in their own lives. They wouldn't be here if they were mean or cruel. Why don't you tell me your story? I sense a sadness. Did you die young?"

"I did." And with that Jolie, for that was her name, talked openly as they walked along.

"My baby is only ten months old, and I'm pretty sure she's living with my mother in Manchester. Mum was not a good mother to me, and she'll be just as bad for Aggie. She put her own needs ahead of everybody else."

"What about Aggie's father?"

"Oh my God, no! He's a good person, but he's incompetent. He wouldn't know how to burp Aggie, let alone change her diaper. He's totally into games. That's what brought us together."

"You were into games? You mean video games?"

"Yeah. At least when mum wasn't hiding my phone. She thought he was bad for me. She was always trying to separate us."

"I see. What do you think needs to happen? Is there anything we can do from here? Maybe I can help."

"Help? From here?"

"I don't know, let's see."

"I need to get back into her life."

"That won't be easy."

"There has to be a way for me to mother her from over here. There has to be, right?"

"Jolene, you've died. Aggie is back on Earth."

"I know, I know, but you can figure out a way, I'm sure you can. You said you could."

"I said maybe."

She went on. "There've been people who've come back from the dead, I know that, you know that, I know you know that, tell me how."

"Yes, there have been countless people who come back from the dead—as ghosts. Is that what you mean?"

"No, I mean, well, maybe. I don't know. Whatever works. Whatever puts me back into Aggie's world."

"You can visit Aggie, but you can't mother her. You can't burp her or change her diaper. And she probably won't see you. And if you stick around long enough, you'll harm yourself. Her world is not your world."

"Well, people talk about reincarnation. That's a way to come back, right? And be seen, right? Do you know how to set that up?"

"You do move fast! Yes, reincarnation is very common. But what does that have to do with Aggie?"

"But for me that would be the solution, so can we consider it? I might look a little different, but it wouldn't take long before she knew I was her mother."

Sephia began to wonder if the woman was sane. "Jolene, would you explain to me how she would know you were her mother?"

"By the love I give her. There's nothing like a mother's love, you know that."

"Wait a minute. You do realize, don't you, that you'd come back as a baby, right? The best you could do is come back as Aggie's baby sister—or half sister. With your boyfriend as your father. How could you be her mother?"

Jolene's brow knit. She was staggered by the complexity of it all.

Sephia continued: "Did you think you could be reincarnated as a grown-up woman? That's what it sounds like."

Jolene bowed her head and walked silently ahead. Looking up, she said, "I don't know what I was thinking. I'm just so miserable I can't think straight. I can't bear losing my baby. I hate being dead!"

"Your mother didn't do so bad a job raising you. She must have showed you a lot of love. She thought taking your phone away would help you. That was one way of showing love. Not a good way maybe, but her way. That's why you have so much love to give to your baby. So try to be content knowing Aggie is well cared for. If she turns out like you, how can that be so bad, right?"

Jolene looked down and shook her head.

"And I've got a job for you to do that will make you *like* being dead." She looked up, startled but hopeful. "You do?"

"Mothering ten-month-old babies over here. I can easily set that up."

This recommendation was Sephis's trump card. She knew what Jolene could not have known: if she declined, she would quickly sink into the Shadows or reincarnate randomly and hurriedly into an unselected body. "We are all called to serve. This would be your way of serving. What do you say?"

A sad smile broke out on her face.

That evening Numen and Sephia sat on the veranda looking out over their beautiful world. She told him about the dazed girl who wondered if she could return to Earth as her child's mother.

"On Sirius you almost could," said Numen. "The barrier between the living and dead was so thin that sometimes spirits advertised their services to parents seeking a babysitter. And if the baby happened to be yours, as sometimes happened, a temporary reunification was possible."

"How strange."

"But it led to problems. Sometimes the child started to reject her real mother. Eventually laws prohibiting kindred babysitting were passed. The dead had to forfeit all rights to their orphaned children. Even ghosting was outlawed."

"Ghosting?"

"Dead parents watching their children. Remember that ghosts are easily seen on Sirius."

"Ah, yes. So that would be like stalking someone?"

A solitary owl hooted in the woods far below and beyond the garden, and a cricket hidden in a nearby lantana bush chirped endlessly.

"Listen to that cricket. Such a solitary being," said Numen.

"No, husband. The female cricket is nearby, silently charmed by her mate's ballad. He is not alone."

"Really. How do you know such things, Princess? The poor male never stops chirping. Have you noticed? Is she that hard to get?"

She looked up at him. "Did you think I was hard to get?"

He looked down at her and chuckled. "Very."

Sephia slapped her hands in glee and laughed merrily.

"Listen, the cricket has stopped," Numen said when she quieted.

It was true. The cricket had stopped. He took her hand.

"Did you know that yours is the second hand I've held today?" she teased.

"Really?"

"Yes, I took the strange girl's hand. She needed love."

"Do you need love, Princess?"

"I do, husband. I do."

18

Wild Animals

Animal rights activists were crossing over in greater numbers than at any time in Earth's history. So were wildlife poachers from Africa and India who made a living by selling elephant tusks, rhino horns, tiger pelts, pangolin scales, and a lot more. Slaughter of Earth's animals—on land, in the oceans, and in the air—was rampant. Voices of outrage and grief had reached the Capitol. Specialists calling themselves post-humanists asked for time with the Regents; so did those with opposing views. Numen and Sephia decided to bring all these discordant voices together and hear both sides in open debate. It was not televised—there was no telling how rowdy it would get. For the sake of privacy they staged the meeting close to their home. An arboretum with different experimental tree formations not found on Earth was the site. The attendees were asked to imagine whatever they chose to sit on, if they wanted to sit.

The Guardians had scanned the planet and done behind-the-scenes research on the subject. Already they felt somewhat informed and had reached tentative conclusions.

They opened the meeting with holographic videos of slaughtered African elephants, suppliers stuffing pangolins by the thousands into crates in Nigeria, and users sipping powdered rhino horn at a party in Vietnam. A tiger pelt spread out as a rug in an American mansion brought the preliminaries to a close.

Numen introduced the twenty-five speakers. The first was a poacher from Zimbabwe who lost his life hunting rhinos. Poachers usually landed in the Shadowlands at death, and Bheka was no exception. But he rode his good heart, with help from his saintly grandmother, into the astral light and gradually got used to it.

"I never wanted to kill animals, but I was desperate. My wife kept prodding me to do something for my kids, get them out of poverty, put them in a private school. And my friends razzed me for being a coward. 'You could make in a day what you now make in a month,' they said. "They were right: a horn would get two-hundred dollars. Two hundred American dollars. One of them let me use his AK-47. I spent a day in the bush before I got close enough to shoot one. I fired everything I had and he dropped. I sawed off his horn and put it in my knapsack. I managed to get back to town without being seen and showed it to my wife. She was thrilled, but I felt sick to my stomach. I kept thinking about that dying animal lying on the ground screaming. I'd never heard that sound from a rhino. Yeah, it made me sick to my stomach."

"Where did the money come from?" Sephia asked.

"An organized crime syndicate."

"They paid you?"

"Yes."

"How did you end up here? You were a young man with children."

"I was shot."

"Shot while looking for a horn?"

"Shot on sight. That's what they do in Zimbabwe. You shoot them, and they shoot you."

"You knew this going in?"

"I did it for my kids."

"How do you feel about it now?"

"It was a terrible mistake. Now my kids don't have their father."

"And the animals you killed?"

"I feel bad for them. They had kids too."

"Would you describe yourself as having repented?"

"Yes. I have. It was the only way out of the Shadows."

"Thank you, Bheka. We are happy to have you with us."

"Thank you."

Another spirit, from India, said he had never known a poacher who wasn't a bad man. "They do it for greed—nothing forces them. And they enjoy it. For them it's a sport. The only way to stop them is to put them in prison for life or kill them. This man got what he deserved."

"It's not as simple as that," said another spirit, a Chilean from Patagonia who herded sheep. "People kill animals for other reasons. Pumas killed my sheep, each worth a hundred dollars. Every rancher hates them. We had no choice but to kill them. But tourists love them and pay good money to see them. What were we to do?"

"And tigers kill *people*," said another.

"Oh, come on!" objected a fair-haired American woman, a dedicated, volatile animal rights activist. "Of course there are exceptions. But this wanton slaughter goes on because men get rich off it. The real bastards are the syndicates and users—rich Asians believe tiger parts will cure baldness, toothache, arthritis. Even laziness! They even sip penis soup for better bedtime performance. It's sick and stupid. We ought to do everything possible to end it. But the poachers like Bekha aren't the real problem. It's the users. For God sake, let's not pretend." Her aura flamed fiery red by now. She sat down.

"I'm all against poaching," said a South African white man. "But hunting is another matter. Hunting protects animals."

The woman who just spoke flung up her arms and groaned. A few others muttered in disbelief.

The man bravely went on: "In South Africa we have wildlife habitats where big animals roam free. Big-game hunters from all over the world pay great sums to go on safari and kill a lion or buffalo. That's their trophy. They bring it home and mount it. The money they pay helps preserve the habitat and pay the salaries of men who hunt down poachers. Poachers know better than to enter the preserves. I know it sounds crazy, but hunting, if managed well, helps the populations grow."

"There are other times you can hunt down a wild animal," said an Indian. "If a man-eater kills someone or an elephant goes berserk and destroys property, you can legally kill it. You can kill in self-defense. Or if the animal is disabled or too diseased to recover."

"But these are exceptions," cried another woman, a friend of the first. "You are muddying the water. For some reason that I can't fathom you stand on the side of a man's right to kill an animal for sport. You—"

"That's not true, Madame."

"Oh, blather."

"Let's try to listen respectfully to all views," stepped in Numen.

"I'm merely pointing out that we're up against a complex problem," said the Indian. "We'd better grasp its complexity before adopting a policy that tries to fix it."

"It gets even trickier," said an American naturalist. "In 1900 there were only 500,000 deer in the U.S. People killed to eat or hunted unregulated for fun. In the 1970s the various states passed laws to build the herds back up. You had to get a license, restrict your kill, and hunt only in specified seasons. Today the deer population is over 30 million. Now the states have to cull the deer to keep the populations down. This is to keep them from starving. So, you see, hunting wild animals is sometimes not only not bad, but even good—or even necessary." He sat down.

A British ex-army man who fought in the Second World War and had seen the horror of warfare stood up. He did not speak immediately but seemed to be controlling an anger that was about to burst. "I have seen many men die on the battlefield," he began. "I have seen what a bullet can do to a man. I have seen the wild terror in their eyes, heard their piercing wails and moans of agony. When the guns stop firing, the fields are full of the noises of the dying. In movies men who are shot die instantly and all is quiet. In real life they die slowly. Soft, ebbing sobs follow the screams. They might whisper their mother's or wife's name when the end is very near. Don't imagine that battlefields are quiet places when the guns stop firing, no. In real battles the wounded scream out their pain. Only the lucky ones die outright."

He had his audience riveted. Then he came to the point.

"Do you think a deer's death is any less horrifying to the poor animal? Taken by surprise, it feels a bullet, maybe several, slamming into its flank or neck. Mammals don't die instantly. Their organs fight for life until the very end. They may be as sensitive to pain as you and I. Imagine the deer twitching on the ground, defecating, blood spurting out of the wound. This is what it means to cull. This is what it means to cull, my friends. I want no part of it. Nature knows how to cull. It doesn't need our help." He sat down.

"What's worse," said another man fidgeting with his hands, "the killing of deer by hunters in prescribed seasons or slow starvation of whole herds due to lack of habitat? They need our help. Hunting solves problems they can't solve by themselves."

"Before we entered the scene they seem to have managed quite well," said the World War II veteran.

"That's an assumption, and probably a false one. In any case, they must share space with us. We have to help them do that."

Opinions rattled back and forth with little progress. Finally Numen stood and took over.

"Friends, in one way or another you all want to protect Earth's wildlife. We can disagree on how to do it. To cull or not to cull. To hunt or not to hunt. We have heard different views and will never agree on everything. But we all agree that poaching must be stopped. Killing tigers for their claws or rhinos for their horns is a stupid and despicable act. It's a crime. Make no mistake: if it were stopped, the plains of Africa and the forests of India and Indonesia would once again thrive as breeding grounds for our finest beasts. Let's not niggle over the wisdom of culling or managed hunting. Let's bring together all our ideas to stop poaching. What can we do in the Astral to grow the herds of lion, elephant, tiger, leopard, and buffalo on our beloved, confused planet? Take a half hour break to think it over."

"Feel free to wander over the grounds," Sephia added. "You might look for the exotic birds that love this place and listen to their songs. Fly over the gardens with their thousands of specimens or perch in one of the trees. Or huddle in one of the many grottoes tucked in shadow by hedges and thickets of flowering shrubbery. Enjoy this place."

"Back in a half hour," said Numen.

When they regathered, a bearded, blue-eyed Norwegian spoke first. "Send down ideas to artists making picture books for children. Prompt them to tell the story of a lion being hunted down. Show how the lion escapes from the evil poacher. In this way a whole generation of future adults will learn to value the lion. We can't do anything about their parents, but we can reach their kids."

"A wonderful idea," said an African with blue-black skin. "But by the time they grow up there might not be any more lions—or rhinos. Do you know that a company in San Francisco is fabricating rhino horns? They can't be distinguished from the real thing, not by appearance, not even chemically. They intend to flood the world with artificial horns until they are so cheap that poachers can't get rich by killing rhinos. This is where our efforts should go."

"How?" said a voice.

"In the old-fashioned way: through prompts. People don't know about this company. We could help spread the word."

"To whom?"

"To goodhearted entrepreneurs who want to beat the syndicates at their game."

"Excuse me if I offend," said the fair-haired woman who spoke before the intermission. "I don't think the monsters who traffic animal parts deserve to live. Tell their spirit guardians to fall back and leave them unprotected. We all know the perils of such a state. Maybe they can learn how to be human in the Shadowlands once they get here. And the sooner the better."

"Would you be willing to descend into those twilight regions and tutor them?" said Numen.

She hesitated, then said, with a hint of shame in her voice, "I'd have to think about that."

"We're like people back on Earth who complain about the heat when it's hot and the cold when it's cold," said a man who described himself as a realist. "There really isn't much we can do about it from our side. Perhaps the world's governments will educate their citizens before it's too late. That's all we can hope for."

"Nothing from our side, then?" said Numen.

"Not from what I've heard here."

"Suppose," said Sephia, who levitated in her excitement a foot above the ground as she stood up, "suppose we build zoos all over the Astral, hundreds of them. A zoo for each sector on all seven levels. And fill them, not with mythical or exotic animals as is the custom now, but with all the noble and fascinating beasts of Earth, from elephants to pangolins to great apes. We'll open our world to their astral forms instead letting their energy dissipate in their species archetype. Dolphins and walruses and octopuses. Even blue whales in giant aquariums. They would have an afterlife of their own. We have the technology; we just must think big. They'll become so familiar to us that we'll learn to treat them as our friends, even our pets. Killing them for any reason won't occur to us. What do you say?"

The audience seemed stunned and sat for a moment in silence. Numen looked at her with admiring approval. This was the solution that the two of them had discussed at length and saved for last.

"That's fantastic," said a voice."

"But it will still take 40 years before it has any impact on Earth," said the realist.

"Less if the children influence their parents," said Sephia.

So it was decided. An entirely new industry was introduced to the Astral—zoo building and expansion. The spirits of wild animals and aquatic beasts who died were inventoried and put into service. Such was the enthusiasm for "Sephia's madness"—the name originally given it by her critics, but then adopted as a rallying cry by her supporters— that many postponed their rebirth so they could participate in the project. It was the most exciting thing to happen in the Astral since the discovery of astral travel to distant planets.

19

Spiritual Blue

A day of rest on the last day of the month, the 28th, arrived. Sephia was breaking in a new gardener, a Benedictine monk who had tended the gardens of his monastery in France until arthritis made work impossible. He was getting used to his new youthful body, which he clothed much as on Earth, except that he didn't have to pull up his trousers or stretch his arms through shirt sleeves. "You don't need a spade, Marcel. You don't need to stoop," she said laughingly. "You don't need to dig. You need to imagine. Imagine the flower you want to place there, just as you imagined your clothes on your body. Go ahead, imagine."

He couldn't resist stooping as he meditated on where the nasturtiums would go.

"Well done," she said while bringing her hands together in a glad, soundless clap. "You see, there it is. You can stand now."

He stood up and nodded his head.

"How's it going, Marcel?" said Numen, touching down on the scene like an eagle.

"Oh, hello. She's a good teacher. How are you today?"

"I've been renovating a forgotten region down at Level 5. The trees are suffering a psychic wilt for lack of attention. Hopefully you'll take on this kind of work in a few years. You'd be good at it, and I could use the help. By the way, how's your arthritis?"

"Gone," he said, laughing at the joke.

"You may call me Numen. I'm afraid I'm going to take your teacher away. Can you manage on your own?"

"Sure. I know how to do it now."

"What is it, husband?"

"How about a little trip?"

"You know me. I love trips."

He looked into her wonderful brown eyes and took her hand. "We're going to a town in the Austrian Alps named St. Gilgen."

"Really? All the way down to Earth?"

"Earth at its most beautiful, I'm told."

"What a surprise. What brings you to this, husband?"

"Schubert told me about it. He said it was the place where the most loved movie ever made was shot."

"A movie?"

"*The Sound of Music* it's called. He said it's on a beautiful lake, and we like lakes."

"What do you intend to do there?"

"Just hang out. Hover. Maybe descend. I guess I'm ready for a little taste of Earth. Can you stand it?"

"Of course I can, though I'll have to rearrange my schedule. But it's so unlike you."

They lifted off, tacked over to one of the corridors leading down to Austria, and descended. Thick, sticky-feeling clouds parted as they broke through into a sunlit blue sky.

They scudded sideways toward St. Gilgen, then descended farther onto a walkway alongside Lake Wolfgang, a blue inland sea hemmed in by steep mountains. The town appeared with its little gardens of edelweiss, gentian, and Alpine rose and its chalets with their gabled roofs. People walked by them wearing sweaters as wind blew hair back across their faces. The snow-topped Alps rising beyond the lake, and the thick forests of fir, larch, and pine climbing up the slopes made an agreeable impression. Except for a little girl who stared at them as they glided by, no one saw them.

"Schubert was right. It's an appealing place for a physical planet," Sephia said.

"Yes. Let's lift off and have another look from above."

"All right."

They rose to a height of about 2000 feet and planted themselves. No floaters hovered around them. The panorama was all theirs for the moment.

"Isn't it fun to snoop," said Sephia in a relaxed, fun-loving mood. They felt no discomfort from the wind and chill on their bodies, but they could see and hear, though not as sharply as in the Astral.

"This takes me back to Sirius, Princess. I almost miss it."

"Really? What do you miss most?"

"I don't know. The whole physical experience, I suppose. Not that I'd trade away what we have now. But there were many good moments, much joy. Sometimes I get nostalgic thinking of my kids. Two boys especially, one from my first life, one from my third and last. We were very close. But, as so often happens, they drifted away after they started their own families."

"Finally, you are telling me about your past. You say, 'drifted away.' Weren't there grandchildren?"

"Oh, sure. But I enjoyed teaching my boys, guiding them, watching them form. We didn't see as much of each other once they married. They became the teachers of their own children."

"Do you miss your parents? What about your wives? Any divorce?"

"My last wife and I were very close. When I died, I made a point of preparing a home for us. But even after she came over I felt something was missing."

"Is that why you took this assignment?"

"Not exactly. I took it for the same reason we all jump at a bigger challenge when it comes our way. Out of curiosity we want to see how we manage. And we relish being honored with so great a responsibility—being chosen over so many others. We crave recognition."

"But you still feel you're missing something."

"No, Princess. With you I am entirely happy, as I've said before."

"Seriously, Numen, tell me the truth. Are you really happy?"

He looked at her warm, loving eyes as they studied him. "There is nothing like you, not in all the Afterworld."

Their bodies shimmered and melted into each other. An onlooker would have seen, not two bodies hovering close together, but a single oval of a color unknown to Earth, the color known as "spiritual blue," the color of the soul.

20

Earth Addictions

Ever since the Regents took up their post, complaints steadily rolled in over the harm being done to Earth by Earth-addicted spirits." Many of the complaints came from grandparents whose grandchildren were their victims. Others came from the victims themselves.

Sephia and Numen decided to set up a commission to study it more deeply. The commission interviewed thousands of spirits from dozens of different sectors and selected a few to present their case in writing to the Regents. Of nine presentations, one especially stood out. The speaker was not a relative or intimate friend of the victim, but his psychiatrist, who died three years ago. The characters in his account are Poles from Krakow, all of them alive on Earth. This is the written document:

My name is Piotr Nosek. I was a licensed psychiatrist practicing in Krakow, Poland, until 2016, when I retired. Dr. Alex Adamski, still alive, was a long-time critic of my "unprofessional and risky" therapies, as he called them, and had done serious damage to my reputation with our fellow colleagues and some of my clients. My son, Jan, and Alex's son, Milan, both sixteen at the time, were in the same grade and had known each other since playing in a football league for children. A mishap deepened the already strained relationship between me and Alex: In a match Jan collided hard with Milan, a tall, slight, rather small-boned boy, and Milan fell to the ground groaning with a broken collarbone. Alex claimed, absurdly, that the hit was excessive and intentional. Since then we avoided each other whenever possible. The boys themselves continued as friends, Milan feeling his injury was just part of the game.

"So these are your digs," Alex said rather insolently as he walk into my office unannounced one afternoon during lunch hour, the first time in eleven years he set foot in it, though it was just down the hall.

"Yep, this is my Corsica," I said in surprise, referring to the island that the Roman sage Seneca had been exiled to. "What brings you here?"

Alex sat down. "Our sons are friends, as you know. Has Jan mentioned anything about Milan lately?"

"No, I don't think so. But I've noticed he hasn't been around. Why?"

Alex looked troubled and a little embarrassed. "In the last month or so, Milan's complained of hearing voices in his head. From what I can gather, they aren't good voices—he said they torture him. I put him on an antipsychotic right away that he hates and refuses to take. He says it makes him feel like a zombie, the usual complaint. He says the voices don't come from within him, the usual claim. Where they come from he can't say, or at least he won't tell me. At this point he refuses to talk about it anymore. Inga is out of her mind with worry, and, frankly, so am I." Alex paused, looked out of the lone window, and summoned the strength to proceed. "I know you've made a point of—this might surprise you, but I've quietly noted out of curiosity, at times even bordering on respect, well, let's call it your eccentric views on things. I once overheard you say to someone, it was several years ago, maybe at a party, that you thought the voices schizophrenics heard might come from spirits. Though I thought it farfetched, almost ridiculous at the time, it stuck in my mind, and when Milan told me about his problem, I remembered it. Maybe you could talk to him and let me know what's going on. Maybe he'll open to you. He certainly won't to me. You know how sons can get with their fathers—or maybe you don't."

"Oh, I do." I was thunderstruck that Alex, my old nemesis, the man I thought despised me beyond help, would trust me with his son's mental health. All I could say was, "No, Jan hasn't said a word about this." I looked at Alex in a new way. I saw his suffering, how prematurely grey he was, how wretched and beaten up. My heart softened. "Yeah, I'd be happy to talk to him. But my weird views don't make me a miracle worker. I'll just try to help him open up. And, Alex, I'm terribly sorry. I really am." I couldn't help but notice the moisture in his eyes.

Alex stood up, looked again out the window of my small office at the end of the hall, and left with a quick "thanks" as he passed through the doorway.

After he left, I thought back to a boy in my high school class who thought he was Jesus—that's what the voices were telling him—I can't remember his name now. He was an attractive boy and the star of his debate team. But the voices drove him into a full-blown case of schizophrenia, from which he never recovered. He got a scholarship to Jagiellonian University in Krakow, but he lasted less than a year and killed himself when he was 20.

Two days after Alex's surprise visit, a feeble knock that I'd been expecting got my attention. "Milan, it's good to see you." I extended my hand to the boy, who took it limply and let me shake it. "Sit down."

I had spent the previous weekend looking for hints of openness to the sprit hypothesis in the professional literature. Of course I knew that psychiatrists regarded and treated the disease as a series of hallucinations, but might there be a maverick voice out there somewhere? I also knew that the Catholic Church designated specialists—each diocese had an exorcist, a priest—to deal with demonic possession. It was clear that Christ himself did not regard possession as a hallucination. But what inclined me to question the standard prognosis was not what the Bible reported, but my exploration of poltergeist phenomena that I had been doing on the side. I knew that poltergeists were real and figured that if a spirit could possess a home, it could possess a person. As the years passed, I had grown more and more suspicious of theories that reduced all mental disease to purely physical causes, but I was far from sure that Milan was being hounded by a demon. After all, medication did have a very real impact on the brain of the person afflicted, and the brain and the drug were entirely physical. Why would the drug work if a spirit was the cause? For a number of reasons I wanted to believe that Christ knew what he was doing—I was a practicing Catholic—but I remained agnostic on the question of demonic interference. Definitely open, but agnostic. With Milan I was open to anything.

The first thing I wanted to find out was whether Milan had taken a drug to get high. I knew that methamphetamine was a well-known gateway to mental illness. The second was the possibility of some repressed trauma that Milan might have lived through—another gateway. I realized I was treading on ground that was potentially treacherous. Suggesting that he might be bothered by a dark spirit could send him over the edge. But I also felt that opening his mind to that possibility could be a liberating insight. I really didn't know what to do, except pray. "Let me do no harm to this boy," I prayed with unusual fervor to anyone listening as Milan sat in front of me with a scowl on his face. After a little small talk, I asked, "Are the voices with you now?"

"No, they told me not to come."

"Did they? When did they tell you?"

"All morning long. They wouldn't let up. I wouldn't have come if Dad hadn't brought me."

"Is he outside?"

"Somewhere. I'm not sure."

"That's okay. Tell me, do you know who the voices belong to? Let me put it this way. Do they come from within you? Do you produce them? Or do they come from someplace else?"

He stared into space as if zoned out, as if he hadn't understood the question, then whispered, "I don't know."

"Let me try again, Milan. What do they feel like? Do they feel like your own thoughts?"

"No, but my other doctor tells me they are."

"Forget the doctor. What do they *feel* like, Milan?"

"They feel like—they feel like—they feel like somebody else."

"Milan, I want to tell you something that might surprise you. I think you might be right."

Milan looked surprised, then said faintly, as if relieved, "So you understand."

"I think I do." I closed my eyes and sent up another prayer. "Let me ask you something else. I'm going to ask you to be completely honest with me. To trust me. You might not be ready to do this, and that's okay. But, well, let's give it a try. I want you to think back to something that might have happened to you a long time ago. Something that might have horrified you, maybe when you were a little boy, maybe something that scared you to death, that you just couldn't face, some kind of trauma—do you know that word?"

"Of course. I'm not stupid."

"Sorry. Can you remember anything like that, something that was traumatic?"

A pained, pensive look spread over Milan's face as he searched into his past. "No," he finally said.

"Are you sure?"

"Yeah, I'm sure."

"Good. That's what I was hoping for."

"Nothing worse than being bashed into by my son?" I joked.

A wispy smile broke over Milan's face. "Jan's a good dude," he said, nodding his head with its unkempt, shaggy brown hair.

After a pause I continued: "Milan, there is something else I need to know if I'm going to be of help. Are you on drugs?"

"Uh, uh, yyyyeah."

"Is it meth?"

"Uh, yeah."

"Is Milan on it too?"

"No. Not that I know of. Not the last time we talked."

I slowed down my delivery. "Let's get back to the voices. Do you know who they might belong to? Do they have a name?"

"Not exactly."

"Not exactly. What do you mean?"

"Do you know who Kurt Cobain is, the American rock star?"

"Jan has mentioned him a few times. He plays his music. Why?"

"He's a god to me. He's the best. Did you know he killed himself about a month ago?"

"Did he? No. Jan never said a word."

"Well, one of Kurt's friends is calling me to come over."

"What do you mean?"

"Yeah. He tells me Kurt is waiting for me."

"Waiting for you? What does that mean?"

"He says that if I don't I'll be a complete failure at everything I do. I'll never be respected. I'll be human scum. No one will like me. No one will ever hire me for a job. But if I come over, I'll be welcomed by Kurt. He's waiting for me. I'll be part of his inner circle. This was my destiny even before I was born. That's what they say."

I was speechless. "They're asking you to kill yourself."

"Yeah."

"What else do they say?"

"I hear other voices in the background, calling me over, threatening me if I don't. Horrible, frightening voices that keep jabbering on and on."

I had heard this kind of testimony before, especially from adolescent boys. I pressed on, changing the subject. "Your father told me you don't take your meds. Why is that?"

"They told me not to."

"The voices told you not to take your meds?"

"I hate how they make me feel. It's like pouring sludge into my brain."

"That sounds pretty awful. But what's worse? Listening to the voices, or taking your meds?"

"The voices. They torture me. They never shut up. It's hard to sleep. And the dreams, oh my God! And I feel totally exhausted after they leave. Like I can barely sit up."

"So why don't you take your meds, the lesser of two evils?"

Milan looked confused. "I don't know. I guess because they tell me not to. They tell me it's poison. I have to obey, or else. They scare the shit out of me."

"So you take meth to escape the pain."

"Yeah. But it's killing me, I know that. I know that. I just don't know how to stop."

By now I had what I needed to know. Milan was a classic schizophrenic just like my high school classmate many years ago. I decided to bring the session to a close.

"What about next Wednesday at the same time?"

"Is that all? I mean, aren't you going to do something for me?"

"You mean like prescribe a drug?"

"I don't know."

"You already have the drug from your other doctor, right?"

"Yeah."

"Milan, the therapy I offer is different from what you've had up till now."

"What is it?"

"I'll let you know next Wednesday. I want you to trust me."

A sickening frown came over his face.

"What is it?" I said.

"They're back. They're screaming at me. They're telling me you're trying to destroy me. They say they've taken over the world, that you don't know anything. They say I must go home to Kurt. He is waiting, they say." His whole body shuddered as he threw his head back in a rigid, terrified stare.

I decided to take the plunge, to say what I had come to suspect. "Milan, listen to me. Listen to me. The voices are lying. Don't obey them. Reject everything they say. They laugh at you when you take them seriously. They are trying to destroy you. They are trying to get at you through Cobain. They see your weakness. They see your attachment, your addiction to him. Do you understand?"

Milan scowled and looked menacingly at me. Then, in an instant, his face contorted, and out of his mouth came a horrible sound, half scream and half growl. His eyes bulged. His expression changed. I had the impression that the face wasn't Milan's. Goose flesh covered my entire body.

He jerked up out of the chair and cursed me with language straight out of hell. As he spoke, spit flew. He then turned and fled howling from the office.

He came back a week later, and I continued counseling him. I told him the voices were not coming from within but from demonic spirits—by now I was convinced of this. I told him that everything they said was a lie. "When you hear the voices, say to them, 'That's a lie.' Over and over, 'That's a lie.' If they persist—and they did—'then shut them out with a prayer.' I recommended memorizing the 23rd Psalm from the Bible beginning with 'The Lord is my shepherd.' They hated religion and cursed God. Ironically they denied the existence of an afterlife despite living in it themselves. I told him to treat the voices as idiots, bullies, frauds, to jeer at them, to see if they would leave him alone when it became clear he wouldn't play their game.

The voices subsided. He was winning the battle. He made such progress that he flushed his antipsychotic pills down the toilet one morning. This went against the advice I gave—I was afraid he might still need them from time to time. By now I understood why the pills worked: The demons couldn't control the victim's thoughts so long as the brain was so fogged up. So the pills were useful in the short run. Short of a complete healing, they temporarily removed symptoms. They were like armor and shield during a single pitched battle. I was right—Milan broke down. The voices attacked him in a new way—they made themselves visible. Three-dimensional shadow people began to haunt him. He saw the color of their eyes—red or lime-green—and they could walk through walls. Sometimes they wore capes, sometimes hats. Sometimes they made feints toward him, but then backed off. Always they threatened him with death if he continued to see me. 'He's insane,' they yelled. 'He only wants to destroy you.'

Seeing his tormentors led to desperate phone calls to me at night. "Turn the light on," I said. "Say your prayers. Recite the 23rd Psalm over and over, just like we discussed. Storm heaven with your prayers. Crowd out the voices any way you can. We'll talk tomorrow. Tomorrow is not far off, Milan. Hang in there."

When I invited him to church and he accepted, the voices amped up to a new level. "A bunch of crap!" they shrieked. "The Bible is shit! Stay home and listen to your music. Go get some meth. That's what Cobain wants you to do. Meth, man!" Milan tried to resist them, and when Sunday came around, his head felt like it was caught in a vise, and he whimpered an apology to me over the phone. The next Sunday he fought off the demons and sat at the back of the church with me. Sosamma, my wife, was afraid of him and sat up front with Jan next to the twelfth station of the cross.

Eventually Milan destroyed all his Cobain tapes and defied the voices. Whenever they erupted, he recited the 23rd Psalm, which sent them into a fury. He knew now without a doubt that the voices came from the outside, not his own mind, and he knew he was fighting for his life. With that incentive he found a strength he never had when he thought the voices came from within. With my dogged support, one day the voices stopped. Hardly daring to hope, his parents watched the transformation. A week passed, and the voices still hadn't reappeared. A month later, Alex asked what he could do for me. "Do you realize what you did? My God, you worked a miracle." Milan never relapsed again and lives with his partner in a gay marriage in Warsaw, where he works as a public school guidance counselor.

Piotr's account ended here.

However, it left several questions unanswered, and Numen and Sephia called him back. He wore his brown hair in waves that half covered his ears and hung down the back of his neck, a different look from the close cut he wore at the group interview. Sephia wondered at the change.

"We cannot thank you enough for the document," she began. "It's now in every library; and, as you know, everyone who worked in your field has been alerted. Much good work is underway. But we have some questions. First, where were the guardian spirits in Milan's case? We would have expected them to protect him."

"This is my own conclusion," Piotr began. "In cases like this their helpful prompts are ignored. In time it becomes clear to the guardians that they're wasting their time trying to help. Other spirits, not many, battle away until they are worn down by the sheer persistence or size of the gang—in Milan's case there were several demons. So you see, not all guardians are equally committed. They all have other duties and concerns. They can be distracted. In Milan's case his addiction probably drove his guardians away fairly quickly. I suspect he had been going through life unprotected for quite a while."

"This is what we suspected. So what do you advise us to do?" she said.

"Many of us have professional friends we left behind. A few of them thought their patient might be possessed. The patent's behavior was so extreme it was hard not to. But they didn't know how to treat it; spirit therapy is forbidden territory. So with a half-guilty conscience they prescribed a drug, which of course only masked the symptoms.

I think these fellows can be reached and changed. They can be urged to attend one of the few conferences that dare to consider possession. I remember one I attended. A very courageous therapist blew us all away with story after story of successful treatment using what he called spirit release therapy."

"You mean exorcism."

"That's not what he called it."

"Did it work?"

"Absolutely. The woman was completely cleared and rejoiced in her release. But the demon sneaked back in a few days later. She didn't know how to keep it out. And the shrink didn't either."

Numen broke in. "Must you call them demons, Piotr? It's a term loaded with religion. Why not call them Earth-addicted spirits prowling the planet? Something milder that we're all familiar with?"

Piotr looked puzzled. "Well, they seem worse than that. They seem more than confused. They seem evil. As if they get pleasure from winning the battle over good. As if they get pleasure in exercising their power. But try telling that to Earth. Psychiatrists keep telling themselves the cause is a chemical imbalance in the brain. Which when translated means they don't know what the real cause is."

"Is the real cause of schizophrenia always these dark spirits?"

"No. You might say the term covers too much. Only in some cases are spirits involved."

"Do all psychiatrists once they come over here, once they die, admit spiritual causes in some cases--in cases like Milan's?"

"Most do. It comes as quite a surprise to them."

Sephia joined in: "Do any of them go down and confront these spirits—wage war with them you might say?" the demons?"

"Go down to Earth and confront them? Yes, I know of such cases. But it's brutal work. Most of us don't have the stomach for it." Piotr gazed at the blue sky. "It's selfish, I know." He hung his head, then lifted it with agitation written on his face. "I'll tell you what. I'll give it a try. I'll do it for you."

"Please do it for the victim," Sephia said.

He looked back up at the sky and pushed his hair back away from his face. "Of course. But the inspiration comes from you."

She reached out and grasped his hand, smiling.

"But that's a short-term solution," he said. "Long-term we must be patient. Most of us here see our error and won't make it again when we land again on the planet. That is, if we get into psychiatric work again."

"So you are planning to return? You aren't planning to ascend, Piotr?"

He let out a long sigh. "I don't think I'm ready."

"But you make yourself ready by service, and what you are about to do is heroic service."

He laughed gently, as if to himself. Was he really capable of change, of finding happiness in service, of becoming a servant? He didn't know. He didn't know.

21

Democracy

Another psychiatrist pleaded over and over for an interview with the Regents. Their perimeter guards, both mental and physical, got tired of confronting "the impudent trespasser," as one of them called him.

"Let's see what he has to say," said Numen, who was never afraid of an old-fashioned dog fight.

The man brought his wife, a woman he recently met in the Astral and married, over the heated objections of his Earth wife.

"Women must like him," Sephia joked. "Maybe there is more to him than bad behavior."

Tall, tanned, blonde, and with facial features that didn't deviate by a millimeter from Earth's idea of good looks, Rufus had practiced psychiatry in Perth, Australia. His new wife was a female version of himself, so much so that Sephia wondered if he had required her to take on the resemblance before marrying her. Or maybe she was a robot he had fashioned. But the woman's aura left no doubt, and it didn't resemble her husband's aura at all. Sephia wondered what she had looked like down on the planet.

The two couples met in the cupola that sat atop one of the visitors' houses spread out over the vast grounds. The house was surrounded by a forest of tall trees that blocked a vista even from the height of the cupola. The building was designed for introspection and soul-searching.

After the usual formalities of greeting, Rufus came quickly to the point. His wife, Rosemary, sat smiling next to him. Both were dressed in white, she in a full-length gown and he, surprisingly, in V-neck, collared medical scrubs.

"I have watched," he began, looking at Numen, "with growing annoyance at the propaganda against us psychiatrists. We did the best we could with our drugs. Resorting to exorcism would have done more harm than good and gotten us disbarred, and with good reason. Earth is a physical planet, not some grand toy for spirits to play with." He looked over at his wife, apparently for support.

Numen looked puzzled, as if having trouble gathering his thoughts. Sephia jumped in. "Are you saying that drugs—are you saying that Earth should always be content to treat psychotics with drugs, when all they do is mask symptoms rather than provide the cure?"

"Drugs are the best we have. There is nothing else."

"They are not the cure," Numen said with force. "They keep the spirits at bay, that's true, but they keep coming back. And the drugs destroy whatever chance many of the victims have of leading a normal, happy life. They prefer the demons over the horrible side-effects of the medication. How can you call drugs the cure?"

"Sir, you've never lived on Earth. I suggest you go down there to see what it's really like. Take a vote. See how many of us would choose exorcism over drug therapy."

"Let me make sure I follow you," Numen went on. "You do admit that the voices schizophrenics hear are not their own thoughts, but belong to hostile spirits. Is that correct?"

"Yes, but that's irrelevant. That's what we know from here, but it's not what we can know from down there."

"There are exceptions. I am told that spirit release therapy is being practiced by a small number of psychiatrists. We should do all we can to turn them into the majority."

"Through exorcism?"

"No, through spirit release therapy."

"What's the difference?"

"None. But the word *exorcism* is associated with superstition rather than good science."

"And rightly so," said Rufus, his voice beginning to rise. "I like that word. It's more honest. Exorcism isn't progress. It's not even medicine. It's going back to the Dark Ages, not forward."

"Rufus, those are ignorant thoughts, the thoughts of Earth at its worst. You admit that the voices come from dark spirits. With drugs you're fighting spirit with matter. If you don't fight spirit with spirit, they'll win every time."

"You are not listening. I suggest you go spin your yarns on some other planet."

"Rufus!" said his wife.

"Take a vote. Take a vote, I say," Rufus continued. "Not one in a hundred psychiatrists will agree with you."

"On Earth, that's true. But here in the Astral, where we know better—"

"We're not talking about the Astral. We're talking about Earth."

"We're talking about a higher truth than Earth has been able to reach. We have an obligation to help her catch up. Schizophrenia is a lifelong condition unless you vanquish the spirits."

"Sir, we have over 50 medications to treat it." His voice was shaking with rage.

"They might help a little in the short run, but they will never cure the condition. Demons hate and fear spirit release, or what you prefer to call exorcism. With proper guidance and a strong will, the freed soul can resume a totally normal life."

"I say again, conduct a vote. Conduct a vote!"

"Rufus, this is not a democracy."

"Well, it should be. Then at least we'd be governed by spirits who know what they are doing." He spat these words out.

"Friend, you are putting yourself over the will of our Galactic Parents."

"Let's go," pleaded Rosemary, who blanched with every word spoken by her husband.

Sephia suddenly reached out and took Rosemary's hands. Their eyes met for an instant, as only two women's can. No words were necessary.

Moments later Rufus wrapped his arm around his wife's waist, stepped out from under the canopy of the cupola, and rose quickly. They vanished like two fast-flying birds into the pure blue sky.

"Well, husband, tell me how you would have dealt with Rufus's challenge if he had given you the time. Why not democracy?"

"I would have told him democracy is best for a messy planet like Earth, or even Sirius. But for the Astral? This stopover world? The truth is much plainer to see. We are closer to the Source. A democracy would only introduce clamor and inefficiency."

"But we must be open to all points of view, don't you think?"

"Absolutely. And then decide."

"Then how do we differ from tyrants who can do anything they want?" she pushed on.

"By having nothing to gain."

"Except the approval of our Parents?"

"That doesn't motivate me," he said. "Does it you?"

"Yes. Definitely."

"As a side effect, sure. But the good is good no matter who approves it. Doing it is what motivates me."

"Really, husband, you are too good for this world." She looked up at him with an ambiguous smile.

He fluttered inwardly under her gaze. He realized that without her his never-ending call to duty would weigh on him like a backache on Sirius that never went away.

22

The Sun

The Russian Natalie Stepanian and the American Carolyn Shoemaker became friends shortly after Carolyn's death in August 2021. Natalie, who died in 2018, specialized in the study of large-scale solar flares and was especially interested in predicting their occurrence. Carolyn discovered 32 comets—one of them named after her—and over 500 asteroids. Once Carolyn learned the universal language, Natalie looked her up. Thus began a close collaboration on the subject that had been percolating in Natalie's mind since shortly before her passing, a subject introduced to her by the intriguing speculations of the Englishman Rupert Sheldrake, a biochemist and holistic philosopher. Sheldrake, still alive on the mother planet, believed that all self-organizing systems emerging from nature—animals, humans, planets, suns, galaxies—had souls. Unlike things made by earthlings, such as light bulbs, chairs, computers, or skyscrapers, these soulful systems were conscious and were able to choose their future.

Natalie and Carolyn hypothesized that the Earth's sun, having a soul, was free to choose its activity. Earth's scientists had known for more than a century that solar storms posed a catastrophic threat to life as it had evolved on Earth since the technological revolution. They had evidence that such an event—known as a coronal mass ejection—would probably happen within the next hundred years. They wondered if the sun consciously controlled these events.

They asked for a meeting with the Regents and got it.

Numen opened the meeting: "So you are saying that our sun is a living system with a mind of its own—do I have this right?" He and Sephia and the two scientists sat on chairs under a banyan tree that covered an acre—"a big tree for a big idea," Sephia said.

"Yes, we think so," said Carolyn, a 40ish looking brunette with a quick smile under twinkling dark eyes. She looked over at Natalie, a rather dowdy 50ish white-haired woman, lovely in her own way, but lacking Carolyn's charm. Natalie, who was the expert, began:

"Earth assumes that the sun runs like a clock, so the solar wind, or what we call daylight, is dependable and predictable. Most of us here in the Astral assume it too. But this isn't true. Even back on Earth, scientists knew it wasn't true a long time ago. Eruptions occur frequently and unpredictably. In 1859 a storm of such magnitude occurred that Earth's telegraph machines shut down. Superheated gas, solar flares, rocketed down to Earth in such mass and with such speed that the Earth's entire electrical grid would have been damaged if that event had happened today. We would have been thrown back into the Dark Ages. Chaos would result. Starvation would be rampant. People would die of disease and injury without access to medicine. Carolyn and I want to do something about this." Natalie's placid expression had become suddenly excited.

"On July 23, 2012," Carolyn continued, "such an event did occur. If it had happened one week earlier, Earth would have been in the line of fire. As it turned out, the deadly plasmic ejection shot harmlessly out into space like an arrow that just missed its target. We missed the Dark Ages by one week."

Natalie added: "Earth's scientists did a statistical survey on these episodes and came up with a prediction: there was a 12% chance of such an event in the next ten years. That is pretty scary. Can we help Earth avoid such a cataclysm?"

Sephia looked puzzled. "Why didn't we hear about this during orientation? How can you explain this?"

Carolyn looked over at Natalie. "We can't. Perhaps because no such collision has occurred in modern times. There's no history of it. We've been lucky."

"So what do you think we should do about it?"

Carolyn: "Well, before we get to that, let's get used to the idea that the sun we see might be the body of the soul we don't see. Let's get used to the idea that the sun is free to shoot down flares, that it actually chooses to shoot down flares in whatever direction it pleases. Let's get used to the idea that both the miss in 2012 and the hit in 1859 might have been intentional."

Natalie: "Or, to look at it in another way, that the sunspots that cause these flares might not be controllable, anymore than ulcerative colitis or prostatitis are for us."

Numen: "Very strange. What a frightening hypothesis."

Sephia: "If you're right, what use is it to us? It seems like one more problem with no obvious solution, like hurricanes or tornados."

Natalie: "We think there might be a solution. If the sun is a conscious being, if the sun we see is only its body, then maybe we can communicate with it. Maybe it can hear us. Maybe it can be persuaded to go soft on us, to shut down those deadly flares until they are no longer aimed at us. After all, the sun rotates on its own axis every 25 days. Maybe it can control an ejection until we are out of the way. Maybe it actually did in 2012."

Carolyn: "In other words, maybe it's a star with free will that can be influenced. Isn't that what earthlings do when they pray—try to influence their god? Or their saint?"

Numen: "It's an interesting hypothesis, but is it testable?"

Natalie: "We think it is. That's what we want your permission to do."

Sephia: "Are you saying we might be able to persuade the sun to withhold these flares until the Earth is not in the line of fire? Do I understand you correctly?"

Carolyn: "Exactly. Yes. Do you see this as a worthy goal?"

Numen looked over at Sephia, whose expression was indicating approval: "It would seem so. But the sun might have other ideas. Have you considered the possibility that, well, that these ejections might be a means of cutting back our dependence on too much technology, like social media?"

Natalie: "Good God, no. But let's not underestimate all the great things technology has done. Keep in mind that the Sun wouldn't be able to choose what systems to shut down and what to leave untouched."

Numen: "Or, God forbid, reduce the planet's population for its ultimate good. Or something beyond our imagining."

Sephia: "Husband, why so gloomy? They debated with each other and fretted over what to do, only asking for permission to test. What can be the harm in that?"

Numen: "I'm just trying to be thorough. All right, so what will you need?"

Carolyn: "Tens of thousands of volunteers. We want to mass our thoughts into a single ensemble, a single prayer, and send it to the sun. That's the plan."

Numen: "Interesting. But how will you know you've been heard?"

Carolyn: "Well, that's the challenge."

Natalie: "But in theory it's testable. We could compare what happened when we prayed to what happened when we didn't. Would periods of prayer coincide with prosperity and periods of non-prayer with catastrophe?"

Sephia: "A little like a test involving placebos, right?"

Natalie: "Exactly."

Numen: "But it would take hundreds of years. Maybe if you—no, that wouldn't work. There must be another way. Can you shorten the test?"

Carolyn: "It might be as simple as getting a response. After all, no one has ever asked for one. We will ask. Wouldn't *that* be nice?"

Numen: "In what form would a response come? Do you imagine the sun communicating its thoughts? How would that work?"

Natalie: "Actually, people have been praying to the sun since time immemorial. Millions of Hindus worship the sun, they call it Surya, every morning. They pray to it for a good crop and give thanks when it comes. The unanswerable question is—did it actually help with the harvest? And Americans and Europeans do sun salutations as part of their daily yoga routine. That complicates the problem."

Numen: "That's exactly my point."

There was silence for a moment.

Numen: "So go and find out. Your research could save the planet. Forgive my earlier skepticism. A sun with a mind of its own but no 3½ pound squishy brain—as you said, it takes getting used to. Well, you've helped me get there." He looked over at Sephia, who nodded her head. "You have our blessings and support. Keep us informed every step of the way."

As they stood up and said their goodbyes, a large snake crawled out from under one of the roots of the great tree that shaded them. The two scientists shrank back and yelped. "Don't worry. It won't bite," said Sephia, who bent over and gently lifted the snake by its hooded neck while stroking the top of its head. "Good Mr. Snake," she purred.

23

The Shadowlands

A long tradition in the Astral was an annual Fair that paralleled Earth's autumnal equinox. On September 22 the celebration began. Tournaments with games ranging from three-dimensional chess to concerts with instruments and sounds unknown to Earth; dances featuring ballet artists whose controlled stretching of arms, legs, and neck had developed an art form unique to the Astral; historical theater placing side by side events as reported by Earth's historians and those same events staged as they actually happened, sometimes with the actual participants doing the acting; comedy routines making great fun of the stupidities of Earth, which left their audiences laughing uproariously at how seriously they took themselves; and costume contests designed to bring out the most beautiful, the most bizarre, or the most hilarious inventions were all part of the fun.

Those more inclined to religion, crowded into their sanctuaries to listen to glorious sacred music: Bach, Mozart, and Beethoven were staples, but also popular were great works of astral composers unknown to Earth. Hindus would act out episodes from their great epics and Muslims Muhammad's ascent to paradise. The newer music and rituals from the Universal Religion appealed to a different set of spirits. Science was a big part of the Fair. Members of the Einstein Circle demonstrated how astral light differed from material, and neuroscientists explained how the mind used the material brain as its instrument until it was shed at death. These and other demonstrations, including the latest inventions being readied for telepathic export to Earth's inventors, were crowd favorites. But nothing captured interest so much as the galactic voyage, a treat for the very few lucky winners of an annual lottery. Specially trained guides would take clusters of these winners to the Andromeda Galaxy to view a planet similar to Earth. Dipping down into the physical atmosphere of the planet required careful herding against getting lost, but meeting their like in that planet's astral world was a fascinating and joyous event without danger. Meanwhile back home, visitors from Andromeda with their weird heads and faces, their bizarre vocal expressions of merriment and grief, the universal astral language they spoke that was so close to Earth's, close enough to be considered a dialect, and their odd bird-like movement when walking intrigued hundreds of millions of viewers. A remnant of life on Earth, not encouraged but tolerated, was the war game. Such games were favorites for some of the men, and famous battles were reenacted on the elysian fields of the Astral, though without injury to anyone.

The Astral's beaches and lakes with crystalline water that seemed like condensed light were the favorite destinations of children. Their teachers, most of them motherly spirits beloved as parents, would tell them about picnics back on Earth where food and drink were taken in through their mouths—which led to cutups giggling and choking. Boat races provided great fun, with the children rooting for this one with the yellow streamers or that one named "Peaches," a fruit said to be a favorite with "the swallowers" on Earth. Some of the children who had memories of Earth enjoyed teaching their big-eyed little peers who didn't. Christmas trees and Easter egg hunts were favorite topics for children from a Christian background; their teachers materialized trees and eggs, then taught the children themselves how to do it. Meanwhile, in Hindu sectors, children enjoyed throwing colored powder at their teachers in memory of the Holi Festival, while Jews taught the young victims of Tay-Sachs disease the Passover rituals that their early deaths had stolen from them.

All this merriment and celebration was followed by the Day of Penance, a worldwide call to descend into the Shadows. Why the equinox? Two Guardians, whose reign is described in the astral histories, thought that the equal night and day was a perfect symbol of the timeless dance between two equally appealing partners, good and evil, and set up the Fair as a reminder of their differing destinies. In some ways the festival resembled the fun-loving Mardi Gras followed by the penitential

Ash Wednesday in the Earth's Christian tradition. The second day had always been regarded as more important for spirits aspiring to higher worlds. In 2027 a record number, about 330 million descended into the world of shadows to teach and hopefully lead out souls stuck there. In 2018 a record number, 17 million, were redeemed—a "bumper crop for God," as one author put it.

No one expected the Guardians to wallow in such a "dirty business," but some in the past had. Now in their fifth year, Numen and Sephia talked it over and decided to descend.

Against everyone's advice, Numen had decided to descend alone. "Perhaps it's my arrogance, but on Sirius I learned that safety concerns were overrated and enfeebled the population."

"But there's a whole class of spirits trained to protect those who go down," said Sephia.

"I know all about the Escorts."

"You're being foolish, husband."

"There aren't nearly enough to go around, Princess, and besides, I can't see how anyone in the pits could overpower me. Can you imagine that happening?"

"It's the environment that might overpower you. That's what concerns me."

Numen shook his head.

They descended through each of the lower spheres and noted how the purity of the light and the splendor of the trees and flowers dimmed slightly as a sphere gave way to the next below it, though by Earth's standards, even the lowest of the seven was grand. They moved lower and entered a land of mist. Pushing on, the mist lifted, but the familiar light didn't return. The sky was overcast, and the usual warmth missing. The soil was rocky and the trees less lofty. Flowers were smaller and gave off no scent.

They came upon a town with rundown houses. Spirits were about, but they didn't seem to be doing anything, and they shrank back as the couple passed them on the way to the center of town, which was marked by a large clock tower in the middle of the main intersection.

A crowd stood near the tower, a few wearing spirit robes and the rest the street clothes of Earth. Robed spirits exhorted the others to accept their help and rise above the mist into the Astral. It was from groups like these that conversions were made. They lived in the upper Shadows and typically were just a single act of humility—usually of forgiveness, either of self or another—away from breaking free. The residents looked stupefied as they listened to the messages of love that poured forth from their robed saviors.

"They've grown so accustomed to their soul sickness that they can't let themselves change," Sephia said.

"We could reach them, wake them up from their stupor," said Numen.

"Then why don't we?"

"We'd be interfering. And it would be too easy."

"Where are the Escorts? I haven't noticed any."

"No danger at this level. We need to go deeper."

At the next lower level an Escort approached and offered help. He carried a staff and wore a red robe with a big cross on it that looked like the flag of Switzerland.

"So it's getting dangerous already?" Sephia said.

"Not for someone as brilliant as you two." His face was ruddy and his hair thick and curly. "Only some discomfort."

"Then you would advise we go deeper?"

"Yes, if you don't mind a challenge. They can get quite ugly down there."

"Thank you, brother. By the way, which level is your home?"

"The second. But I'm going all out for the third."

"You intend to ascend?"

"I hope to. But I still feel the pull of Earth. At times I miss it sorely."

Sephia reached out, took his hands in hers, and gave him that incredible look that could melt a statue. "Thank you," she said.

They continued down to a level where there was much commotion. Robed descenders were going from resident to resident looking for prospects. Others huddled in corners with clients and tried to get them to acknowledge and repent their crimes. The light was very dim at this level, the houses ramshackle or abandoned, and the streets crooked, wide in places and narrow in others for no discernible reason. Leafless trees stood like scarecrows on both sides of the street.

"Look at that woman over there," Sephia said, pointing to a spirit with a face that sagged at the lips in a most pitiful, tragic way. "You go on, husband."

"I'll watch to see if she's receptive, then go."

"Don't be silly. You go on. I'll see you back at the Capitol. Good luck."

Delfina, that was her name, came from Buenos Aires. She had lived with her husband in a marriage that shook the foundations of their home when they argued. "He was a terrible lover from the start," she began, "and was too stupid to learn. And he drank heavily when he came home from the bank. He was a trust officer if you can believe that. His name was Diego." Delfina spit his name out. "So of course I took a lover. Who wouldn't?"

"Did you love him?"

"The lover? Hell no! Actually several. I got addicted to sex, good sex, just a good screw, nothing more."

"No children?"

"Yes, Juan. He was eleven when it happened. When Diego started assaulting me again for enjoying what he couldn't give me, I snapped. I ran to the kitchen and got an ice pick. He was drunk, and when he came at me I stabbed him in the eye, then the neck, then the heart." She paused as she relived the moment.

"Where was Juan when all this happened?"

"Watching television. He came running in."

"What happened next?"

"I was accused of murder, but my saintly mother took the blame. She went to prison for me. She told me to look after Juan."

"You let her do that? Did you protest?"

"No. But it wouldn't have made any difference. She insisted. But I am ashamed."

"It's good that you are. So you live down here in this dark world to punish yourself for your crime."

She was quiet for a moment. "Not exactly."

"What do you mean?"

"I used to beat Juan when I was drunk because he disobeyed me. He was a small, sickly boy. But one night as I was sleeping, he came into my room with a knife. I woke up as the knife plunged into my throat. I looked into his eyes and saw my husband's face. He was in my son's body. My son was too weak to do it. My husband got his revenge."

"My God. What a terrible thing you have been through. I am so sorry."

"I am sorry only for what I did to my son."

"But it was Diego you killed. Do you not feel sorry for what you did to him?"

"What? After what he did to me? He left my son an orphan. What are you saying?"

"Well, can you at least stop hating him? That will keep you here for as long as—"

"Stop hating? I'll hunt him down until—it's the whole meaning of my life down here, don't you see?"

"Delfina, do you want to leave this place?"

"This shithole? Of course I do."

"There is a way."

"A way?"

"You must forgive Diego and yourself."

"Forgive? That's that Catholic shit I grew up with. It's for fools and chumps—and nuns."

"No, Delfina, it's the way out of this place, the only way."

Sephia's eyes narrowed.

"The only way, Delfina."

But there was no response from her to Sephia's kind, loving eyes, misting over with emotion. "The only way," she said one more time, then left.

Meanwhile Numen descended farther into dark, cavernous space. He saw terrible sights on the way down but kept descending. He wanted to get to the very bottom of the world beyond death, not only to better understand the obstacles that stood in the way of redemption, but, as always, because he was curious—curious to experience true hell, the worst that intelligent, sentient life could ever know. He prayed to his Galactic Parents for help. "These are all your children, Father. Help me to love them as you do, Mother. Make me a humble instrument of your will."

He reached a land of jagged rock formations wrapped in a darkness that his eyes could barely penetrate. *Could this be the bottom?* he wondered. Strange screeches, at first distant, echoed around him as if he were in a cave. Moving steadily forward, he came upon a sizable crater with a fetid watery substance in it suggestive of a swamp. Something was thrashing around and making the screeching noise. He thought at first it was some kind of aquatic beast but then realized that two spirits were dueling each other. Around the crater other spirits seemed to be watching the battle but with little apparent interest.

Numen came upon a spirit seated higher up. "Excuse me, sir, but what's going on down there?"

"What! Who are you?" said the man, shocked, drawing back in alarm. "You're burning me."

"An observer."

"You don't belong here. Get away from here."

"What's brought you to this wretched place?"

"Wretched?"

"Are those your friends?"

"Where?"

"Down there, seated along the bank. The spectators."

"Spectators? They're not spectators. They're blind."

Numen noted the man's clothing, no better than rags. He saw how the man never met his gaze and realized the man was blind too.

The man spluttered contemptuously, "Get out of here. Go back where you came from."

"First tell me, what do you all share? What has brought you together in this place? What did you do on Earth?"

"You are hurting me. You are hurting me, I tell you. Go. Go."

"I will if you tell me. What has brought you to this place?"

The man yelled, "We kidnapped children and blinded them, okay?"

"My God, man. Why did you do that?"

"You promised. Go away. Go away, you are hurting me!"

"Tell me why and I will."

"They made good beggars. We lived off the money they brought us. That's how we survived. We took care of them, fed and clothed them, took them to the temple or mosque to do their work. It was an honest living. Without them we would have all been beggars. No one seemed to understand that and they threw me into prison. I hanged myself and ended up here."

"Wouldn't you prefer sight? I can help you regain it."

"Get away. You're a torturer. Get away, far away. Leave this place."

Numen left the spirit and began his ascent out. Not happy with his failure, he decided to try again, this time at a higher level, before putting the Equinox to rest. He was surprised that so narrow an activity as blinding children should result in a common confinement. He wondered if there were many such places in the Shadowlands and realized that he didn't know. He had always assumed that the gravity of the crime, the evil intent leading to the crime, not the specific nature of the crime, dictated where the soul would end up. He wondered now what kind of criminal he would like to interview and where he could be of most help. He disliked the idea of coming home without "a catch." He imagined Sephia coming home with hers.

When studying Earth's history before taking up his assignment, he had been intrigued by the Cambodian dictator Pol Pot, who killed a quarter of his own people and claimed to die with a clean conscience. Numen found it hard to believe and for a while wondered if earthlings were an inferior race until counterexamples of great heroism and sanctity removed his bias. He wondered now if dictators from all over the world and from different time periods were housed in a common ghetto, like the ghetto of the blind he had just left. Perhaps one of the Escorts would know, so he began asking around. One thought he knew where such a place might be. "I once led a spirit to Stalin, one of his grandchildren," he said, "but didn't find out if there were others like him. I wish I had asked."

"Can you take me to that place? I'm not interested in Stalin in particular."

The Guardian led Numen through a maze of dungeon-like ghettoes, dozens of them. They had reached a higher level where numerous descenders and their warrior guards were busy at work.

"We're too high," the Escort said in frustration.

"Don't give up," Numen said. "I think we might be just above the place. Let's go this way."

"Lead on. I'm not in a hurry."

"Is it possible, sir, that you are the Guardian?"

"I am very sorry. I didn't mean to inflict myself on anyone. Yes, I am, but please don't concern yourself with that. I am in your hands. You are the guardian for the moment. It's all a matter of context."

"I can't wait to tell my friends, sir. Oh, here we are."

It was unlike the other ghettos Numen had seen. The shabbiness and gray gloom he saw everywhere was missing here. So was the moldy smell. Dark it was, but the light was strange, not so much diminished as unnatural; it imparted a sharp, glinty edge to objects rather than lighting them up more generally. His second impression was a feeling. It was as if a shadowy but penetrating fear pervaded the atmosphere—not the hatred he expected, but fear. Looking farther out, he saw a bottomless chasm of blackness encircled by a narrow, ascending trail of slippery, loose shale hugging the side of a vertical cliff. The sound of a distant rockslide growled. Where did the trail lead to? It looped around like a horseshoe and continued climbing, but towards what was unclear. Numen learned that the murderer of twenty million serfs did indeed live here. As he suspected, there were others like him. Adolf Hitler, Pol Pot, Mao Zedong, and Joseph Stalin were inmates—that was the word the informant, himself a resident, used. "The Big Four," he added with a sneer.

Numen wondered how he might get an interview with Pol Pot. Should he politely ask? Should he tell them who he was and use the currency these aggressors understood, the threat of greatly superior strength? He decided to mask his status. Hitler, Stalin, and a dozen others were walking the trail. Pol Pot was available and agreed, even eagerly, to an interview.

"I can see by the light you give off that you are a spirit from a much higher world," Pol Pot began. "Unlike the others who have paid us a visit. That is why I am giving you my time, the only reason. Who are you, anyway? Your aura is strange, unnatural, unpleasant."

They stood at the door of one of the many small homes bunched back away from the edge of the chasm, as far back as possible.

"I'm from Sirius, a planet on the other side of the galaxy."

"That explains it. So what brings you here?"

"I'm studying Earth's recent dictators—if that's the correct word?"

"What is your real purpose? What's in it for you?" he asked suspiciously.

"Just as I say. A need to understand."

"So let's say you understand. What then? What does either of us have to gain from this little chat?"

"I'm not sure. Maybe nothing. But let's see what comes of it. Tell me why you—I take it you know how you are regarded on Earth today."

"What, as the ruthless killer of my own people, as an unprincipled tyrant, a psychopathic murderer?"

"That's what people say. That is your legacy. Is it fair?"

"Everything I did I did for my country."

"But there was all the killing. Thousands of mass graves scar the countryside. Two million dead. You were the leader when all this happened. You gave the orders."

"Are you really so ignorant? Surely you know why all this was necessary. There were bad elements everywhere, intellectuals, capitalists, and individualists who refused to step down from their high horse and work the fields to make Cambodia self-sufficient. They stood in the way of a perfect classless society, a shining model for the world to follow."

"So you had them killed."

"To keep them alive brought no profit. To destroy them brought no loss."

Numen stared at Pol Pot as if he couldn't believe what he heard, then said, "Would you say that again?"

"To keep them alive brought no profit. To destroy them brought no loss."

"So you saw all this killing as a necessary evil."

"On the contrary. Bloodshed for a noble cause brings a sense of exultation. There is nothing evil about it."

"Bloodshed brings exaltation? Do you really mean that? I understand you had many of the dead buried next to the fields for use as fertilizer."

Pol Pot changed the subject. "Are you aware that common people still visit my grave and bring rice offerings during the Festival of the

Dead? I feel their pity and am relieved of my suffering. At least a few understand what I was trying to do."

"You died many years ago," Numen continued. "You seem to have only one occupation, walking the trail. Why do you do it?"

"Do I really have to explain that to you? It's the only way out."

"The way out? Yet it's forever out of your reach."

"So far. But I've gotten close, very close. I just have to keep trying. I never give up. I never gave up in life. Why should I give up now?"

"What do you feel as you walk?"

"Fear, fear of slipping into the void. Disappearing into nothingness. The horror of ceasing to exist. Terror. We all live with fear when we walk. But we don't have anything else to do. And there is always the chance that—that we'll make it."

At this point Numen put it all together. He understood why these dictators lived in this strange world. "Tell me, what do you think awaits you when you reach the summit?"

"Rebirth. Another chance."

"There is no other way?"

"What would that be?"

"Repentance. For all the killing you did. For exulting in the killing. There is nothing at the summit, Pol Pot. It's as illusory as the perfect society you murdered your countrymen for Repentance, Pol Pot."

The dictator looked at Numen as if he had seen a wrathful deity who had come to carry him off to hell. Stuttering, rejecting, hoping, horrified, he gaped at Numen, gaped and gaped. Then he fell to his knees and wept. He wept profusely, choking and coughing and blubbering, then screamed, "I meant well! I meant well! Oh my God! I meant well!" His fellows stared in horror at the strange scene.

Numen let him weep, then lifted him up. Pitiful, desperate, utterly miserable, he gazed up at Numen in terror. "Can you get me out of here?" he said in a shuddering, barely audible whisper.

"Only if you stop justifying yourself, Pol Pot. Look underneath that cry, 'I meant well.' Repudiate that delusion. Acknowledge your crime. Then I can help you."

He stood stock still with mouth open, confusion on his face, his whole body quivering. Numen felt his distress as the truth began to dawn on him.

Three days later Sephia and Numen found the time to review their Equinox experiences.

"You went out of your way to help a mass murderer? Why?" said Sephia.

"I hadn't intended it. I just wanted to better understand what drove him. I was completely amazed at his conversion."

"But is he changed? Wouldn't he do the same thing if he had the chance?"

"He would be afraid to." Numen described Pol Pot's fear of falling into the pit and dying. "His basic flaw was not so much a love of power as a lack of fellow feeling. Whether one lived or died was insignificant to him. People were just objects to be used and discarded. But there is hope for him. He took no joy in the killing of people for its own sake, as a sadist would. He was a textbook follower of Mao Zedong: killing the bad elements was the only way to realize his goal, which was to make Cambodia a perfect society, a utopia. I see him as a crazed idealist and deep down a victim of a flawed upbringing which left him with a deep-rooted sense of inferiority and no room for compassion. Is he on the brink of freeing himself from that terrible dungeon? If he is, I dread to think what his next incarnation might bring."

"I hadn't seen until now the merciful side of your nature, husband."

"I looked into the records to see if my thinking was consistent with the originator of that strange ghetto. Guess what turned up. Prima, your predecessor, conceived and designed it. She referred to it as a "boutique dungeon for human monsters." Her desire was not to punish them but to change them. The ticket out was repentance. If sincere, the rest was forgiven. I think Pol Pot might be capable of repentance."

"Surely there were a million others more worthy of your loving interference. Why him?

"I'm sure you're right. But I didn't meet those other millions. I met him."

"Will you be checking in on your monster?"

"Yes, I have no choice. It's not easy going down there, as you know. But I got myself into it. I gave him my word. I'll see it through."

"Just as Fruva warned you not to. Remember the Monsignor?"

"All too well, Princess. All too well. Maybe I'm still being punished for some long- forgotten misdeed, some failure to practice mercy. Poor me."

"Poor husband indeed." She smiled at him, nuzzled up against him, and branded him with a look of love so sweet that his eyelids fluttered like an aspen leaf in spring.

24

Poverty

One of the most admired spirits in the astral world was Sir Leslie Kirkley, the founder of Oxfam. He asked for a private meeting with the Guardians a few days before his ascension "to get some things off my mind." Leslie, who died in 1989, joked in his easygoing manner that he had worked his "mischief long enough for an interim world. But the charm of the place seduced me to overstay."

"We are fortunate you did," said Sephia, while Numen nodded his head. They sat on a porch under a flower-bedecked trellis and looked out over the world he would be leaving. A bluebird with an orange breast sang a sweet melody while peering down at them from the trellis.

"I have closely followed you, both of you, since you arrived some six or seven years ago," Leslie said. I congratulate you on the fresh approaches you've taken to solve problems, both here and on Earth. But Earth's greatest problem, the one thing that grieves me the most, is the poverty of its innocent masses, especially its children. Poverty, and everything that leads up to it—that's what should concern you, as Guardians, the most, if you don't mind my saying so."

"Please go on," said Numen.

"Let me tell you a story." Wearing a purple chemise hanging down to sandaled feet, he rose from his chair and began to amble slowly back and forth while talking. "Meet Flora, a 19-year-old South Sudanese mother living in a Ugandan refugee camp. Why is she there? To keep it simple, her country's two largest ethnic groups are fighting a civil war. Their leaders are both men, one the president of the country, the other the vice-president, mortal enemies. So far 400,000 have died from violence, famine, and sickness. These two men have rigid, undeviating egos. Their main victims are the women and children of their own country.

"Flora fled her village after seeing her friends, including women and girls, gunned down point blank in their homes because their men fought for the wrong side. 'They would enter your home, rape, then kill. My husband and I and our baby fled into the bush just in time and worked our way south to the border. My mother didn't make it. She died of wounds from successive rapes. We finally entered Uganda.'

"That's how she put it to one of our workers. She lives in crowded conditions but is grateful for shelter. She has always wanted to be a tailor but can't get training. Most of her energy is spent carrying water on her head back to the camp and bartering it for food. Other than keeping herself and child alive, there is nothing else for her to do. She is terrified of going back home but doesn't see any future in Uganda either. She is thin, tall, 110 pounds, in good health. Of the 95,000 in the camp, there is not one soul who is overweight.

"Hers is the story of the typical refugee: South Sudan, Syria, Yemen— these are just the worst cases. The world's homeless are refugees from their surrounding societies. They are everywhere, and they need our help. Who set up the camp where Flora is living? Donors. Without donors Flora would have died. That is the good side of the story. So are the efforts by outside agencies to bring the warring sides together and talk peace. The United States is committed to peacekeeping and has the resources to give to it. But that is not enough. It isn't close to enough.

"Maybe we can do something here in the Astral for the Floras of Earth. That is what I want you to consider."

The only sound for a few seconds was the repetitive song of the bluebird. Then Sephia: "Thank you, Sir Leslie, for so thoughtful a presentation. As you were speaking, I found myself wondering about the causes of poverty, and it occurred to me there were many. In Flora's case it was war. But in others it might be a natural disaster or lack of education or even the color of your skin."

"Or being a female."

"I take it you're saying that, whatever the cause, the worst disease of the planet is poverty. There is nothing worse than poverty. It's the ultimate scourge of the planet, and that's where our attention should go. But I'm not convinced."

"You're not?" Leslie glanced at Sephia with a puzzled frown.
"I'm thinking of inequality."
"Really?"
"Think of it this way. What makes people miserable is seeing that others around them have so much more."
"You have a point. But, well, let me put it this way," Sir Leslie went on. "In affluent societies, yes. Where there is very little poverty, that can cause a great deal of suffering. It's called envy, and advertising incites it. But in places like South Sudan, envy is no more than a footnote. When your stomach is growling day after day without letup, you don't envy the man living in the mansion. All you want is a roof over your head and some food in your belly. Yes, there is gross inequality, and it's grossly wrong, but first let's get rid of the poverty. Do you follow me?"
"Hmm. But in the developed world they go together. We should try to eliminate both."
"I agree. But we should keep our priorities straight. First eliminate poverty. Then reduce inequality. Do you agree?"
"Hmm, yes, I follow you." Sephia then turned to Numen. "Husband, you have said nothing. How unlike you."
"My mind is whirring. I'm thinking of the many different causes of poverty. That's where our efforts should go—eliminating those. We'll need plenty of help. What about calling together the cabinet?"
Two days later the Guardians convened the cabinet to discuss Earth's poverty. By now they had dismissed Divinus and Prima's cabinet and chosen their own. These included four men and three women with shining credentials who were admired by thousands, sometimes millions while on Earth: U Thant, the Burmese Secretary General of the United Nations, and a Buddhist; Vaclav Havel, the first president of the Czech Republic; Viktor Frankl, Holocaust survivor and author of the famous book *Man's Search for Meaning*; China-born Chien-Shiung Wu, universally regarded as the First Lady of Physics; Dr. Paul Farmer, celebrated for his heroic dedication to the poor, especially in Haiti; Anandamayi Ma, a Hindu mystic regarded by many Indians as "the living embodiment of the divine"; and Rev. Barbara Harris, the first American bishop in the Episcopal Church and African-American freedom fighter. They lived far apart in their various astral communities but came together when called by the Guardians.
When Sephia summarized the meeting with Sir Leslie and asked for ideas about removing the young woman's suffering, Barbara seemed less enthusiastic than the others. Seated at the right end of a semicircle facing

the Guardians under the great vault in the mountaintop statehouse, she said, "Friends, I have lived here for only seven years and am the last to join the cabinet. I expect to learn more than I teach, so please regard what I say as tentative." She had risen from her seat and clasped her hands as if momentarily in prayer. "I have experienced oppression in many forms and have grown from it. We Christians expect to suffer—we don't see it as contrary to God's will for us—that's why he made the world like it is. We Christians believe so deeply in the value of suffering that we sometimes let it take its course rather than put a stop to it. Every wise parent knows what I am talking about. Without a steady diet of disappointment, the child never becomes a moral being. Suffering is a universal condition. We find it in the animal world, the human world, even the angelic world. I assume it exists everywhere in the universe, even in the heart-mind of God. So let us not be too quick to remove it. Let us reduce it where it clearly stunts the victim but leave it alone when it doesn't, as when on Earth we let a flu virus run its course rather than trying to kill it with medication. Thank you, friends, for hearing me out."

Numen was impressed by her analogy and couldn't help saying, "A boat load, Sister?"

"A thimbleful will do nicely," she said with a smile. "I hope you were taking me seriously."

"Absolutely. Our goal is to figure out a way to reduce suffering when appropriate. The death of her mother, the murder of her friends, the loss of her home, and all the rest—this is suffering we want to relieve."

"Yes. But worse is that she has no way to serve the world—she wanted to be a tailor and can't find a teacher. And there is no way to educate her child properly. She lives without hope. Those are tragedies. But just as bad, possibly worse, is the damage done to children of wealthy parents in the so-called Developed World. Do you see my point? There are worse things than poverty."

"A worthy preamble. Thank you, Bishop Barbara," said Vaclav Havel.

"Just Barbara will do. I haven't found any bishops up here," she said ironically.

"Would anyone object to the use of first names?" said Numen.

No one did.

"Well," Vaclav continued, "can we talk now of how to deal with the problem? First, is it within our means? As a politician I came to appreciate straight talk, all too rare in my experience."

"Viktor?"

"Mind-to-mind prompting—we target either an individual or a group. Our mental power is far greater than on Earth. We don't need words to help Earth solve its problems. We need concentration."

"I have never been good at that, Viktor," said Chien-Shiung. "I don't even—if I may speak frankly as a scientist to a psychologist—I'm not even sure I believe in it. Is there any proof that ideas slung down from the Astral to the Earth have any impact? Do they really reach a target and change things?"

"Before addressing that very interesting question," said Dr. Paul, "can we first draw up a list of the targets? In field work there is doctor and patient. Do we send our prompts—I believe that's the word in use, though I would prefer prayer—do we send them to the Floras of the world or to her providers?"

"Can you be clearer about what you mean by providers?" said U Thant. "How would that work? On Earth I began each day with Buddhist meditation and prayer. I prayed for the whole suffering world. Would I be considered a provider?"

"Spiritually, yes," Paul answered, "but that isn't what I had in mind. In Haiti I could never get enough helpers in the field. I was thinking of sending down a prayer to a possible recruit. Maybe your prayer would serve as inspiration for him to serve. It would jumpstart him to sign on. So I see prayer as targeting potential providers as well as present victims."

"So you can choose to pray either for the sufferer or his helper," said U.

"Or you can pray *to God* to bring relief to the sufferer, let us not forget," said Barbara. "Or to prod the would-be helper into service. You might think of God as the Big Helper."

"But we are talking about what we can do, right here, from the Astral," interjected Numen. "That doesn't rule out God, of course."

"Please, brothers and sisters," pleaded Chien-Shiung, "where is the evidence that all this praying or prompting does any good?"

"Dear sister," spoke Ma for the first time, "I've been here for 47 years, and all I do all day is pray. I pray for anyone a friend asks me to pray for, usually a relative down on Earth, someone who is suffering. I also pray to the gods and saints dwelling in the higher worlds to help. They love to help. They can't wait to hear from me."

"You pray all day? You never rest? You never enjoy yourself?" said Chien-Shiung.

"Oh, sister, prayer fills me with joy. To pray is to love, and is there anything better than love? Oh, sister, you must come with me and I will teach you how to pray. Then you will have no more doubts."

"But, well, yes, I might do that."

"Don't hesitate, sister. Come with me to my sector and I will teach you."

"Can I come too?" said Viktor with a smile and a wink.

"Everybody, come, come!" said Ma, who mistook Viktor's gentle joke.

A moment of solemnity settled over the group. No one knew exactly what to make of Ma, dressed in a white robe with a smudge on her forehead under long straight black hair and the serene eyes of a saint, but all felt blessed by her uncanny beauty. Numen, ever curious, wondered silently why she lived on the Fourth Level rather than the Seventh and decided to ask her privately once the meeting was over.

"Can we be specific?" said Paul. "There is famine in East Africa. Whom do we pray to—and for?"

"Send your prayer to a desperate mother whose child is dying in her arms of starvation," counseled Sephia. "She will feel less alone in her despair. Or to the exhausted nurse or aides workers at wit's end. Your prayers can save lives."

"Or tap into the generous heart of a major donor," added Numen, "and ask them to give even more. Money also saves lives. There are thousands of ways to send all this unseen help. We are connected to each other through the One Mind of the Creator that dwells in all of us. We are like neurons passing and receiving information and feelings through a network of synapses. What the receptor does with it we can't control, but we can try to influence."

"So you are confident we can actually make a difference," said Chien-Shiung.

"Yes. We believe that without help from us the planet would be a chaotic wasteland. Our support is essential. The mystic power of Ma to keep it going, to keep it from destroying itself in this nuclear age, is crucial. It's indispensable. You might have wondered what she was doing among you more celebrated world-movers. Now you know."

"I suggest," spoke up Paul, "that we not sit around and analyze, but get busy. I suggest we rouse our brothers and sisters to send aid on a massive, well organized scale. I don't think most of them realize what an impact their prompts can have. I didn't. How many are following the great regional tragedies raging on the planet this very moment? How many have opened their hearts to the food crises in parts of the world they barely knew existed, or the diseases that cripple children for lack of medical intervention? I have seen it all, friends. If we can make a difference from our end, let's do it." Paul riveted Numen with his intense expression, rubbed his hands together, and said, "Where do I sign up?"

"We could start a campaign like the annual Equinox," said Barbara. "We could set aside an annual day. We could call it Giving Day or something like that and tell our spirit population about the planet's current catastrophes. We could set aside areas where givers interested in a particular disaster gather to mass their prayers and send forth the energy they produce."

"Like electrons absorbing and radiating energy in a laser," said the suddenly energized Chien-Shiung.

"We could call it Laser Day," said a beaming Barbara.

"Laser Day," said Numen. "How rewarding to see you all so enthusiastic."

"So can we set you seven up as a Committee to get it going?" said Sephia.

"It would mean diverting some of your attention from your present activities," said Numen. "If we take this on, we must give it our absolute best. No half measures. Are you all up for it?"

It was hard to resist Numen's powerful charisma. At moments like this the dynamism vested in him by Fruva shone like a meteor. His influence reached a point where it was barely distinguishable from control. A consensus quickly formed, and when U suggested that the other equinox, the Vernal, be set aside as the day, the movement was officially born. It had a name, a date, and a momentum guided by Numen and Sephia that was unstoppable.

Working over the next month the committee identified sixty-three focus groups for the inaugural event, ranging from the rising rates of suicide in the West to the plight of sixteen distinct refugee groups around the world. Earth's many addictions that led to poverty, including gambling, alcoholism, narcotics, and the rampant, unchecked use of social media, drew especially large numbers. The Committee had hoped to attract a billion or more to the thousands of "prayer sites" spread across the astral world but had to settle for 780 million: about a tenth of the total population.

Was the world changed for the better? Were conditions improved compared with the previous year before there was a Laser Day? Wars and nuclear threats continued to roil the world, weather extremes wrought their usual destruction, and addictions worked their fatal mischief; but the number of the dying who landed in the Shadowlands decreased. Still, that was no proof. The committee was working on a placebo for the second event that they hoped would scientifically show a decline in the planet's misery index. Meanwhile Ma had moved on and up. She ascended from the Fourth Level without touching base at the Seventh, a rare achievement. The Guardians were looking to India for a replacement from the same spiritual stock.

25

The Aliens

B y the year 2030 it was clear to qualified authorities on Earth, ranging from high-ranking military specialists to professional ufologists, that aliens were monitoring and studying Earth. Most of the planet's population was either unacquainted with the evidence or seldom gave it a thought. There had never been a decisive event that no one could deny and would change forever the way the world perceived itself. Until October 13, 2030.

At 12:58 Eastern Daylight Time in six American cities, a grey avocado-shaped object approximately fifteen feet high and fifty feet long dropped quickly from the sky and landed softly on a National Football League field surrounded by 60,000 or more fans minutes before the kickoff. Stunned, amazed, frightened, disbelieving, sounds leapt from the stands unlike anything heard at a game as a portal opened from the object and three humanoid beings slightly less than four feet tall stepped out with arms raised. What happened next varied from city to city. In Washington D.C., for the first half minute the three beings stood, their arms now lowered, and waited to be taken. No one moved toward them until five policemen, guns drawn, moved cautiously forward. As they approached the beings, an assistant coach from the Washington team rushed up and stepped in front of the police, as if protecting the intruders. Five minutes later the aliens were whisked into an ambulance and driven to Andrews Air Force Base. The craft, with five more aliens still inside, was allowed to take off and led by helicopter to the same base, where it landed in front of FBI agents, military brass, a platoon of soldiers with weapons held in the patrol position across their chests, and several Air Force reporters and photographers. Five of the six football games were postponed until the next night, a Monday. Astonishingly, the New York Giants game commenced only 55 minutes behind schedule, as if one of the greatest events in world history deserved to take a back seat to a football game.

News of the event reached Numen as he was overseeing a Meaning of Life conference televised across the Astral, and Sephia as she conducted a conference to address the bitterness that the Uyghur Chinese felt against their Han masters. Both were shocked and dismayed. Who were these beings, and if well-meaning why hadn't they given a friendly warning? Sephia remembered seeing beings small in stature and put out an all-points bulletin across the Astral to see if any resided locally. Aliens had always been welcomed—after all, Numen and Sephia were aliens themselves. Why no consultation, no warning?

Eighteen hours later a delegation claiming to speak for the intruders signaled by telepathy to Numen that they were responsible and could explain the situation. The Guardians told them to report to the Capitol at once.

Five spirits looking like earthlings met the couple in a walled-in clearing surrounded by soaring dark-needled trees resembling spruce. The spirits knew the universal language. They said they came from a planet in a different galaxy but in the same galactic cluster. The name of their planet sounded like Teejiv.

Numen began by explaining the setting. "These magnificent trees have always inspired feelings in me of ancient friends. I seem to feel their welcome as I sit in their shade and sniff their resin. Of course, we created them—or rather our distant astral ancestors did. We would like to regard you as friends. You know our language and apparently have resided with us for quite a while. You don't have the bodies of those unannounced visitors down on Earth—you resemble us. Please assume them now if you can."

All five shape-shifted into the small-bodied creatures they claimed to be; the process was almost instantaneous and validated their identity. Their large, black, almond-shaped eyes, tiny mouth, and large bald head matched Sephia's memory.

"You may put back on your Earth uniform if you like," Sephia said, but not before she noted how difficult it was to tell them apart.

They struggled to suit up in their disguise.

"Are you all male?" said Numen.

"No, we are all female," said one of them.

"I see. So tell us what your intentions are, and why you didn't consult us before undertaking something so momentous, and with such an unpredictable outcome. Your friends in flesh might have been shot."

"We knew that. Frankly, we thought you might tell us to go slowly, or not proceed at all, but that is what we'd been doing for almost a century. We felt the time to act had arrived. We understood the risks and advised the commander of the expedition to proceed."

"How did you advise him?" Numen was suspicious.

"Through the medium on the lead ship."

"What you did," Sephia jumped in, "shows disrespect for our ways. I speak to you female to female. It suggests you are beings to fear rather than friends. You're obviously far ahead of Earth. You must think of them as savages with their endless wars, religious feuds, and primitive technology. You could probably take over the planet in the wink of one of your big beautiful eyes. Is that your intention? Keep in mind that Numen and I are both aliens ourselves, so you are not threatening our native planets. But never doubt that we'll do everything we can to thwart an invasion. We will not cooperate with you."

"Madame, you misunderstand us. We hale from a planet that almost destroyed itself seven centuries ago. It still hasn't recovered its native beauty—it never will. We come as models not to follow. We see the way you throw around your threats to annihilate each other, and you have the bombs to do it. Our devices were cleaner; they didn't come with radioactive fallout, but in every other way they were just as crushing. They wiped out a third of the population. Your devices would end by destroying the aggressors themselves and leaving most of the planet uninhabitable. Men and women live among you who let reason control their emotions, but they are too few, and they are never your leaders. They are your sages. They are the people you don't listen to. Will you listen to us? That is our hope."

"Do you have a name?"

"Not one you could pronounce. I have taken the name Kiah."

"And the others?"

Kiah introduced them.

"Explain your method. The planet is in an uproar."

"A healthy uproar. One we anticipated and planned. One that went off exactly as planned."

"How so?"

"For once Earth has forgotten its wars. Your media, those endless news channels on your television sets, your endless replays of the latest atrocities that enflame hatred and desire for revenge, your military gurus who counsel retaliation rather than negotiation and reconciliation, your politicians who refuse to trust the enemy long enough to sit down with them and listen to what they have to say, your arms manufacturers who get rich selling bombs that end by destroying the country in a supposed war of liberation, the death toll that sends mothers to their graves mourning sons they outlive—all of this is suddenly old news. Now, thanks to us, Earth is uniting against what it perceives as a greater threat. The very size of the threat dwarfs all those lesser threats and makes them seem like petty skirmishes. This is exactly what we hoped to accomplish."

"It seems like substituting a greater paranoia for a lesser one," said the unconvinced Numen. "Hysteria might lead to planet-wide madness."

"We don't think it will because we are just getting started."

"Started?"

"We will tell Earth's leaders that if they don't destroy their nuclear arsenals we will do it for them."

"That is a direct violation of our Galactic Parents' regulations," said Numen heatedly.

"We would call them guidelines."

"Then let yourself be guided. You are defying them."

"Guidelines allow for exceptions. Regulations do not."

"Surely you know why the universe is so vast and the planets so far apart. The whole purpose was to prevent meddling by more developed alien worlds, which is what you are doing."

"We haven't come to conquer," Kiah replied, "but to save you from yourselves so you can carry on. You have reached an inflection point where your very survival is in question. I am surprised. We thought you, being fellow aliens, would receive us as friends. We see ourselves as a big brother taking our squabbling junior siblings under our wings. Once we stop the fighting, we'll depart and leave you alone. We have no intention of controlling you. We understand and endorse our Parent's guidelines, or what you Earthlings like to call "the prime directive."

Numen looked at Sephia for help. She stared back blankly as a breeze caressed the branches of the surrounding trees, who seemed to Numen to serve as witnesses of whatever deal might be struck.

"It doesn't matter even if you are well-intentioned," he said. "In cases like this the results are disastrous. You would be treating us like children, taking away the responsibility we must use to solve our own problems. Our morale, our very self-respect, would suffer disastrously." He looked again at Sephia, saw her nod her head, and took a deep breath. "We appreciate your offer and don't doubt your good intentions. But we forbid you to proceed."

The visitors looked shocked, and a few seconds of silence followed. The leader turned to the others and began speaking in their own language as the Guardians apprehensively looked on. "Well," said the leader, turning back around, "what will you permit us to do?"

"Nothing. You have made your point. It's enough for us all to know you exist and are watching us. Earth's ego has suffered a healthy deflation. You can watch all you want, but you cannot interfere."

"Husband," Sephia broke in, "perhaps we can allow them to tell their story."

"Excuse us for a minute," Numen said.

They stepped back and huddled. "That would still be interference, Princess."

"It would, but our Parents gave us discretion. They wanted us to grow as much as those we govern. Following rules is not always the best way to grow. Making exceptions, if undertaken wisely, would please our Parents."

"Let's not rush. Let's bring this to the cabinet."

"No, husband. I know this would help our world, like any good history lesson, not hurt it."

"Is this your intuition speaking again?"

"You may call it that."

Numen began to remonstrate, then fell silent. Shaking his head, he finally gave in and said, "Have it your way."

Their decision was greeted with great relief by the delegation, who dreaded reporting back to those on the ground that they had failed to get a single concession.

Over the next week the Guardians busied themselves preparing the presentation, first for the astral world, then for Earth itself. The Astral had long known other worlds existed because aliens shared their stories and even escorted Earth's astral citizens to their worlds during the Equinox festival. Still, there was great excitement over a televised historical account of a planet's near destruction, especially one outside the home galaxy.

The Guardians asked for a rehearsal before the presentation, and Kiah agreed. They invited her to the Capitol along with her all-female entourage.

They gathered in a grotto featuring a pond into which a thin waterfall flowed down the side of a rock. The aliens showed up in their native attire—small beings grey in color with large, strangely arresting eyes. Kiah's voice was higher than when in her Earth disguise. She began: "Teejiv's gravitational pull is seventh-tenths Earth's. It rotates around two suns and is itself encircled by three moons. A Teejivian year is the equivalent of thirty-one Earth months, and the seasonal variation between winter and summer is less extreme than Earth's." She apologized for cutting short background information about racial differences among its population and the great variety of its subhuman species. What mattered for now, she said, was what led to the crisis that almost destroyed their world. Using the same holography familiar to the Earth's Astral, she showed the planet's undamaged areas—great forests, rivers winding through green plains, rugged snow-capped mountains, white beaches embracing blue-grey seas, skyscraper cities and quaint smaller towns—then turned to the ashen ruins of the two ground-zeroes, where the warring sides incinerated the planet's finest and proudest population centers, the capitals of each country.

Then she told why it happened. "Briffs were humanoid creatures that resembled Earth's apes. Here is a close-up of a typical herd. Their numbers were huge—they bred like your rabbits. From the beginning of historical time they were the primary Teejivian food source, comparable to that of the buffalo for North American natives, except that the Briffs had a somewhat bigger brain. Eventually the plains people, the Shraves, with their vast tracts of arable land, became vegetarians and condemned the meat-eaters of the forested and mountainous hinterlands, known as Drofes. The technology of both cultures was equally advanced. In a moment of self-righteous rage over the plight of the Briffs, the Shrave president's wife, his queen, compared the consumption of Briffs to cannibalism, then compared her counterpart, the wife of the Drofe president, there she is, an ardent defender of the traditional practice, to a vulture-like creature from ancient Teejivian mythology that lived on ordure. There she is. It was an offense that the Drofes could not tolerate, even after an official apology. A Drofe mob burned down the queen's private chamber, a national treasure the equal of the Earth's Taj Mahal. There it is before its destruction. There are some of its art treasures. Three Teejivian years later—eight Earth years—after a string of broken peace treaties, the Drofes, assuming the gentrified Shraves lacked the courage to retaliate, dropped the first bomb on a small Shrave city. They miscalculated. The Shraves immediately targeted a city similar in size. Niney-five days later emotion triumphed over reason, insanity over sound judgment, and half the planet lay in smoking ruins, as you can see."

"Good god, what a story," said Numen, shaking his head after Kiah ended her account.

Sephia stared at the narrator and shook her head in compassion and disbelief. "And it all started over a personal insult?"

"It was more than personal. The Drofe First Lady, as you might call her, stood for her entire people. And there are many backstories that fed into the feud, too many to go into. The insult was simply the trigger. What we want to show Earth is that anything can lead to a catastrophe. Your World War I is a case in point: a disproportionate reaction: 18 million deaths over the assassination of a future leader, not even a present one, by a nineteen-year-old student. You would agree?"

"Of course. By the way," Sephia continued, "Who exactly are you? We never thought to ask. Do you hold an official title?"

"I'm the equivalent of the Cabinet Secretary in the British government, except that I'm a spirit. I'm the senior post-mortem advisor to our president on the ground."

"So you are the official representative of your government," said Numen, "the official advisor from the land of the dead to the land of the living. Did I understand this correctly?"

"You could put it that way."

"And your president," continued Numen, "what is he, or she, the president of?"

"The whole world. We are a one-world planet. A democracy with many countries, but all united in a single system, with all voting from a list of the same candidates, which might be from anywhere in the world, and without party affiliation."

"Incredible!" said Numen. "How in the world did you manage such a thing? It sounds like a recipe for tyranny."

"Except that it's a democracy."

"Well," said Sephia, looking over at her husband, "what do you think?"

"Well, yes." He looked back at Kiah. "I think we can let you go ahead. The trick will be to get Earth to listen to you. How can you quell their suspicions enough to get a hearing?"

"We'll leave that to the troops below. Mixed in with the pilots are some of our best diplomats, a mixture of male and female."

"Are you considered part of the team?"

"Yes, the post-mortem team."

"That's what I assumed but wasn't sure. But you are in close communication with the living, with the troops, as you call them?"

"Indirectly, yes. That is where our mediums come in. We have a clear channel with them. They are trained to let our messages come through without contamination or coloring. And our diplomats are standing by, waiting for our counsel, waiting for the go-ahead. You see, our planet honors the mediums we use. They even have a budget for their development and training. They sift out the gifted from the mediocre. On Teejiv there is a readiness, a planet-wide readiness, to listen to them, and to us through them. We get our messages across to the living with a minimum of static."

"Then they will tell the same story you told us?"

"Yes, it's quite certain. But first we had to get your permission. And now that we have it, we can move ahead. All our study of Earth over the past eighty years is culminating in this present great moment. If we get our message across, if we give Earth our warning, we can return home content."

"But you wanted more," said Numen.

"Yes, and our fleet will be watching. They will not be going home. If Earth reaches a point where a nuclear war seems inevitable, well, I cannot promise you we will not interfere."

"Those words trouble me greatly, Kiah."

"I understand. But we think the message we deliver will make that event much less likely. Your permission should be enough to save the planet. That is our hope."

"I'm not so sure. What would you do if your hopes were disappointed?"

Kiah didn't answer.

"Kiah?"

Again she didn't answer.

November 10 was set as the day of the address. After fractious debate, The General Assembly Hall in the United Nations Building in New York was chosen as the site. For reasons much speculated on but never determined, the lead diplomat chosen to give the address and his two assistants, both robed in dark, somber colors, asked for a quiet moment in the UN interfaith chapel. They were then led to the great hall with its 1800 seats and 75-foot-high ceiling. In an extraordinary demonstration of humility and respect, the President of the General Assembly, the Secretary-General, and the Under-Secretary-General gave up their accustomed seats at the podium behind the green marble desk. Standing on a makeshift platform to be seen better by his audience, the main speaker, who identified himself as his government's Secretary of Alien Development but declined to give a name, addressed a waiting Earth. He supplied the same background and told the same story that Kiah told the Guardians. Then he added:

"I can feel your puzzlement over the notion of a one-world democracy. As you have heard, we were once like you, divided into many countries, each speaking its own language, each with its unique culture or religion, each with its own idea of where boundaries were to be drawn, each with its own way of doing things, each thinking its way was best. It was this way of thinking that led to war. After our Great War, we came to our senses. We saw that our very existence depended on our willingness to cede our national egos to a greater collective enterprise. Only the threat of annihilation could have inspired such an act of generosity for the common good. It took four turbulent centuries to complete the transformation. We put aside our competing ideologies and found an uneasy compromise between the extremes of freedom and control. We urge you to follow this example. Many of us still know our ancient pre-war traditions, but we don't cling to them as if they define us. We have moved on.

"You might say this is asking too much of a people. Would it not lead to tyranny under a demagogue, even an elected demagogue? How could any single authority over a whole world not succumb to the temptation to do as they pleased? Can the natures of Teejivians really be so different from that of earthlings? You might ask what this one-world compromise actually involves. It begins with the way we indoctrinate our children—yes, indoctrinate, I will not use a pretty word to disguise what we do. We instill in them from a very young age thoughts of unity and harmony. We tell them what to think, how to think, and how to live well. We take no chances. And if as adults they deviate, we recalibrate them. If they persist in their individualism, we punish them, usually by caning, as in your Singapore—we do not believe in prisons. If even that does not work, although this is very rare, we execute them. We do not tolerate hardened, uncorrectable criminals.

"'But where is there freedom in your society?' you might ask. Within the boundaries we set there is plenty of freedom. In our arts we do not tolerate ugly or degenerate license, but we recognize and encourage a wide palette of tastes. In our athletic games we delight in sports of many kinds, both those suited for males and for females, like your baseball and volleyball, but never those that rely on violence to entertain, like your boxing. We have no guns, either for combat or hunting. We have what you call social media but regulate it strictly; adolescents are caned for bad behavior, usually with their parents' approval and even gratitude. Sexual expression is reserved for marriage; and sex, while immensely enjoyable, is designed, ideally, for reproduction, not hedonism; we see to it that partners are found for everyone who desires to marry. We have compassion for homosexuals. Racism does exist, but not to the degree we find on Earth: the smooth, unblemished gray of our bodies varies little from person to person, and the variations in the shapes of our bodies, especially facial features, are less extreme and less likely to inspire disesteem or revulsion.

"Health care and education at all levels are free for all, and taxes are high. Salaries are regulated. A salary cap amounting to five million of your American dollars applies to everyone, No one becomes excessively wealthy. The salaries that our athletes or movie stars or inventors or CEOs make never exceed that amount. We have found that five million is enough to inspire ambition and unlock genius without leading to arrogance. On the other hand, we provide a living wage for even the humblest occupations. We regard extremes of material inequality as one of your planet's greatest evils. We regard the bloated egos of your superrich as moral debris.

"We are saddened by the immense disparity in wealth and resources between your rich and poor countries. We look down from our ships at the towering cities that your emirates have built out of the desert with their petrodollars. Then we shift our gaze westward to the parched African landscapes where men wear themselves out trying to coax food out of the hard earth and babies starve. We were once like you, so we don't condemn. But this terrible disparity is our first concern.

"From our ships we cannot see the spiritual factors that make up your psyches, and we are too strange looking to live among you and see for ourselves; but our ancestors, our beloved dead, whose spirits walk unseen among you, tell us much about your societies through our mediums. They say that most children in wealthier countries are not educated to carry the responsibilities of a favored people. Instead they waste their lives chasing pleasure and wealth and never develop compassion for their wretched co-inhabitants. The One-World philosophy that we encourage is alien to them, so Earth's problems are passed along from one generation to the next without getting closer to a solution. They also tell us that your religions, instead of bringing peace to the world, too often breed dissention, especially when they claim to have a monopoly on truth. Our people suffered from similar delusions before the Great War, and in fact the warring religions whipped up the final catastrophe. It took ten generations to substitute the one religion that we all share today for the carcasses of the various creeds that we study in our museums. Only the best among you have climbed out from under the dead weight of narrow convictions and work toward a common purpose in a unified world.

"These are our concerns. We hope that you will learn from the mistakes we made seven of your centuries ago. We have not come to conquer, but to help. In a few days we will lift off, and you will not see us again."

The two emissaries seated beside the speaker stood and, as the crowd was on the verge of applauding, began to sing. Each sang a different note in a high-pitched harmony in the Teejivian tongue that was neither beautiful nor ugly by Earth's standards, but strange and inaccessible—like the sound of a cello to an Amazonian tribesman. Less than a minute later the three singers stopped. Did they smile? Some would later say they did. Together they saluted the crowd, or so it seemed, by raising their left hand, palm down, a few inches directly over their head, as if sheltering it from rain or sun. Standing in this way, they listened as the crowd began a steady but unboisterous applause, as if not sure how it really felt. Police then led the aliens off the platform.

Three days later, the avocado-shaped ships silently lifted off and, having reached a height of approximately 400 feet, disappeared in an instant as earthlings watched on their television sets.

In the following weeks the world bristled with a new kind of conversation. The jaded old stories about politics and war disappeared from the air waves, and the "Teejivian visit" became the only game in town. Most of the world welcomed it, but some called it an "invasion" with dangerous implications. Almost all opinion setters wondered if a Teejivian-style uniformity was feasible on a planet like Earth. Conservatives thought it wasn't and compared it to China, where thought was controlled by a single party. Great numbers wondered how a world could exist without prisons, with only the threat of corporal punishment controlling the criminal element. Western European women overwhelmingly condemned the practice of caning, while Chinese males thought it deterred crime. Some commentators suspected that the aliens had put a pretty face on their world in order to inspire better behavior from Earth. Others advanced a "conspiracy theory" which claimed that the aliens would be coming back to do what they said they would not do: conquer the Earth and set up an administration with those they conspired with. A few even claimed the visit never happened and was a governmental scam perpetrated by "globalists."

Back in the Astral the Guardians congratulated Kiah and her associates as they strolled along one of the Capitol's garden paths. "But I still think you went too far," said Numen. "This was more than influence."

Kiah turned to her associates and said something in their language. "How did we control?" she said, turning back.

"Well, you controlled the media. Earth's media can talk of nothing else. You must have known that would happen."

"But we didn't control what the media would say. Their opinions vary widely. If controlled, they would all be saying the same thing."

"But the very fact that your ships descended to the planet and made themselves visible at a football field left no doubt. No one, a least no one sane, could say they weren't real. Do you think our Parents would endorse so blatant an interference?"

"I think they would," interrupted Sephia. "Teejivians are part of the natural world. When Columbus appeared to the American natives, they were just as surprised. They were influenced and had to adjust. Would you say they were controlled?"

Numen stared at an oversized red flower on a hibiscus bush bordering the path. "Columbus had guns that belched fire as big as that flower. It was more than influence."

Sephia smiled at Kiah and said, "I've never won an argument with him, but he respects my intuition. He's a generous winner."

With that ambivalent comment their dispute dissipated like fog under sunlight, and the meeting came to an end. As for Earth itself, it had become, as an editorialist for The *Guardian* put it, "a little less lofty, a great deal more modest."

26

The Seven Vices

T he ordination of a new cabinet member brought the Guardians and the rest of the cabinet to one of the Hindu sectors of the Astral. Orange banners and tapestries decorated many of the homes that clung tightly together along both sides of a narrow street framed by camphor trees that wove through the quaint old town where Archanapuri Ma lived. Sephia had chosen Ma, this new Ma to replace the former Ma, after weeks of seeking and interviewing. Poet, playwright, singer, and celibate saint, Ma had guided hundreds along the path of total devotion to world renunciation. No one could have been better prepared for death than Ma. She saw it as the gateway to the very world she found herself in now. It was this trait, along with her proven leadership, that attracted Sephia.

Ma had as many devotees in the Astral as on Earth, and they turned out for the ceremony. Now they had gone home, and at last Ma was free to meet her new colleagues. Dressed in a humble white sari and with a bindi the color of pumpkin on her forehead, she bubbled over with joy. Just looking at her brought smiles to the Guardians and other cabinet members except for Chien-Shiung Wu, whose lovely face wore the look of puzzlement.

"We've gathered you here," Sephia said, "not only to greet our new Ma, but to address problems Numen and I have been studying for a long time. Not the problems on Earth that never cease, but here in the Astral, level by level. You seven are beings of great power and competence, each in your own field. What can you do to make our world, the "land of the dead," better? What frailty can you identify and help weed out? Do we encourage too many to come up from the Shadows into our precious country—are we too liberal? Are we too slow to send them back when they obviously don't belong? Are we too reluctant to advise unhappy misfits who never should have gotten here in the first place to try the upper Shadows? Are their presences in the Astral corrupting influences? Some of you know how inclined by nature I am toward mercy—Numen is always reminding me of that—well, he might have a point. So I ask you to keep your eyes and ears open."

"There are seven levels in the Astral and seven of you," Numen continued. "We would like to give each of you free reign, without coaching from us, to identify the chief problem, or, I should say, the most fundamental form of decay at your level. Then let us know what you find. And get as much help as you need, thousands if you can organize them. Think of it as a giant census. We need information. If we don't sweep the floor from time to time, we might end up no better than Earth. Let's set a deadline for a final decision, say, three months from now. Sephia and I won't expect updates. We want to stay out of it. We have our biases and want them challenged."

"This might be difficult," Sephia continued. "All of you but Ma live at the highest level and are used to dwelling in an atmosphere free of sectors. You'd have to spend a lot of your time on a lower sphere, and this would require sacrifice. Would you be willing to take this on? And if so, how would we decide who went where?"

"Fear not, dear Sephia. I'll gladly take the lowest. That's what I did on Earth. I'm good at it," said Paul Farmer with an accommodating smile. "Besides, the Astral is full of charms at every level."

"I'll take the second. We Christians aren't happy unless we suffer at least a little," said Barbara Harris with an ironic grin.

"We Buddhists see suffering everywhere," said U Thant. "I'll take the third level if I can't trade it for the second with our good sister."

One by one they all spoke up, each trying to outdo the others for the "honor" of serving the lowest. They agreed that Ma should stay where she was, at the fourth, and that Chien-Shiung Wu would better fit at the seventh. "I don't mind a bit," Wu said with a chuckle. Vaclav Havel and Viktor Frankl took what was left.

"We should have known," said Sephia. "Thank you. Thank you ever so much for your generosity."

The party broke up and left Ma alone in her Hindu world. Thakur, her guru, had been waiting for over forty years for her to die and take his place. Now he could ascend.

The Guardians had an agenda of their own. The tenth anniversary of their rule approached, and they wanted to show, both to their subjects and themselves, that they had not been sleeping on the job.

When the three months had passed, the Guardians and the cabinet met in secret near Wu's home. She had chosen a spot imagined and sculpted from the ether by ancestors far back in time. Its beauty was stunning. The party of nine looked out on mountains rising vertically from a bottomless depth shrouded in mist. Waterfalls rushed down their sides and disappeared. The nine sat on a flat, smooth, moss-matted rock that stuck out like a giant tongue over the edge of the chasm. Over the rock two ancient, crooked pine trees waved their dark green needles in the misty breeze and filled the air with their scent. Orchids grew out of the crags to the left and right of the tongue, and birdsong reached them from a line of cypress trees guarding the path to it. Wu chose this spot because it reminded her of the vacations she took with her family and the landscape paintings she studied in school. "Sometimes I get homesick for Earth," she said as they sat in a semicircle, gazed at the spectacle and listened to the rush of the waterfalls and the chirps of the birds that cut through the sound.

Everyone sat in silence and absorbed the beauty of the place—sat and gazed, as if reluctant to spoil the moment with the news they each brought.

"Thank you for this moment, Chien-Shiung," said Numen. "We will never forget it."

With that the meeting got underway. They reformed in a circle as Numen asked each to state in a few words what they discovered.

Viktor suggested they go in order from the lowest to the highest, and all agreed. Paul spoke first. "It was sad to see how little ambition there is at this level. The talk tended to be of lives led, not lives dreamed of. There are times for introspective self-analysis, of course, and when done right it's hard work because it leads to regret, repentance, and, hopefully, growth. Very hard work, I would say. But I didn't find much of this at Level One. I saw friendships, dedication to jobs assigned, fun-loving games, every kind of entertainment, many good things. But also boredom. And no wonder. Without goals to reach, high goals, entertainment and small talk grow tiresome. These were decent souls. They wouldn't be in the Astral unless they were. If I had to choose a word that summed it up, I would choose sloth: contentment with where they were, with too little momentum to carry them forward."

"Do you think they are headed for rebirth?" said U.

"Most of them. I don't see what would propel them upward."

"That is very illuminating, Paul. It's what we suspected. Thank you."

"Barbara, tell us what you found at Level Two," said Numen.

"Much of what Paul found is what we found too. This was partly due to a kind of homesickness for the basic comforts of Earth. Take food for example. Many here experienced serious hunger on Earth, even starvation, and they carried a longing for food right into the afterlife, where of course it's not needed or available. There were others who had never known hunger—Americans especially—whose social lives revolved around eating and drinking, sometimes bordering on gluttony. Some of these missed the routine—decent people who lived from pleasure to pleasure 'until death grinned in at the banquet,' to quote William James. Many of them show little interest in joyful service or spiritual growth. Will they rise to the next level? I am no one to judge, but it seems more likely they'll return to Earth—even though many don't even believe in reincarnation. So where will they be ten years from now? Will boredom ignite a spark of interest in higher pursuits? And is there anything we can do to ignite it? Is it even worth trying? Well, friends, that is my report."

"Thank you, Barbara," said Numen. "How powerful the pull of Earth! U, you are next. Tell us about Level 3.'

"Level three, yes. The third sphere. Well, I found a lot here that Paul and Barbara described, an awful lot. But it took on an accent they didn't mention. My assistants, hundreds spread all over this lovely sphere, kept bringing me back accounts of sexual play. Mostly good memories, nothing perverse, no rapes, and almost no pornography. But too much loveless sex, both within and outside of marriage. I personally did many interviews when I kept getting this feedback. I asked questions like, 'Was sex without love a good thing in your memory?' Mostly no, they admitted. I talked to celibates to get their impression. I wanted to know if they had risen above their need for sex, or did they feel they had missed something basic, something essential to the human experience? The answers varied. I talked to homosexuals, and their enjoyment of sex tended to be quite intense. Yet most of them said the desire to have children was fundamental rather than sexual pleasure. Many wanted to go back to raise a family. I got answers from all over the place. But one thing stood out. Those old couples who were contentedly married and some of the old celibates felt no desire for it, but many of the others felt it strongly—call it lust—strong enough to deter them from ascending. The Buddha said the cause of suffering is *tanha,* selfish desire. I think he was right. All of this is not to say that sex was the only predominating memory. Far from it. But it showed up more frequently than I imagined.

"So do you think those old married couples and lifelong celibates were ripe for ascension?" said Numen.

"Not as a rule. There were plenty of other longings holding them back," said U.

"Thank you, U. Now it's your turn, Ma."

"Thank you. Like all the levels before the highest, religion figured. I sent my assistants all over the sphere. We observed every major religion, even broke them down by sect. We focused especially on how they converged as the dogmas that defined them and kept them distinct tended to decay. This confirmed what we already believed: that as the lower astral zones gave way to the mid-range, souls showed signs of spiritual maturity. But there was still quite a difference between the Fourth and the Seventh. For example, in my own Hindu sector, casual conversation between friends often turned to the money they made back on Earth. They told tales of conquest in business or how grand their houses were once they emigrated to America or the millions they sent back to their relatives in India or left behind at death. How does this manifest itself at Level 4? By the palaces they have built for themselves. For me this is embarrassing. It certainly doesn't suggest that our great saints of the past with their emphasis on world renunciation have much sway here. Or that the souls living in these mansions are serious about freeing themselves from rebirth, which is the whole point of our religion. But young souls outnumber old ones in every religion. So, in the last analysis, I guess all is as it should be. I can say with that great Christian saint Julian of Norwich, 'All shall be well, and all shall be well, and all manner of thing shall be well.'"

"Let us hope so, Sister. Again, this confirms what we suspected. Thank you. Viktor, what stood out at your level?"

"Level Five is not a realm where all is well, that is certain. Energetic souls with powerful egos and often a record of high achievement on Earth are common here. Sparkling cities and grand amphitheaters for concerts and games dot the vast landscapes, whose natural beauty rivals that of even the Seventh. All this competitive energy has made the Fifth, as we all know, the leading tourist destination of the astral world. It brings delight to countless millions before they dive back into matter. However, all this creative energy has given rise to unhealthy competition. Imagine this sphere divided into city states claiming bragging rights for being the best and attracting the most. What began as a friendly contest among brotherly factions has evolved into a sometimes rancorous war of words, with entire communities united in competition against others, as if they were back on Earth trying to win an election. This is shameful for any level—it's what you would expect in the Shadowlands. In my view, drastic measures are required."

"We are aware of the situation, Viktor," said Numen. "If the leaders of these factions can't govern themselves and live in harmony among themselves, we'll seal off the boundaries, and there won't be any tourists for them to entertain. But already there is movement toward a truce. Let us remember that these are not bad spirits. I'd be surprised if, once they regain their sanity, they won't change their habits. Even so, we'll ask them to go through a ritual of public apology, televised to the entire sphere. If they remain uncontrite, not likely, we won't hesitate to escort them to the Shadows. Well, Vaclav, I trust you have better news from Level Six."

"Ah, the Sixth. In general we found a keener intelligence and greater emotional range than on the lower five. This showed itself in many ways, negative and positive. Deep emotional attachments abound here, as we've always known. Ideas on Earth like *Soul Mates* wedded for eternity probably come from memories of having lived at this level. These couples are beautiful to observe but left me, personally, feeling a little envious, for I have not found her, or perhaps it's more correct to say she hasn't found me. That brings me to the negative. By now cultural, religious, class, and racial identifications are in full retreat. The qualities of one's inner character have taken their place, and auras leave little doubt about it. This is good, of course, but there is a dark side. In place of competition between more visible attributes, we found a subtler form leading to a sadness that one's virtues and talents haven't been recognized as much as those of others. We all hunger for recognition, but when its absence turns into resentment over the good fortune of another—a better job, a more esteemed appointment, especially a coveted friendship—envy sours the joy of life at this high level. We found quite a bit of this. I think it requires our attention."

"Very interesting—and to me surprising. Definitely something to be looked into. Thank you, Vaklav. That brings us to the seventh and last sphere where most of us live. Is there anything more to say that we don't already know? If there is, I suspect that our scientist, Chien-Shiung, has found it. Chien-Shiung?"

"Thank you, comrade. At this highest level, where most of us are steeped in the spirit of service and aspire for ascension, one must peer through a microscope, so to speak, to find a flaw. I should tell you that I had fewer than fifty assistants to help me. I could have arrived at my diagnosis without them. I only needed to search my own heart. After I tell you what I found, I will excuse you for concluding that my own actions prove my thesis. As you focus the microscope on your own heart, will you not find what I found? Do we not possess a sense of self, of self-worth, that is slightly out of phase with reality? Are we not tempted to think that we deserve what we have attained and that others do not? Do we forget that we owe so much of what we have attained to good fortune, and they to bad? Unless I remind myself, I do forget. Forgetting is my default position. That is all I have to say."

"I don't think we can be reminded too often of this great truth," said Numen. "Humility and gratitude are the antidotes. Thank you, Chien-Shiung. Well, we have much work ahead of us."

"Can we take a break before considering what to do about all this?" said Sephia.

"Perhaps at a later meeting after we've had time to think it over?" said Paul.

Sephia looked at Numen, who nodded.

"All right. Let's reconvene next month. We'll be in touch."

"Well," said Paul, suddenly standing, "Whooooooo!" He leapt into the misty void with this happy shout and flew like a hawk toward the mountains far off. The company looked in astonishment at each other and wondered what to do. Then Sephia took off with a whoop of her own. The rest followed except for Ma. When they returned to their eyrie on the rock, they laughed gleefully like children at play.

Paul teased Ma for not joining in. All Ma would say was, "I felt stuck. I've spent half my life seated in meditation. I just couldn't bring myself to get up."

At this, Paul picked her up—she was as light as a ghost—and took off with her in his arms. Then he let her go; and they flew side by side toward the mountains, then back. They landed on the rock with Ma wearing a face of utter exhilaration. From that point she and Paul formed a friendship that neither of them had known on Earth. His colleagues whispered among themselves that he might have found a soul mate at last.

The nine left their eyrie, full of joy but pondering what lay ahead of them, like vacationers returning to homes that had weathered a storm in their absence.

27

Sun and Moons

Sephia and Numen enjoyed reading. After a series of meetings over the civil war in South Africa, they sequestered themselves in the public library near their home. Large and spacious with high vaulted ceilings, as if made to resemble a church, they settled into their favorite chairs side by side with a small table between them. The regular patrons knew them and felt honored to share space with their Guardians but didn't dare disturb them. Sephia was reading a book just released by a novelist who on Earth had practiced psychiatry. He hadn't found the time to write a book but found plenty of it after death as a Level 5 resident. He titled it *Freud's Nightmare*. If books were for sale on the Astral, it would have been a bestseller.

"I must make a point of hearing him lecture—such a fascinating thesis," she said in a low voice approaching a whisper.

"Tell me about it," Numen said as he laid his reader—a device resembling a Kindle—on his lap.

"He's created a society on a fictional planet in which the sex organs of a few dozen newborns appeared on their chests. Seen as freaks by almost everybody, a cadre of psychiatrists, neuroscientists, and theologians wondered if they presaged the future of the species and studied them as they matured into adults and cohabited. I won't tell you where this is going, only that the book is suggesting that someday Earth might evolve to a point where sex and urination are not physically connected. You know how children are astonished, even revolted when they hear about this for the first time. That's because—well, I don't have to explain it. Anyway, the book is a serious evaluation of the Creator's wisdom in linking creation and waste at this stage of their evolution. And a most interesting speculation on what disentangling the two would mean for a more evolved society."

"How utterly bizarre. I should think the only evolution needed is what we have here," said Numen. "Profound love, even passionate love, but without sex organs to express it or any waste matter. Perhaps the book is halfway there. By the way, where do the newborns come out?"

"From the breast."

"Interesting. I should have guessed."

"Well, husband, how is your book going?"

"A bit sludgy, but fascinating to a geek like me."

She laughed. "Tell me about it."

"It's a debate between two theologians, a Scot named McManus and an Indian named Das Gupta. It's based on a series of letters they wrote exploring the subject. Das Gupta thinks our Ur-Parents experience all time as an eternal changeless present—there is no past or future. McManus thinks the past is past and the future hasn't happened yet and can't be deduced, not even by the Creator. In other words, our Ur-Parents are a little like us."

"What do you think?"

"For me, Princess, existence is meaningful only if there are things that need to get done, things in the future. If everything is already set, life is pointless, even for our Parents. I imagine them as observers, planners, doers who enjoy or suffer with every unforeseeable oscillation of the universe. What about you?"

"For me God, if you'll excuse me, God is a zero point. Do you remember Ma quoting that Christian mystic, 'All shall be well'? For God, all *is* well. The future is always full of surprises for us, but I don't think our Parents can be surprised. If they could, that would mean they were limited in knowledge. I think of them as free from limitation of any kind."

"So what would be the meaning of their life."

"That question doesn't compute. As you say, meaning implies an unpredictable future that beings like us seek to control. Isn't that what we, you and I, are doing, trying to control the future of the astral world, even trying to influence events on Earth, trying to make everything better?"

"Don't you think that's what God is doing? Anyway, this is getting interesting. Do you mind if we fly back home?"

They alighted at a grotto they called the birdbath after a sculpture of St. Francis holding above his head with outstretched arms a circular dish filled with water. Birds resembling those from different regions of the Earth flocked to it, not to drink, but to bathe. Songs rose from it as if from a concert, with tones as varied as a tuba from a piccolo. Sephia was especially fond of the place.

"As you were talking, husband, I suddenly became aware that all the problems of Earth spring from a single source, a lack of anything to do worth doing. Isn't that the way it is? People drift through life from pleasure to pleasure never giving a thought to what they should be doing. And without a sense of life's meaning, its purpose, they'll never *know* what they should be doing."

"And what, Princess, is that meaning? You say there is only one. That's a tall claim."

"I think there is ultimately only one. Lesser meanings come from it, but they are like moons that circle the sun."

"Moons circle planets."

"Sometimes you can be so infuriating, Numen, such a know-it-all. I think you get my point."

"I apologize. So what is the sun?"

"I'm not going to tell you, not yet."

"Not tell me?" Numen looked at the fountain, where birds were fluttering their wings. "You're like those birds flitting their wings and throwing off spray. You're giving me only spray."

"Be patient, husband."

"All right, so what are the moons?"

"Well, let's make an inventory of what's gone wrong on Earth and what's worth doing. Where would you start?"

"Well, I might start with the climate crisis. Earth can do something about that, and they should. For some people it's become their religion. A good religion, but not, according to you, the best. Not the sun."

"No, not the sun. Social media is another problem, a very grave one. Users write things they'd never dare say out in the open. Feelings are hurt, reputations destroyed, lies told. Criminals operate undetected in lawless space. Thieves prey on the elderly. Advertisers make outrageous claims. Fixing that problem is another moon."

"And young people live on their phones," Numen added, "instead of in their books. Earth has become a circus of distraction. How do we fix all this?"

"Then there is the entertainment industry. Movies for the masses are full of violence and sex, with every producer interested only in some novel way to shock the audience. And sex is made to seem as if it's just another form of entertainment, like a game of bowling or a dish of ice cream. It's completely cut off from what the Creator made it for."

"Now that you've got me started," said Numen, "another problem is illiteracy. It's rampant, not only in undeveloped nations, but everywhere else to a lesser degree. Thousands who can't sign their names come to us every day. We teach them the universal tongue once they get here, how to read as well as speak. We need a moon to shine on them, to use your metaphor, before they get here—a big, bright moon."

"So true. Another is the decline of the arts—music, painting, storytelling. The crasser, the angrier, the uglier it is, the more attention it gets. Jaded critics find classical expressions of true beauty boring. They deflect young minds away from them before they've had a chance to discover them. Sometimes I wonder if illiteracy is always a bad thing."

"That's going too far, I think."

"Of course. But the damage done by well-educated, depraved intellectuals is disastrous.

Then there is the manufacture of weapons on such a scale that they create great wealth for the countries producing them. Millions of children have stepped on mines left behind in war zones and lost a leg or their lives. For me that's unspeakable."

"So you are saying, Sephia, that a single remedy can fix all these problems."

"No. There will always be evil. But it would have the best chance of keeping it in check."

"I'm intrigued. Please, don't keep me waiting."

"What Earth needs is a Meaning Brigade that marches under the banner of true religion."

"That's the sun?"

"That's the sun."

"And what is true religion?"

"You know it already. You've been practicing it since your last life on Sirius, and probably long before. You pledged your life to save it from self-destruction. What made you do it, husband?"

"Well, I saw what needed to be done and did it."

"Of course. But why, and at such great cost?"

"Well, because I saw myself as a servant to my people."

"You didn't do it for something you had to gain?"

"Well, I did have much to gain, my life along with everybody else's, but that wasn't especially in my thoughts."

"Your people, the whole planet, was in your thoughts, correct?"

"Yes."

"Let me ask you to go deeper. Why was it important to be of service to your people?"

"Well, because it's the right thing to do, Princess. It helps the people you influence have better, happier lives. Rising above selfishness and healing others—for me that's the sun. Isn't it yours?"

"But you overlook one thing, Numen. Why is it good for you to rise above selfishness and help others?"

"What a question!"

"If you can answer it, you have found the sun."

Numen frowned. He had never witnessed this side of his wife, more like an inquisition than a friendly conversation.

"It's because our Parents have fashioned us in such a way that to do anything less leads to futility and unhappiness," she said.

"Is that all? Isn't that what I've been saying all along?"

"No, husband. You left out any mention of our Parents. You left out any mention of a divine plan. And in that you failed to give religion its proper due."

"Are you saying that religion is the sun?"

"True religion. What else prods humans to better themselves? What else assures them there is a reward for making the effort? Where else do they get the incentive?"

"I see where you're going. But this all boils down to a proper understanding of the divine will—to a true theology rather than what you call true religion."

"But theology is housed in religion. It's a subset of religion. And religion is more than intellectual. With its rituals and stories and commandments and gatherings of souls in a common purpose it nurses the whole person. It's a wise therapist who knows how to help a soul heal and grow. It plants the seeds for ascendancy rather than another life on Earth."

"Getting back to the moons—"

"—yes, the moons, they are never the ultimate source of light. But once they reflect the sun's light, they are powerful drivers toward human solutions. They empower souls to solve all those problems we mentioned earlier. Without them humans procrastinate or leave the work for others to do. And those that do power ahead often forget the original goal and end by creating monsters instead."

"Monsters?"

"Yes. Think back to the day we were walking in the rose garden on the south side, admiring its beauty. You told me about some medical geniuses working toward wiping out diseases that shorten the human lifespan, a noble enough goal. But then they got carried away and embarked on research to prevent physical death. You said this madness is driven by the desperate conviction that physical life is the only life they'll ever know. And this dread drives them toward madness. You then said true religion—those were your words—would show them that death is a portal to a better life, not annihilation. Do you remember?"

"Yes, but we weren't walking at all. We were flying over a new mosque on the Third Level we'd been invited to inspect."

"No husband, we were flying over the rose garden."

He shook his head but didn't answer. "Well, that leaves us with the question of what to do about all this. We see religion on the decline all over Earth. If you're right, and you've made a pretty good argument, then the solution is to find a way to turn Earth back toward religion."

"To true religion," Sephia said.

"That's a tall order, Princess. Earth is not updating its religions. They sound ridiculous to people with scientific backgrounds, and that's a great loss both for them and those they ridicule. You want reform, and so do I. But that's not the way Earth is tending."

"We can only do what's possible, Numen. That's our job. What's important is that we know where to start. I think we've found that. Are you with me?"

"I'm not opposed. We could begin with the cabinet, then spread our ideas across the Sixth and Seventh levels? We could put together that Meaning Brigade you mentioned and bombard Earth with the most powerful spiritual energy we can muster. How does that sound?"

"Great."

"Do you really think it'll work? That it will change the whole world for the better?"

"Numen, my intuition is ringing like a bell in my head and telling me Earth will return to religion, a new religion, something that makes sense and inspires what's best in us: compassion, service, cooperation, harmony, hospitality, and a passion for justice. Let that become the planet's new currency. There will always be the darkness of evildoers, but the moons will outshine them."

Her face took on a beatific expression as if she were witnessing angels. "I see our Galactic Parents looking down upon Earth as if they were standing beside me. And they are smiling."

28

A Strange Coincidence

By an arrangement made centuries earlier for convenience and followed ever since, "Graduation Day" coincided with Earth's full moon. This was a time for celebrating the souls who were moving up, millions of them, either from a lower to a higher sphere, or up and out of the astral world altogether. This was also the day that the Guardians most looked forward to—a recess from work every twenty-eighth day, a holiday on which they customarily visited two or three of the 100,000 sites where the celebrations were staged. Seated in the place of honor, they would listen patiently to the names of the graduates and take note of the places they came from, as distant geographically and culturally as a Japanese statesman from Kyoto to a trekking guide from el Chaltén, Argentina. It was their habit to interview, sometimes at length, selected graduates following the ceremony. On one of their visits—to a Third-Level site as it happened—a strange thing happened.

"Did you hear that name, Princess? 'Pascal Debrisson, Catholic priest from Fresno, California.'"

"I'm sorry, I was daydreaming. What did you say?"

"Pascal Debrisson. Do you recognize that name?"

He repeated the name, then added, "That's the priest who—"

"—oh yes, who got lost in the mountains, of course. He's here?"

"I've always wondered what happened to him. Yes, they called out his name. I'll never forget it."

Following the formalities they wound their way through the adoring crowd and found Pascal. He was astonished that the Guardians of his new world—he had died more than thirty years ago—knew who he was; even more when they embraced him like a long lost relative and Numen said, "Congratulations, Pascal, on your promotion. We have some questions for you."

They lifted off and found a secluded spot next to a brook where two boys were fishing for trout.

"Hello, boys," Sephia sang out, "Catching anything?"

The boys looked startled but didn't recognize the adults. "Plenty," said the bigger boy. "They just swim up and hang on to the lure. Not like home. No bait and no hook."

"Have fun," said Sephia. They walked upstream a little and sat down in the grass.

Pascal told a typical story of joyous surprise when he came over: how his mother, maternal grandfather whom he had never known, and more than thirty of his former parishioners welcomed him. He described the new friends he had made and the first assignment he was given as pastor of a Catholic church, then how he "outgrew" it.

"So they made use of the skills you developed on Earth. You didn't want to do something different?" said Numen.

He described his interest in higher mathematics: "I finally understood calculus," he said, "really understood it. It was thrilling to have such a good mind—the fog of Earth was lifted. But I missed preaching. So back into the Church I went until I realized that most of the dogma wasn't true. The Virgin Mary, Jesus seated at the right hand of the Father, heaven as a place of rest and perpetual adoration, a second coming at the world's end—no, none of this fit. But on the big issues—God, afterlife, loving one's neighbor, accountability for one's actions—that squared with what was best. And that's what the Universal Church was teaching, minus all the other stuff, so I began attending."

"So you weren't disappointed that Jesus didn't meet you and lead you to a place of unending, changeless bliss?"

He thought for a few seconds. "Only at first. And just a little. This is certainly not a place where you can goof off. You have jobs to do and schools to attend if you want to advance. But the whole atmosphere is so pleasant and the people around you so encouraging and friendly and honest and vulnerable—and no one is in a rush, and you're never tired, and it's so beautiful, so many good things."

"I take it you've not visited the Shadowlands," said Sephia.

A shadow fell across his face. "That was one of my duties as a pastor." He shook his head as if chasing away a frightening memory.

"Pascal—we've been curious about this for a long time—did you escape death when stranded on that rock?"

"You know about that?" Again he was astonished.

"Our teacher described your dilemma as a teaching exercise when we first arrived. She went into great detail and told us you had recorded the whole story. But she didn't tell us whether … and we never got around to researching it ourselves. Did you manage to escape death?"

"So you know the whole story that I described for the archives."

"Except whether you survived."

"I had given up, prepared myself to die. But a bear hunter wandered up my way. I thought I was hallucinating but called out. He was real. I was taken out by helicopter."

"Amazing. I think your prayer was heard. The story our teacher told left very little room for hope," said Sephia. "We assumed you died. But you died later."

"Much later. Of cancer."

"Well, what are your plans now?" said Numen. "Will you lead another church?"

"Not right away. I want to fight the Bulge."

"Really?" Numen studied Pascal as if seeing him for the first time. "That's brutal work for a priest. Especially with Fourth-Level sensibilities. Are you sure?"

"Both my French grandfathers joined the Resistance and died defending their country in the Second World War. Now this is my country, and I want to defend it. And I won't even have to die."

"But you will have to suffer."

"Don't worry, sir. I'm pretty good at that."

29

The Bulge

The event Pascal referred to got its name from the Battle of the Bulge, Hitler's last major offensive against the Allies' Western Front. Periodically, usually every forty to sixty years, rebellious spirits from the Shadowlands stormed the Astral at a weak point. Usually united under a powerful leader, they tried to set up a confederacy of disgruntled, resentful spirits who felt they had been misunderstood and unjustly condemned to a miserable existence. In past invasions they managed to annex territory inside the boundaries of the Astral, where they squatted for periods ranging from a few months to a year. Their number reached 700,000 in the last insurrection.

The Astral had a regular process for admitting reformed souls into the regions of light and took great satisfaction in providing this service of love. Its goal was to empty the Shadowlands, but in an orderly way. In the most damaging recent invasion, in 1974, a band of rebels stormed a Level-One sector noted for liberal views and the absence of any particular religious or cultural identity worth vigorously defending. After a nine-month siege the rebels began fighting each other for hegemony, and many began retreating into a more comfortable climate— back where they had come from—where the light did not burn. But the damage had been done. The sector's psychic structure showed signs of disintegrating; many of its proudest buildings had begun to crumble or lean, as if damaged by an earthquake, and its beautiful trees to wither. The chaos of unregulated, indifferent concern for the country they mismanaged was reflected everywhere. Divinus and Prima were sickened by what they saw and resolved never to let it happen again. Now it was up to Numen and Sephia to follow through.

The rebels, this time numbering around half a million, first penetrated the thick nebula that separated the worlds of light from the shadowy spheres below. Their uprising could be compared to lava coming out of the ground, then flowing horizontally across the territory they invaded, creating a bulge about 35 miles across and 40 deep. Volunteers like Pascal answered the call that Sephia and Numen put out. The volunteer leaders came mostly from the Fifth Level, where the fiercely competitive spirit noted in the census found its home. The semicircular line of advance by the marauders came to 110 miles, and volunteers in the hundreds of thousands stood in the way of the bulge, where spirit met spirit in psychic warfare. The weapons weren't made of steel or gunpowder but the stuff of minds massed in powerful swaths of concentration.

Pascal was a member of a company of spirits on the front lines that a column of rebels had overrun. Some of the more sensitive defenders felt their bodies had been walked through, with pain reaching levels of psychic torture. Pascal, one of them, remembered Numen's warning that he would suffer.

Astral reserves in greater number massed their minds in determined opposition and held. The column of invaders fell back. Pascal's company watched as they retreated.

The defenders were of two types: one the type that Pascal was attached to. These thought of themselves as soldiers inspired by a common loathing of the enemy. The second, a majority of them females, refused to hate; their resistance came from deep meditative states calling down divine energy—they called it grace—from the higher heavens. If massed sufficiently, it created a wall of support for the infantry in the front lines. Radical meditators, massed in the tens of thousands well behind enemy lines, claimed that without their aid the war would be lost and the entire Astral overrun. According to their teaching, grace intensified light to such an extent that it became unbearable to shadowed spirits. They thought of themselves as pacifists; many came from the Seventh Level.

Infantry leaders relied on bravery and a capacity to tolerate suffering and often doubted the claims of their more spiritual combatants, whom they regarded as ancillary to the outcome of the combat, like military chaplains on Earth.

Pascal, grandson of fighters who had given their lives as soldiers but a priest by calling, valued the meditators. Ever on the watch for another assault but with plenty of time to do little more than wait, he sometimes got into debates with his fellow soldiers, several of them well educated with doctoral degrees and a few even aspiring for ascension, while others made fun of "the intellectuals" with their mastery of the universal tongue and their "dainty" wartime sensibilities.

"Ancillary, you say," one of the less refined soldiers challenged, "what does that mean?"

"It means chaplains don't win wars," said one of the intellectuals with a chuckle.

Pascal jumped in. "But they do. They're like faithful dogs that come to the aid of their masters."

"What do you know about dogs, Padre?" said another. "Did you ever have one?"

"He might know more than you think," said a witty Moldavian pretending to come to the padre's defense. "Isn't there a famous dog in the Bible?"

"There's no famous dog in the Bible, Marius," said an evangelical Christian from Texas. "They were regarded as wild and dirty."

"I bet Jesus didn't think they were wild and dirty. If he did, he never met Heidi, my chihuahua."

"They didn't have chihuahuas in ancient Israel. What are you saying?"

Rambling, ridiculous soldier talk helped the time to pass. But, at other times, "Here they come again" rang out across the plains. On a good day the rebels piled up like debris behind a dam, shouted insults, and eventually pulled back. Pascal used these times to parlay with any rebel who would shut up and listen.

Once he got into a conversation with an anti-ET racist from Germany who claimed they wanted to remove the Guardians. "How can you allow yourself to be led by aliens? They don't understand Earth, yet they condemn me to hell. Have you been down there?"

Another time he came up against an Iraqi who bristled when the conversation turned to his wife. "She was a bitch who took pleasure in defying my orders. Even when I beat her, she carried on as if nothing had happened. I always followed the Quran, yet look where it got me." Further talk revealed that the man had standards of housekeeping so exacting that no one could have followed them. Eventually it became clear that he was a sadist who treated his wife savagely for the pleasure it brought him.

"You were not following the Quran, friend," Pascal dared to say.

A bolt of hatred raged out of the man. Pascal fell back in pain and retreated to the safety of his fellows.

Another time it was more difficult to pry out the flaw that had landed the perpetrator in the world of shadows. Eric, an American property lawyer, fit that description.

"So you say you spent time away from the family in the privacy of your study," Pascal said. "You made your wife deal with the kids. You didn't help her."

"She didn't work. So, no, I didn't. I had to book my hours at the office and came home to my study, late, exhausted."

"I take it you made good money."

"You could say that."

"So what did you do in your study? How did you unwind?"

Eventually Eric admitted he allowed himself to "indulge in a little porn."

"Did your wife know?"

"Oh, come on, man. You're not going to tell me I should have told her."

"That's not for me to say. But why porn? Of all the things you might have been doing, why porn?"

"You really want to know the truth? My wife bored me silly. Now, can I help that? Am I to blame?"

"So you just stuck it out?"

"No, how could I? How could any man who was surrounded by beautiful women at his beck and call?"

"Are you talking about your assistants at the office?"

"You're goddam right I am."

"And your wife knew?"

"I tried to protect her, but, well, you can't keep things like that under wraps forever."

"No, I guess not. And your kids. How did they take all this?"

"They didn't come to my funeral, I can tell you that. They took her side after the divorce. They disowned me, and I had no choice but to disown them. I left them nothing, gave most of it to the schools I graduated from."

"Any to a mistress by any chance?"

"Well, yes, a little. Strange you should ask."

"You said you had no choice. Tell me, did you have a choice to forgive them, your wife and kids and anyone else who sided against you? No choice? Really?"

A good-looking man even as he squinted in the stinging brightness of astral daylight, Eric looked reflective. "You are asking for the impossible," he said.

"The impossible might be the only way out for you, Eric."

He looked shocked. "I hate hypocrisy more than anything in the world. That's why I've answered you truthfully. No. I can't forgive them. I can't pretend that I forgive them. I don't feel it. Forgiveness would be—inauthentic. It would be unmanly. I was honest with myself and her. And with you."

"I think it might be the most manly thing you ever did. It would take tremendous humility, and humility isn't hypocrisy. Do you know what you lack?"

"What?"

"Courage. The courage not only to forgive, but even more, to apologize."

Eric swung his head around as if chasing away a migraine. "Apologize? You want me to apologize to *them?*" Then he let his head drop. He looked as if he felt no one in the world understood him; as if he were alone, utterly alone in defeat. Mortified, he said, "If you are correct, then I have been a fool, the biggest fool Earth ever saw. And I don't believe I am."

"Go back to the early days of your marriage. Can you see the cracks? Can you see what you might have done to cause them?"

He shook his head in long, exaggerated swings.

"Nothing? Not one thing?"

He looked up at the horizon. "Of course there were things, for God sake! We hurt each other. I hurt her, yes. For Christ sake, we were married. What do you expect?"

"I don't doubt it. But do you have to keep hating her? Try to see how you hurt her, and let the hatred go."

Again he looked reflective, then again shook his head in exasperation.

"It's not necessary to hate yourself, Eric. There is nothing manly about that either. Is your wife over here yet?"

"When did I say I hated myself?"

"Is your wife over here yet?"

"No."

"Will you do yourself a favor?"

"What?"

"Make a date with her when she gets here. Let her see your regret, your acknowledgement that you were a cad. Let her hear your apology. From the heart. No hypocrisy. No conditions. And one more thing."

"A cad? What are you saying? That she was not to blame? That it was all my fault?"

"One more thing. Make a date with me so I can help you out of the hell you're in. I'll come to you in the shadows, you don't have to come to me. I'll stick by you for as long as needed to get you out. In the meantime, go back to your home. Leave off this rebellion."

Pascal reached out and took the poor man's hands.

Astonished, Eric looked at the priest without speaking, then bowed his head. He began to weep quietly, trying to hold in the sobbing. Pascal continued holding his hand until he couldn't contain himself. Minutes later he retreated to his company with a promise to try to forgive everyone he had ever hurt.

It was hard to say whether it was primarily the front line or the backup or the light itself that wore down the rebels, but after six weeks they withdrew. The land's original population drifted back home, repaired the damaged landscape, patched up the buildings, and took up life as before. The Astral was again in safe hands.

30

The Christmas Message

Twenty-five Earth years had passed since Sephia and Numen put on their Earth suits under Fruva's guidance. Under their governance the planet's astral zone had flourished. They took pride in the beauty of its landscapes and buildings, the growth of the Universal Religion, and the increasing ratio of ascending to returning souls, from one in eight to one in seven. The population of Earth had steadied at about nine billion, roughly the same as the Astral and the Shadowlands combined. Equipoise was regarded as healthy.

In the last year a new trend was developing, with more Earth deaths than births being recorded. The main reason was an alarming escalation in warfare. Overcrowded India had had to cap its population at 1.7 billion and passed laws, strictly enforced, to two children per woman. Its growing Muslim population rejected state control of the birth rate and resented high fines and even property confiscation that was imposed on it. Their resentment turned to violence in Kashmir, long a hotspot of tension between Muslim Pakistan and Hindu India, both of which claimed Kashmir as its own. When Pakistan dropped a small nuclear device on a brigade of Indian soldiers clustered at the border, killing all 2900 men and women, national outrage erupted. Even though an equal number of Pakistani infantry died in the same explosion, which Pakistan claimed was an accident, India was unappeased by the prime minister's desperate apology and promise of restitution, including some of the contested territory. It fired a similar sized nuclear device on Pakistan's General Headquarters on the outskirts of Islamabad, which demolished most of the country's military command structure and killed a few thousand civilians. Pakistan, in a lucid moment of sanity, did not retaliate in kind, but a conventional war followed killing tens of thousands on both sides.

Other conflicts were simmering, a few raging. Many Muslim immigrants throughout Europe had long given up trying to acclimate to their host countries and sometimes resorted to violence in their protests for equal rights. The two Koreas were further apart than ever, with the North threatening Seoul with nuclear annihilation and the United States warning that Pyongyang would be reduced to a "heap of ashes" if it dared. Smaller wars were sending souls to the Astral as well. Militias were still killing each other over who had rights to the Donbas along the Russian-Ukrainian border. Israelis were forever feeling squeezed by the burgeoning populations of their Arab neighbors. Lebanon was mired in civil war.

There were a few bright spots, one of them as surprising as it was world-shaking. The United States and China agreed to share each other's technological innovations, especially in the chip industry, for the good of the world, with all past violations of international law forgiven. Beset by a historic drought, and with its new trust of the United States, China agreed to recognize Taiwan as a separate country in return for unlimited shipments of U.S. grain for its hungry, threatening populations. Taiwan's acceptance into the United Nations in November 2047 was hailed by almost all countries, eventually even China, as a victory for the world.

It was against this background that the Guardians a month later reached out to their astral citizens in a Christmas address delivered from Astral Park, a broad, gradually rising first-sphere lawnscape with viewing at either ground or sky level. They had come to celebrate, come all the way down to the Astral's lowest level, come not to warn or criticize or even exhort, but to glow with pride at what had gotten done. Millions attended. Billions watched from their homes.

Sephia, dressed in her traditional Earth colors of orange, brown, and beige, began: "Dear sisters and brothers, let me begin at the beginning. We thank you hospice workers for greeting and sorting and orienting the dead as they come over; most of them expected something completely different or nothing at all. We want you to know how valuable this work is; how much confusion you remove; how psychically exhausting it can be. We understand, for we, both of us, did similar work for our own planets, which are not much different from yours. I next want to thank all you missionary spirits for taking on the most grueling work of all—descending into the twilight world of the Shadowlands. We know how stifling that environment is and how often your efforts are frustrated, even ridiculed and cursed. Yet you go down every day, your hearts heavy but your will determined. Sometimes you come home with a great story to tell, but more often you must wait for the next day, or the next week, or even longer. For that is often how long it takes before the truth is accepted and the soul set free. Bless you. Bless you all."

Numen, clad in silvery blue and white, his lean, austere face startling in its brilliance, spoke: "Citizens of the Astral, we single out you workers in the reincarnation chambers. For rebirth to succeed, your technical training and skills, part spiritual, part neurological, part Astral and part Earth, require the greatest care possible. Any slipup results in a miscarriage. And you see to it that the correct soul is selected when more than one desire the same parents. And your sensitivity in dealing with the disappointed is almost as important as the process itself. So we thank you for this vital service. We also recognize all you judges hearing grievances. Many people—victims of murder or carelessness or cruelty or calumny or selfishness in any of its thousand forms—arrive here seeking revenge. Your intelligence and sensitivity are crucial for saving them from slipping into the Shadows. You specialize in the art of forgiveness, but also of apology. We think of the millions you've rescued from hatred and arrogance. You are amazing souls."

"Then there are all you teachers," Sephia went on, "who educate our orphaned children. Most of them want an Earth existence that was denied them by their untimely death. Others were on track for ascension when they died—just one more Earth life was all they needed. Whatever the need, you lovingly supplied it. But their number is small compared to the souls who die at a riper age. You career counselors help elderly souls find a proper occupation for their skills and wishes. Others of you are great listeners and therapists. You comfort those who miss their loved ones back on Earth or who find themselves forgotten by the one they dreamed of spending eternity with. You console many good souls whose religious convictions didn't pan out and try to show them a better way. You arrange for movement from one sector to another or one level to the next. You spiritual directors maintain our churches and synagogues and mosques, our temples and gurdwaras. You tell the souls in your care to walk in gratitude for the lives they have. You remind them that their lives didn't just happen—they were given. You arouse gratitude in them for the immeasurably great gift of existence. We especially thank you shepherds of the Universal Religion for rescuing them from their sectarian, exclusivist delusions."

"Yes," continued Numen, "then there is the amusement and merrymaking that you organizers and planners bring us, the entertainment and festivals you stage, the live theater, concerts, and hilarious comedy routines that lighten our loads. The art that you fill our museums with; the novels you write that link us to our former homes on Earth; the lectures that stimulate our minds and add to our knowledge; the pioneering music that you compose with the new instruments you find here; the films you keep rolling out that ennoble rather than degrade us; the opinion pieces that keep us thinking; the documentaries about life on other levels and even other planets; the news of events both here and on Earth that you journalists constantly feed us; the fascinating histories of souls who make life on the Astral better in ways I can't name or even imagine—to all of you a huge thanks."

Sephia singled out the contributions of gardeners and builders, architects and engineers, hologram and television technicians, record keepers and archivists, weather makers, time keepers, schedulers, sentinels who patiently observe the planet's many regions, and all the nameless billions in the Astral who empathize with Earth's physical challenges and answer its prayers. "And especially all of you working overtime in the hospices with the crush of souls that war is sending us."

The Guardians ended with a reminder. "We are often asked about the ultimate purpose of our lives. What do our Cosmic Parents want from us. What do they want us to do? Why did they create us? What would please them?

"The short answer is that they created us to be happy. A better one is that we are meant to become great. Great? How does one become great? My wife has shown me in a thousand different ways: through service. When you become a servant, you will become great, truly great. Then happiness, happiness in its highest form, will run up from behind and tap you on the shoulder. 'Here I am,' it will say with a broad smile. It's a by-product that follows as naturally as warmth from fire. But if you seek it selfishly, it will evade you."

Sephia continued: "We flourish when we use our talents to serve the common good—that is the way we have been made. It begins with those closest to us: our children, our parents, our friends. Think about it. We bring them happiness by serving them. And the happiness we feel is an echo of theirs. But service reaches higher—to our ascended helpers, to the great masters and saints, to the angels in the high heavens, all the way up to our Galactic and Cosmic Parents. Dear friends, we serve them by following the laws of the universe that they created for us and oversee. They are joyful when we cut through the confusion and darkness of our worlds and discover them in our hearts like diamonds glistening in sunlight. They are nestled within our very souls. We know them when we grow still, or during the great Creation Ritual when, surrounded by thousands of aspiring souls united in a common purpose, we pour out our thanks in our temples for the way we have been made. Oh, to have discovered this great secret, what joy, what joy! Oh, dear friends, what joy!"

"The road to it isn't easy," Numen continued, "but if we follow it, we will become more than our Parents' servants: we will become their children, loved in a special way, trusted with responsibilities that will merit help from those we aspire to become like."

Sephia then sang the Christian hymn *O Holy Night* in the universal tongue. Millions wept, not so much at the hymn's beauty or even the precious memories of Christmastime on Earth that it called up, but at the otherworldly purity of her voice, which, as a journalist later put it, "made the galaxy hold its breath."

They had decided on a more spontaneous way to close the ceremony. "We are too remote from our subjects"—that's how Numen had put it. Sephia had private reservations about "the experiment." She feared that his directness, as when he used the word "subjects," might require a more sensitive tilt. In the end she gave in. Two weeks before the occasion, they invited citizens to submit questions on any subject to a multi-level sorting committee. They had no idea what the committee had come up with when they remounted the stage following the formal presentation after a brief break.

One stood out among the thirty-one heard. It came from a Second-Level enquirer who died less than a year before and that might have been considered indelicate. It certainly caught the Guardians off-guard. "Why do you call each other 'princess' and 'husband'?"

The couple stared at each other for a few seconds without a word. Then Sephia spoke: "On Pollux, my home planet, it's the custom for married people to address each other by their role, so I call Numen 'husband'. 'It sounds impersonal,' you might say. Not to me. Sometimes I do call him by his name, usually when I want his full attention. But to call him 'Numen' all the time would—how shall I put it?—would use up the force, the bite stored up by using it sparingly. We do have our disagreements, and it's then that I'm likely to call him by his name. Thank you for the question." She turned to Numen. "What about you, husband?"

"Ah, Princess. First let me say we don't have an exact equivalent in Sirian culture. Not long after I arrived here, I read about a sixteenth century princess in India named Meerabai, a woman of extraordinary bravery whose life was constantly threatened when she defied a custom. If you know the story of my wife, you know she lived under death threats for defying a custom on her planet and even spent three years in prison. I was struck by the similarity and almost unconsciously began thinking of her as 'my princess.' Thus she has remained ever since. A strange account, no doubt."

"Let me add," said Sephia, "that the word 'princess' felt odd to me when I first heard it, but I respected my husband enough not to object. Now I've grown used to it and see it as his way of expressing, not only respect, but affection."

The Guardians closed the address to long-lasting applause and began a series of meetings with winners of various awards, ranging from heroism in the trenches of the Shadows to outstanding achievement in musical composition to a "groundbreaking" of some new building. Days unbroken passed before the flood of appreciations given to them had been acknowledged and their duty done. Finally the last ribbon was cut and the last goodbye said, and the couple headed for home.

31

Expansion

Sephia and Numen handed the reigns of government to their cabinet and embarked on a weeklong self-guided meditation retreat. They were thoroughly familiar with the theory behind meditation but hadn't made time for the practice. They each had a short phrase, a mantra, to quiet the mind—like a tidal wave smoothing out all the ripples behind it as it rolls across the sea. The final goal was to release even that phrase and enter the silent, still, vast openness that was one's true self. They remembered one of Fruva's teachings comparing the true self to the light of the sun: you don't seek the sunlight as if it is something you don't have; it is already within you; it is who you are. Fruva told them the light came from our Cosmic Parents. Unlike prayer, which reached out, meditation reached in. Sephia and Numen found themselves struggling to find and dwell in that light.

Each had been sitting alone in a secluded spot on the Capitol grounds, and by the fifth day they had made progress. "But there is only so much I'm good for; my mind is beginning to reel," Numen confided to his wife when they briefly reunited. "How are you doing?"

"Deeply refreshed but ready to get back to work."

"I'd constantly catch myself lost in distractions. I became almost obsessed wondering how we'd been doing all these years. Thoughts like this kept muscling their way into the practice." He fidgeted with his fingers in his beard. "How do you think we've been doing all these years, Princess? Really, what's your honest opinion?"

They were seated in their favorite spot on the platform looking out over the vast, beautiful tract that made up the Astral's highest sphere. "It's too bad this world is so underpopulated," Sephia said. "It seems made for a numberless multitude. How about you? You go first."

Numen didn't answer right away. They gazed at the sunny spectacle of forests, steppes, rivers, lakes, and mountains. They reminisced about the shade they helped create, the campaign to save wild animals, their circumvention of an alien takeover, and other successes. "My main regret," he said, "is how little headway we've made in getting earthlings to realize that there is such a place as this. The futures they work toward all come to an end. They set their goals too low, and the inner work they needed to do never gets done. They arrive here like refugees instead of citizens. Or like boulders in a mudslide, as Ma put it to me the other day. No idea what the Creator expected of them. Lives without a compass."

"I can certainly relate to that. But all this meditation opened a sad place in me—along with the peace, of course." She stared into space as Numen waited for her to go on, but she didn't.

"Are you saying you regret taking our assignment?"

"It's not that. But I have my lonely moments, as you know. I still miss Soopta, the perfect daughter who seemed so much a part of me when I left the heavens over Pollux. And I found myself wondering how my grandchildren down on the planet are doing—do you realize they would be in their thirties by now? In Earth years, I mean. You don't seem to be as attached to your past. Anyway, these were my distractions."

"I'm more attached than you suppose, Princess."

"You keep saying that but never explain."

"I keep some things to myself. Besides, I have you. That's enough to fill my heart."

"You are too kind, husband. And a little too mysterious for my taste."

"What are your latest thoughts about keeping in touch when the assignment ends?"

She didn't answer right away. A silky white and green scarf tied loosely round her neck fluttered in the breeze. "It would be a terribly lonely thing if we didn't," she finally said.

"Why do you say that?"

"No one else will ever understand what we've been through—and what we've given up."

Numen adored his wife but never saw clear evidence that the love was returned to the same degree. He wondered if Polluxian women were less effusive by nature or if he simply didn't inspire the love he sought. "I like your scarf," he said rather oddly.

As if reading his thoughts, seeing his vulnerability, she turned and looked at him. She took his lean hand and rubbed it gently.

"Do you know what I think, Numen?"

"What?"

"That the Creator might have decided not to create anything at all. After all, they had each other. They were never alone. What need had they of creating? Yet they created anyway."

That's the way it is with us, she mused. She thought of Gaia, single, alone at the top—no wonder she felt so helpless. She thought of the way she and Numen plunged into the Shadowlands on the equinox—each inspiring the other to descend.

"I can see why the Creator sends us out in pairs," she said.

"Look carefully, Princess." He pointed toward the horizon, moving his finger slowly from right to left. "Am I imagining it, or can we begin to make out the curvature of the sphere?"

There was also that which she loved: his unbridled curiosity.

She studied him as he scanned the world they now thought of as home and tried to imagine what it would be like to lose him. She had wondered about it before, and even though she sometimes found him annoying, even exasperating, every time she shut out the thought as an impudent intruder.

"Love has a way of expanding," she said.

He looked at her, studied her sitting so close to him as she looked out and up into the sky. "Yes, love has a way of expanding," she repeated. She lowered her glance, turned her head and looked at him. He noted that her wonderful eyes were wet as he stared into them and she stared back. At the same instant, their faces, hers so round and his so lean, broke into smiles.

www.ingramcontent.com/pod-product-compliance
Lightning Source LLC
Chambersburg PA
CBHW020812060726
47498CB00017B/2759